THE LADDER DANCER

Recent Titles from Roz Southey

The Charles Patterson Series

BROKEN HARMONY
CHORDS AND DISCORDS
SECRET LAMENT
SWORD AND SONG
THE LADDER DANCER ★

★ *available from Severn House*

THE LADDER DANCER

Roz Southey

CRÈME de la CRIME

This first world edition published 2011
in Great Britain and the USA by
Crème de la Crime, an imprint of
SEVERN HOUSE PUBLISHERS LTD of
9–15 High Street, Sutton, Surrey, England, SM1 1DF.
Trade paperback edition first published
in Great Britain and the USA 2011.

British Library Cataloguing in Publication Data

Southey, Roz, 1952–
  The ladder dancer.
  1. Patterson, Charles (Fictitious character) – Fiction.
  2. Musicians – England – Newcastle upon Tyne – Fiction.
  3. Great Britain – History – George II, 1727–1760 –
  Fiction. 4. Detective and mystery stories.
  I. Title
  823.9'2-dc22

ISBN-13: 978-1-78029-003-4 (cased)
ISBN-13: 978-1-78029-503-9 (trade paper)

All Severn House titles are printed on acid-free paper.

Severn House Publishers support The Forest Stewardship Council [FSC],
the leading international forest certification organisation. All our titles that
are printed on Greenpeace-approved FSC-certified paper carry the FSC logo.

MIX
Paper from
responsible sources
FSC
www.fsc.org   FSC® C018575

Typeset by Palimpsest Book Production Ltd.,
Falkirk, Stirlingshire, Scotland.
Printed and bound in Great Britain by the
MPG Books Group, Bodmin, Cornwall.

To Jackie, Laura and Anu

WITH THANKS

. . . to Lynne Patrick, without whose help Charles Patterson would never have seen the light of day. I owe her more than I can say. And to Jeff, for his excellent company on many occasions.

. . . to my agent, Juliet Burton, for her wonderfully efficient help and advice.

. . . to Severn House for giving Patterson the chance to range a little further.

. . . and of course to all my family, including my sisters, Wendy and Jennifer, and my brother-in-law, John; Jon and Sonia, and their two recent additions to the family, Billy and Samuel; and Jim and Rachel. And of course to my ever-patient husband Chris, with gratitude for his patience, help and general encouragement throughout (and the never-ending supply of tea).

Charles Patterson's Newcastle

KEY

1: Town walls
2: St Nicholas's Church
3: St Andrew's Church
4: St John's Church
5: All Hallow's Church
6: Castle
7: Guildhall and Sandhill
8: Caroline Square
9: Chares
10: Bigg Market
11: Sandgate
12: The Key
13: The Side

Northumberland Street

Lort Burn

High Bridge

Pilgrim Street

Low Bridge

Westgate

RIVER TYNE

Tyne Bridge

Gateshead

One

A gentleman always behaves with restraint . . .
[A Gentleman's Companion, September 1736]

The day was as filthy as my temper. Gusts of wind swirled the September fog, slapped chill flurries of rain into my face. Passers-by were shadows that flickered into existence as the fog parted then faded as it drifted back again. The hulks of ships moored at the Key were merely dark patches in the murk. Seagulls shrieked overhead.

While I'd been in the houses of the ladies and gentlemen all day, trying to sell them tickets for the winter concerts, the fog had come up the Tyne in thick waves, blanketing the river and the buildings on either side, muffling the clatter of the keelmen loading coal, the barking of dogs, the cries of children. An unseen ballad singer was working her way through a popular song about the latest murder in London. A thin child's voice. Desperation, surely, to be trying to wheedle money out of anyone in this weather.

I turned up the collar of my greatcoat and stepped cautiously along the wet cobbles of the Key. A couple of drunken sailors loomed out of the fog, reeled across my path, laughing hysterically. I jolted back, trying to avoid them, slipped, cursed.

I'd had to spend almost an entire day, in one house or another, talking to ladies who'd only one topic in mind and were determined to raise it. In newly decorated drawing rooms, upholstered with the most fashionable wallpaper and hung with embroideries done by the lady of the house, I'd handed over the freshly printed tickets; lady after lady took them graciously, perused them, asked me who was singing this year – and slipped in a question or two about my wife: 'And how *is* the new Mrs Patterson?' I've never seen a set of people so eager for gossip.

The snide remark made by the maiden lady at my last house-call had been the final straw. 'But my dear Mr Patterson, we didn't expect to see you at all this year. We expected you to be taking it easy at home.' A coy smile. 'A gentleman who marries money has no need—' a simpering hesitation – 'to *toil*.'

Nice of her to avoid the dreaded word *work*, I thought savagely. I'd bowed out of the house and vowed never to go back. A useless resolve, of course; I couldn't afford such a dramatic gesture.

The fog swirled in closer; I twisted a foot on an up-jutting cobble, stood a moment cursing with pain. To make matters worse, I could hear a murmur from my right, from the river itself. A faint keening of grief, a wailing and moaning of distress. Faint lights glittered through the fog, dancing in the water like a hundred stars faintly twinkling.

Each light was the spirit of a man who died in the river, inhabiting the place of their death, as all spirits do. The essence of a man bundled up and concentrated in a single cold gleam of matter, lingering eighty or a hundred years after death, until final dissolution takes it. I know worlds where spirits do not exist, but here we all come to this, eventually: a lonely point of dulled light in a bright vibrant world.

For some people fate is kind. Those who die on solid earth cling to the buildings in which they expire, and can gossip to the living almost as if they have never died; they can feel still part of the world around them. For others, fate is harsh; those who drown in the river or at sea are at the mercies of the tides and swells, and can find themselves drifting forever alone, visible to the living merely as a glimmer of light on a wave. Whenever they come close to land, they cry out and wail and lament their fate, pleading with those who pass for help that cannot be given, that would be years too late. Everybody ignores them, hurries away, afraid that one day this might be their fate too. It is the loneliest, most desolate sound I know.

When it comes to my time to die, I intend it shall be in my bed, or at my own hearth, where my spirit can linger in comfortable commerce with my friends and descendants.

My bed? *My* hearth? *My wife's* bed and *my wife's* hearth, at any rate. As the maiden lady said, I've married money.

The pain in my foot eased; I hobbled forward. The fog thinned, showed me a keel moored at the Keyside. A pig squealed at the bow like an exotic figurehead. Sailors were hurrying about on deck, stowing kegs of water and boxes of biscuits: intending to sail on the next tide, no doubt. The keel bobbed up and down on the choppy waves, drifting away from the Key then bumping back up again, gangplank creaking and mooring ropes straining.

A sailor stopped to call to a woman staggering down the Key. In the trailing wisps of fog, I could see only her back, a ragged shawl, bedraggled hair. As she turned to yell to the sailor, I saw she carried an infant in her arms. Very young, I guessed, by the way its head lolled back. The woman shrieked, cackled with laughter.

No guessing what ailed her. Gin.

The fog drifted back in. I shivered, pulled my coat round me. If I made it as far as the Printing Office without injuring myself, it would be a miracle. And after that, I'd go home. To my wife. My *wealthy* wife. The spirits wailed, and the young ballad singer sang a coarse song that ill-suited her youth. She breathed in all the wrong places; I itched to correct her.

The clop clop of horse's hooves. Moving fast – *too* fast for this weather. I stopped, trying to gauge the horse's direction, not wanting to be ridden down. The fog took up the sound, battered it against the buildings lining the Key and threw it back again confusingly. Was it behind me or—

The horse loomed up ahead, beyond the keel. It was grey as the fog, being ridden hard, breaking into a gallop. On cobbles, in limited visibility, it was folly. The rider was a mere hulk on its back, a bulky figure swaddled in greatcoat and hat. Head down, face almost entirely hidden.

I watched, helpless, as the inevitable disaster struck. The horse came on, tossing its head, struggling against its rider's grip. On, on. One of the sailors shouted. The drunken woman glanced up, almost lazily, obviously befuddled. The horse came on. All the sailors were shouting now.

It was too late. The horse slammed into the woman. Its heavy shoulder caught her, spun her to one side. She shrieked, flung out her hands, dropped the child, grabbed at it again, went down—

The boat, caught by the river swell, drifted away from the Key. The woman went down into the gap between wharf and boat, and was lost from sight.

The sailors were after her instantly, scrambling down, throwing ropes, hauling her sodden and shrieking from the river. Water poured out of her clothes, cascaded down her face, plastered her hair to her head. A burly sailor hugged her tight, swung her up on to the deck. She was beating her fists against his chest, struggling to get away.

The baby had gone.

The horse tore past me, so close I saw the white sweat on its flanks and beneath the saddle. Its breath floated away; its rider's coat skirts drifted out and brushed my shoulder. There was an almost tangible emanation of fury; I caught sight of a hard mouth curling into a snarl. And a glimpse of leather bags hung over the saddle, one embossed with intertwined letters. Then the horse was past and its rider with it, swallowed up by the fog.

Women were running from a nearby tavern. The burly sailor was trying to restrain the woman. She was shrieking over and over, the same word: baby, *baby*. And in the confusion, I heard someone call out, 'Accident!'

It was not an accident. I'd been directly facing the horse. I'd seen the rider tug on the reins, and the horse shift course fractionally to strike against the woman. It had been deliberate.

No accident.

Murder.

Two

A wife is an ornament to any household, provided she
be thrifty and assiduous in the pursuance of her duties.
[*A Gentleman's Companion*, January 1730]

'A ladder dancer?' I echoed incredulously.

Esther smiled mischievously across the breakfast table. Early morning sunlight gleamed on her golden hair and the charming lace cap she has taken to wearing since our marriage. *My wife.* My heart turned over just at the sight of her.

She'd been reading the latest missive from one of her friends in London before she revealed her unpleasant surprise. 'So Maria says.' She shuffled the sheets of the letter obviously looking for something; a three-page letter, I thought, how much had we had to pay for that?

'Ah, here it is.' *It* was a cutting from a London newspaper. 'This is the advertisement for his performance at Drury Lane last month.' She read from the cutting. '*Mr Richard Nightingale, Master Ladder-Dancer of England. He does such wonderful things that have been very surprising to all that ever saw him. He stands on the uppermost Step of the Ladder and turns himself quite round, which no Man ever did, or can do besides himself, while playing on the Violin, with several other things.*'

I groaned and buried my head in my hands. 'And Jenison has hired him for the winter concerts!'

'Now, Charles,' she said, reprovingly. 'Do not despair. It says here the violin has no strings.'

'Then how the devil does he play it?'

'He sings the notes.'

'*Sings?*'

'He imitates the sound of the violin. Oh, and the flageolet, *and* the trumpet. And many other instruments besides. It says he sang the overture to Mr Handel's opera, *Giulio Cesare.*'

I seized my coffee dish. It was, thankfully, very strong coffee.

Esther regarded me sympathetically. 'I know such things can hardly be regarded as *musical*—'

'*Hardly*? Not at all!'

'It will attract the audiences,' she pointed out.

'That's the most depressing thing of all!'

'But if you can get them to listen to Richard Nightingale, perhaps later they will enjoy something more worthwhile, Corelli's music, for instance, or Geminiani's?'

I sighed. 'One can always hope.'

I looked at Esther – *my wife!* – as she scanned the letter for any further information on this paragon of musical virtue. *My wife*: how strange that still seemed. Three weeks was not remotely enough time to become used to it. Or to its consequences.

Three weeks ago, walking into All Hallows' Church with Esther on my arm, I had been ecstatically happy. It had been a quiet wedding, with my patron, Claudius Heron, to support the bride, and my friend Hugh Demsey to support me, the only other witnesses being the organist of All Hallows and his cat, which had wandered in and stayed to wash in a patch of sunshine. We repeated the correct words after the glowing young, romantically inclined curate, accepted congratulations from everyone present, excluding the cat, and went back to

Claudius Heron's elegant home for the wedding breakfast. In the pleasure of good food and good conversation with friends, I'd even forgotten to be nervous about the inevitable intimacies of married life until the carriage set us down in front of Heron's country mansion, loaned to us for a short bridal trip. And, thankfully, there'd been nothing to be nervous about.

That was not the problem. If it had merely been a question of love, and compatibility, there'd have been nothing to worry about, despite the differences in our ages – I've just turned twenty-seven, Esther's twelve years older. But there's more than age between us; there's status and there's wealth.

I expected the disapproval of the ladies and gentlemen; a musician, a mere tradesman, marrying a lady who's related, however distantly, to an earl! What I hadn't bargained for was my own reaction.

Three weeks after the ceremony, immediately after returning from the bridal trip, I'd moved from my lodgings into Esther's house in Caroline Square. With its drawing rooms, dining room, breakfast room, library, half a dozen bedrooms, several dressing rooms and the servants' quarters besides. And a garden. I'd lived previously in one room. I'd had no servants. I'd sent out for my meals or gone to the tavern for them and I'd never had to walk further than a yard or two for my violin or music books. And now, for heaven's sake, I had a room solely set aside for the eating of breakfast! Why the devil could we not simply use the dining room?

The sunshine shone through the windows from the garden and glinted on the strands of hair escaping from the confines of Esther's elegant lace cap to lie across the curve of her neck. Every time I looked at her, I felt a pang of longing and pride that almost overwhelmed me. And every time I looked at her, I saw the jewels in her ears and at her throat, the fine fabric of her dress. And then I looked at the shabby cuffs of my coat.

Esther put the letter down, cleared her throat. 'Charles,' she said carefully. 'You cannot grumble over every little expense. It is a small sum to pay for a letter.'

I gripped my coffee dish. If I could have talked myself out of this ridiculous annoyance, this strange sense of unreality, I would have. I wanted to. No – I wanted to get back to the old easiness I'd felt in Esther's presence, before the question of money raised its ugly head. Had there ever been a time like that? 'I was thinking of the coat you wanted me to buy,' I admitted.

'I mentioned two coats,' she said. 'And new breeches. And some shirts.'

'No, no,' I protested, seizing on the diversion. 'I bought three new shirts only a month ago.'

'Only three?' she said, wincing. 'Charles, you need at least seven – one for every day. More would be better. I will see to it.'

'*You* will?' I said blankly.

She looked surprised. 'Linen is always the wife's responsibility.'

'Well,' I said, speaking before thinking and bitterly regretting it the moment the words were out of my mouth, 'it's your money.'

'No,' she said evenly, 'it is not. When we married, my money became yours.'

'I didn't earn it.'

She took a moment to fold the sheets of the letter away. 'So you intend that when we go out together, I will be dressed expensively, and you will be wearing your old shabby clothes just to prove you are not taking advantage of my wealth?'

I looked at her. She held my gaze steadily. The vision was just too ludicrous; I laughed ruefully. 'That would merely draw attention to the situation, would it not?'

She leant forward, reached out for my hand, her fingers warm on mine. 'People will gossip about our marriage, Charles. They *will* believe you married me for my money; that is inevitable. *We* know it is not true. Surely that is all that matters?'

I wanted to respond. I wanted to say *yes*. I couldn't bring myself to do so. 'I hope to earn a great deal more this year,' I found myself saying. 'The tickets for the subscription series are selling well and the concert directors will be paying me more.' That was true, but not to the extent I was implying; five shillings extra a year was never going to make me rich. 'And I can make more money,' I hurried on, seeing Esther draw back and her smile fade, 'if I take on an apprentice.'

A virulent green gleam shot across the table and climbed to the top of my coffee dish. I jerked back, startled. Coffee splashed on to the tablecloth. 'Master!' the spirit said with an indignant squeak. '*I'm* your apprentice.'

Esther sighed, just audibly. George, who died in this house a year ago, at the age of twelve, had been in life my apprentice, and in some ways, I felt responsible for his death. Which adds a degree of guilt to my feelings towards his spirit. I gritted my teeth. 'You're dead, George,' I pointed out. 'You can't play in concerts and earn me money any more.'

'You don't need another apprentice,' he said obstinately, like the sullen boy he'd been when he died. 'You don't, you *don't!*'

'This is a private conversation, George,' Esther said. 'Please leave us.'

The gleam flickered uncertainly; the green colour faded slightly. George adores Esther with the intensity of a boy's first crush; he told me only a few days ago he was pleased he died in her house so he could stay with her 'for ever and ever'. From the moment I moved in, he's been annoyingly offensive, giving me directions to rooms I already know, introducing me to servants I've been acquainted with for a year or more, and generally trying to give the impression he's the man of the house. In short, showing every sign of jealousy.

Fortunately, mixed in with his adoration of Esther is a healthy dash of adolescent bashfulness which means one disapproving word from her is enough to send him into agonies of guilt. That alone, thankfully, has kept him out of our bedroom at nights.

'*Now*, George,' Esther said.

He mumbled, 'Yes, mistress,' and shot off. I watched until the gleam slid out of the room under the door.

Esther said quietly, 'You are still distressed by that incident on the Key.'

Reluctantly I sat back. 'Yes.'

'The Constable and the coroner both concluded it was an accident.'

'Tell that to the mother.'

She nodded. 'But no blame can attach to her. She was very drunk, admittedly, but there was no way she could have kept hold of the child.'

'It was intentional,' I said. 'He deliberately ran into her.'

'Charles—'

'I don't say he intended to kill her, or the child, but he did intend to hurt them. He was venting his anger on them.'

Esther plainly chose her words carefully. 'I was wondering if perhaps—'

'Yes?' That came out rather more belligerently than I'd intended.

She continued more decisively. 'Over the past year, Charles, you have been involved in four puzzles, and you have proved yourself expert in unravelling the truth. But I am beginning to wonder if that has led you to start seeing mysteries where none exist.'

I took a deep breath. I would not argue with Esther over yet another matter. 'You're not the only person to say so,' I admitted. 'The coroner plainly thought so, and the new constable. But I'm not imagining this, Esther.'

She sat back. 'Very well. Then why not see if you can find any trace of the fellow? Would it not set your mind at rest?'

I saw that leather bag again, jolting at the back of the saddle. The intertwined initials: *CR*. I've always hated leaving puzzles unsolved. Of course, why hadn't I thought of that before? I drained my coffee dish and pushed back my chair. 'You're right. And if I can find nothing, at least I'll feel I've tried.'

She hesitated. 'You will not forget you have to see lawyer Armstrong in the next few days. About the Norfolk estates, that business with the tenant of the Home Farm.'

I dipped to plant a kiss on her forehead. 'You deal with it.'

'Charles, I can't. Not any longer. It's your property now.'

'I'll sign the papers when you've sorted it out.'

'Mr Armstrong will expect to see *you*!'

But like a coward I was already at the door.

Three

Clothes bespeak the man.
[*A Gentleman's Companion*, February 1732]

Walking across town towards the Key, my conscience pricked me horribly. I was behaving like a boor, and Esther's forbearance only made matters worse. At least she wasn't trying to insist I wear a wig; I find them abominably itchy and much prefer wearing my own hair.

I hesitated, then steeled myself and detoured to the shop of

Mr Watson the tailor, at the foot of the Side, where that winding street opens out a little. It was a cramped shop in one of the oldest, most creaking houses in town, but it was elegantly done out. I fancied I smelt money the moment I walked in.

I was served by the man himself, who was dressed in the height of fashion: a reddish-brown coat with huge cuffs and bright buttons. He irritated me before two minutes were out by revealing he'd been expecting me. 'Sooner or later,' he said, with a smirk. 'How *is* Mrs Patterson?'

'I want a new coat,' I said shortly.

He seemed almost gratified by my rudeness, bowing much lower than he had on my first entrance. If he'd not been the best tailor in town, I'd have walked out there and then. My fingers were itching; a voice in the back of my mind was repeating endlessly, *You can't afford this. You can't afford this!*

Watson reached up to the highest shelves and brought down the most expensive, and impractical, satins and silks. 'If I might venture to guide you—' He unrolled a bolt of silk with a flourish. 'With your colouring, sir, you would look very well in puce.'

'I would not,' I said shortly. 'I want a light-brown coat with green cuffs, exactly like the one I'm wearing.' The voice in my head was saying that puce was a dreadful colour but surely there was nothing wrong with that nice dark plum over there . . .

'And a waistcoat?' Watson suggested, unrolling another bolt.

That picture of going out with Esther in her splendid best and me in frayed cuffs came back to haunt me. I took a deep breath to steady myself.

'In dark green, to match the coat.'

'And embroidery?' he asked brightly, his smile a trifle relieved, as if he thought he was winning a battle against a difficult customer. 'We have some very fine embroideresses—'

'Plain.'

'Bumble bees are the latest fashion . . .'

'Plain,' I said. 'With the smallest buttons you have.'

I left the shop having ordered two coats and the waistcoat, with the prospect of a bill larger than any I'd ever received in my life. To be paid out of Esther's money.

Preoccupied, unhappy, I turned towards the Key.

There was no fog today. Sun glinted on the metal fittings of the pulleys, on the iron bands of barrels piled outside a tavern. Few ships were moored, and there was a lazy, desultory air about the place. The ship involved in the rescue of the woman had been allowed to depart, delayed by only a day. I couldn't even be sure I could identify the spot where a child had lost its life before it was aware enough to know the world.

I walked through groups of aged sailors swapping tall tales of peril and audacity, passed Jas Williams' chandlers' shop, which was doing good business. That was where George had grown up, wheezing over every flour barrel and pestering his father for a fiddle. Not that George had ever grown up of course; he'd been murdered while in my charge, and it was only that thought, and the guilt that accompanied it, that gave me any patience with him at all.

On the corner of one of the most disreputable chares, I found the lodging house next to the Old Man Inn, and called for a spirit I knew that had died there. It came, a faint gleam on a windowsill, apparently pleased to meet me again. 'Mr Patterson, sir! You're keeping well, I hope?'

'Alas,' I said with mock sadness, trying to keep the bitterness from my voice. 'Married.'

The spirit burst out laughing. He'd been the landlord of the neighbouring inn in life, and he had a landlord's laugh, round and from the belly. 'Cheer up, sir. There's good things about marriage as well as bad!'

'Yes,' I agreed ruefully. 'You're right.' And I ought to remember, I thought, that there were more good things than bad.

'For one thing,' said the spirit. 'You'll never have to pay for another whore!'

I went on, hurriedly. 'I confess I came for information.'

'One of your mysteries?' The spirit had helped me with another only a month ago. Then it said, more sombrely, 'Not the child?'

I nodded. 'Something about that affair strikes me as not quite right.'

'Didn't see it,' the spirit said, with a note of regret. 'But there were plenty in the inn that did. Went rushing out as soon as they heard the screams.'

Which meant, I reflected, that they'd *not* seen it and probably only had their information at second hand. 'What do they say?'

He chuckled. 'Every possible story under the sun, sir! But

I hear you were there. Did you not give evidence at the inquest?'

I did. And I said unequivocally that the horseman rode straight for the woman. Everyone else had said the fog was so thick no one could see an inch in front of their faces and the fellow was likely not to blame. Anyway, the woman had been drunk and had probably staggered into the path of the horse. The coroner, who'd been in the comfort of his own home at the time and hadn't the slightest idea how foggy it had been, but did know the poor drank too much, had implied it had been the woman's own fault and said that in future she'd do better if she kept out of the way of gentlemen in a hurry.

'Do you know the woman who was knocked down?'

The spirit sniffed. 'I know her kind. She's a whore.'

'She lost a child,' I said. 'I don't know a woman, whore or lady, who'd not be distressed about that.'

The spirit sounded good-humoured. 'With respect, sir, I've known a good many whores in my time. Plenty of them drink in the Old Man. And there's none of them that don't find children a burden.'

I stifled my irritation; annoying him would do no good. Spirits have a tendency to brood on offences and to bear grudges; they have little else to occupy them. 'But the child was an innocent victim,' I pointed out.

'True, true,' he said with an air of philosophy.

I was beginning to think there was nothing to be gained here. 'Do you know of anyone who saw the incident but didn't speak at the inquest?'

'There's Brewer,' the spirit said. 'The pig man. He'd just brought the animal for the ship's crew and was having a beer with them before going home again.'

'Do you know where he lives?'

'Up by St Ann's chapel somewhere.'

'And he didn't testify? Do you know why not?'

'He's dumb, sir. And none too bright, either.'

I sighed.

'There were some whores,' the spirit said. 'One of them had a customer in the alley.' It laughed. 'Couldn't get it up, poor devil. Drunk out of his mind.'

'Did you know him? Or the women?'

'Never saw much,' the spirit said. 'Not in that fog. I heard 'em, but no one used names. No call for it in that kind of transaction.'

I bid him goodbye and wandered across the Key to stare at the river and Gateshead Bank on the other side, with the tower of St Mary's church peeking above the trees. There seemed only one thing to do. I needed to speak to the woman herself. Perhaps she'd known the man on the horse. Perhaps he'd been a customer; some whores are not above threatening a respectable man they'll tell his wife about his activities. Most men are sensible and know the threat can be averted with a shilling or two; to kill the woman seemed a ridiculous over-reaction. But perhaps she'd unluckily picked on a man with a vicious temper. The horseman had been *very* angry; I'd felt the fury coming off him in waves, caught that brief glimpse of furious mouth and set jaw.

So it might pay to talk to her. Which was not a pleasant prospect as, according to the evidence at the inquest, she lived on the Sandgate, just outside the town wall: one of the poorest, and most dangerous, areas of town.

Four

A gentleman is known by the company he keeps.
            [A Gentleman's Companion, July 1732]

The Sandgate lies at the far end of the Key, beyond the ruins of the old town walls. Hovels cluster at the river's edge, dwarfed by the tall ships that moor here. Almost every accent you hear is Scotch and the whole place reeks of gin.

They have their own watchmen here but none of them are elected or paid. They're purely self-appointed but they put the watchmen in the more respectable parts of town to shame. One was following me from the first step I took beyond the ruins of the town wall: a thin young man with a coat so torn and grimy it looked as if it was about to fall off his back. Where I walked, he walked; when I stopped, he stopped.

I looked about in some trepidation. I was unarmed and outnumbered. All around were little knots of people: sailors for the most part, of the worst sort, shouting and laughing together. Women slouched in doorways, watching the street apathetically; children played dully with sticks and stones. All, all stinking of gin.

And not one friendly face amongst them.

Except for one young man hurrying from an alley, who stopped when he saw me and blinked in surprise. A young man so nervous, he clasped his hands together to stop them shaking; he had to clear his throat before he spoke to bring his voice above a whisper. Edward Orrick, curate of All Hallows, who'd married Esther and myself only a month ago.

'Mr—' (The little cough.) 'Mr Patterson. Are you here— Do you come to see—'

'The mother of the baby that died.'

'Indeed,' he said eagerly. His face fell. 'She is, sadly, that is, I'm sure you realize—'

'Distressed.'

'Indeed. And— er—'

'Drunk.'

He looked embarrassed, glanced round, realized we were the centre of curiosity. 'Did you wish to, if you want—' He gestured back into the alley.

'I'd like to see her, yes.'

The alley was narrow and filthy underfoot, littered with dog turds. A dead rat rotted against a wall. On the eaves above, spirits clustered, hanging from broken gutters and slates that teetered perilously on the verge of falling. Orrick was apparently oblivious to it all. He ducked under a low doorway on the right. I followed, hesitated on the threshold to let my eyes adjust to the gloom within.

We'd walked directly into a downstairs room of average size, with one glassless window covered by newspaper, and a biting draught cutting through. A flickering candle was stuck by its own wax to a brick that protruded slightly from the wall; it made no impact on the dimness.

At least fifteen people were crammed inside the gloomy hovel. There was a heap of clothes in the far corner that was probably an elderly man; a dazed-looking child of indeterminate sex leant against him. A woman of middle-age and a youth of about eighteen were lounging against one wall; the young man was idly kicking his toes into the back of a woman hunched on the floor. The rest were children, the youngest barely a year old. And the silence was terrible. So many children ought to be wailing, complaining, scrapping with each other. Instead, they looked at me in sullen dulled silence.

Even a casual glance told me I'd made a pointless journey. No one here would give me any information, as a matter of honour.

Orrick was saying in his soft, gentle voice, 'Now, madam, I've brought you a visitor. Mr Patterson, the gentleman who saw what happened.'

The woman cross-legged on the floor didn't even raise her eyes.

'Gin,' Orrick whispered to me.

'You going to do something useful,' the young man said loudly. 'Or have you just come to gawp?'

The woman beside him said, 'It's a shilling to gawp.'

'Now, now,' Orrick said reprovingly.

She ignored him. 'Shilling to view or out you go.'

'I came to help,' I said.

'Oh, in that case,' the youth said, 'it's an extra sixpence. Cheap at the price. A nice clear conscience you'll have afterwards. Ain't that worth the money?'

'It wasn't her fault,' I said. 'She wasn't to blame for the child's death.'

'Tell that to the crowner,' he said.

The woman on the floor spoke for the first time. 'Gin,' she said.

'Two shillings,' said the lad. 'My last offer, sir.' He sneered.

I glanced round the assembled company. A girl of twelve or thirteen years old stared fixedly back. The old man in the corner broke into sobs.

'I think we'd better,' Orrick murmured. 'Perhaps we should—'

I nodded.

We walked back through the narrow alley into the street. The self-appointed watchman was standing against a wall, still watching, still sneering.

'Sometimes,' Orrick said, gripping his hands together tightly, 'I feel they don't, they refuse—'

I couldn't guess what he wanted to say. I wasn't sure he knew himself. Perhaps just an expression of helplessness or bewilderment.

A noise behind us. I looked back to see the young girl had followed us out on to the street. Her brown hair was lank and unwashed; she was dressed in layer upon layer of rags, with a too-large pair of clogs bound to her bare feet with strips of cloth. She too was watching us, with a calculating smile.

'They don't *want* to be helped,' Orrick said flatly.

We walked back to the town wall together. Orrick's head was bent; he stared at the cobbles under his feet as if examining them for some meaning. The young man still leaned against the wall, although he shifted his position to follow our progress. The girl kept pace with us, a few yards behind. Planning to dip her hand into one of our pockets, no doubt. I didn't feel any inclination to criticize her; in fact, I was rather wishing I had one of Esther's sovereigns in my pocket; the girl clearly needed it more than I did.

Under the ruined town wall Orrick stopped, as if he wanted to say one more thing before he crossed the border into another country. He looked at me directly. '*Was* it an accident?'

'No.'

He nodded, slowly. 'The world is very wicked,' he said, and walked heavily on.

I looked after him for a moment then glanced back. The girl stood in the middle of the road, head lifted, still with that calculating look. I wondered if she'd given up the idea of picking my pocket and was going to beg instead. It would be the height of folly to give her any money; it would all go on gin. But why not? There was probably little else in her life to please her.

She sauntered insolently up to me, hands holding tight to the rags that passed for a shawl. I reached into my pocket, held out a penny on my palm. She stared at it then lifted her eyes to mine. Blue eyes in a face that wore an expression too old for it. She shook her head.

'Nah,' she said. 'I want more than that.'

There was something more than mere insolence there, something that made me uneasy. 'How much then?'

She considered, then smiled wolfishly. She was about to speak when someone behind me started shouting.

I glanced round. A middle-aged man, heavy and red-faced, lumbered towards me. A merchant by the look of him. He shouted at the girl. 'Get away with you! Go back to your hovel now, do you hear me?' The girl gathered her shawl around her, smirked, then turned and walked off, head high.

'Slut, sir,' the merchant said. 'They all are. The mother got so drunk she drowned her own child! Don't have anything to do with them, sir.' And he stalked away to where a boy held a horse for him.

When I looked back, the girl had disappeared.

Five

In the warmth of a well-regulated family circle, true contentment may be found.
[*A Gentleman's Companion*, January 1731]

I was itching to carry on hunting for the man who'd killed the child but tickets for the winter concerts still needed to be sold. I had a living to earn; I was determined to carry out my resolve to match Esther's wealth with my own. And music is more than a profession to me. It's a passion that's survived even the tedium of teaching apathetic children and adults of little or no taste. To run my fingers over a harpsichord keyboard or the neck of a violin is a refuge from the troubles of life. Losing the chance to pass on that passion to other people would be like cutting out part of my soul.

So I walked up from the Key on to the long stretch of Westgate, towards the house of Robert Jenison and his family in the genteel part of town, not far from where I myself now live in Caroline Square. To sell concert subscription tickets to the gentleman who is himself the chief organizer of the concerts and the most assiduous attender. But the Jenisons regard themselves as leaders of Newcastle society and consider it only right they should be formally petitioned, even begged, for their support.

I've never been comfortable in the Jenisons' house. They have a passion for the new. Every time I venture into Mrs Jenison's drawing room there is a new sideboard or a new table, new curtains or new pictures. The pictures are generally productions of the lady herself or one of her three married daughters;

a little while back, they all had a passion for feather pictures,
arranged to simulate landscapes.

The result of all this newness is, somehow, to produce a
room that is supremely uncomfortable and incredibly cluttered.
Footstools hide between chairs to trip you up, miniatures and
ornaments cluster on side tables ready to fall over at the least
jog of your elbow. Even the door to the next room – probably
a private withdrawing room – is decorated with a fan made
of preposterously large feathers. And today I could not help
but contrast the comfort and clutter with the unfurnished hovel
I'd just left.

I took my place with caution on a new blue-upholstered
chair and smiled at the two ladies who confronted me.

'Bring the tea, Simkins,' Mrs Jenison said.

The servant withdrew; Mrs Jenison, a plump middle-aged
woman, fidgeted, straightened an ornament on a table, avoided
my gaze. Her face was flushed.

'I trust you're well,' I said.

'Oh— oh, yes indeed.'

She plainly had not the slightest idea how to address me.
Her old imperious tone – 'Tickets, Mr Patterson? You really
must take the matter up with my husband' – was no longer
suitable and she didn't know what to substitute. I was neither
fish nor fowl, no longer merely a tradesman but not quite a
gentleman either.

'And how is *dear* Mrs Patterson?' her companion asked, with
the most simpering of smiles.

If it was difficult to face Mrs Jenison, it was much worse
to deal with her sister-in-law. Mrs Jenison had simple desires: to
be ahead of her neighbours and relatives in every way possible,
and to have a little peace. But her husband's maiden sister, Mrs
Annabella Jenison – the *Mrs* is, of course, a matter of courtesy
– was a different matter. Sharpened by want, and placed in the
most invidious of positions, she was altogether more unpredict-
able. Dependent relatives are always the very devil to deal with;
they say and do whatever they think will keep them in good
odour with the people they depend upon.

'It's such a while since I saw her,' she said, without waiting
for a reply. 'Not since your marriage, indeed.' A simper. 'So
romantic.'

I smiled, fixedly.

'And I never guessed!' This fact was plainly a source of pleasure to her. 'I never imagined! And Mrs Patterson is not in her first youth . . .'

It occurred to me, as her eyes went misty, that there was a not-so-hidden message behind this remark. Mrs Annabella must be almost sixty, and with no money of her own must long ago have given up hope of a husband. All that was left was love, and Esther's late marriage had apparently given Mrs Annabella one or two ideas.

She hid her mouth behind her hand and murmured again, '*So* romantic.'

Mrs Jenison, secure in her position, her married status and her wealth, seemed unconscious of the undercurrent. She poured tea for me, and plunged into one of her favourite subjects. 'I hope your wife's taking care of her health, Mr Patterson. It's so easy to catch cold at this time of year.'

I allowed her to talk of her eldest daughter's chill (*while she was expecting her second, you know*) then seized an opportunity to praise the new china, which was genuinely beautiful. She glowed and plainly began to feel more at ease. She informed me, in detail, of all the multiplicitous ways *not* to make tea, and warned me to tell Esther to put the milk in the dish first to avoid cracking the china. Then she realized she needed more hot water and paused to speak to the servant.

Mrs Annabella bent towards me. She said, with a significant look, 'Some gentlemen *prefer* mature women.'

Startled, I stuttered a little; I do not regard Esther as mature – at least, not in Mrs Annabella's sense. But was she trying to hint she had a specific gentleman in mind? I wondered if the gentleman in question had her in mind.

'Do you continue to teach, Mr Patterson?' Mrs Jenison asked. She sounded anxious, as if a new worry had occurred to her.

'Indeed.'

'Oh, no,' Mrs Annabella said, shocked, 'that must be such hard work!'

Mrs Jenison frowned then smiled graciously. 'Teaching music cannot surely be described as anything so menial as *work*. Music is a vocation.'

'An Art,' I agreed.

'And a delightful one,' she said, pouring me more tea. 'It

cannot be considered—' a little shudder— '*work* to pass on the pleasures of one of the Creator's greatest gifts.'

And so, I reflected, any disturbing circumstance can be got over with a little effort. Mr Patterson is a gentleman (now, at least) and gentlemen don't work. Therefore his teaching cannot *be* work. I had thought it would go the other way: gentlemen don't work, Mr Patterson *does* work, therefore he's not a gentleman.

Mrs Annabella, clearly put out at being chastised, snatched at a workbox on the table between the two ladies, pulled out a piece of embroidery and regarded it with furious concentration. She took up a pair of delicate engraved scissors, snipped off a length of thread and reached for a needle. Her nose in the air all the time as if she was above such dull things as everyday conversation.

The drawing-room door opened. Mr Robert Jenison stood on the threshold. I rose. He nodded, said, 'Ah! Patterson!' as if he hadn't known I'd be there, although the servants must have told him.

'Tea, dear?' Mrs Jenison asked.

He visibly recoiled. He was a man of medium height and more and more rotund as the years passed, but he compensated for these imperfections with dull businesslike wigs and sombre clothing that made it clear he was a man of good solid worth. But today he was hesitant, not quite meeting my gaze. 'And how *is* Mrs Patterson?'

I sighed inwardly. 'Very well indeed.'

He cleared his throat. 'Good, good.' He covered his obvious unease by fumbling in a pocket as if for a lost coin. 'And to what do we owe this pleasure, Patterson?'

At last! I put down my dish of tea. 'I was wondering whether you and Mrs Jenison, and Mrs Annabella of course, would honour me by subscribing to this winter's concerts.'

His face cleared. This, his manner said at once, was something he knew how to deal with. He took the subscription ticket from me and regarded it approvingly. 'Printer's done a damn fine job, wouldn't you say?'

'Indeed.'

'This fellow we've got coming to sing this year is the real thing!' he said enthusiastically. He put the tickets down on the table, I noticed, which meant he'd accepted them; now all I had to do was to get him to pay for them. 'We saw Mr Nightingale in London last winter, did we not, my dear?'

'Oh indeed,' Mrs Jenison said, without a great deal of warmth. 'He was excellent.'

'So charming,' Mrs Annabella said, simpering. 'So handsome. A fine gentleman.' Her gaze grew misty again; she let the needlework drop to her lap. I wondered if Mr Richard Nightingale was a handsome figure of a young man, with a pleasing way with the ladies.

'Wasted in London,' Jenison said. 'Not properly appreciated.'

'He was so light on his feet,' Mrs Annabella said, with a reminiscent smile. She put a hand on her heart as if to stop it palpitating. 'And when he stood on top of the ladder, I was quite afraid he would fall off!'

There had to be some way to head off the worst excesses of this rapture. 'But is the Assembly Room ceiling quite high enough for ladder dancing?' I wondered.

Jenison frowned. 'Possibly not.' He dismissed the problem with a wave of his hand. 'In any case, the dancing is a mere novelty. I've hired him for his singing.'

'Handel,' Mrs Jenison said. 'And Vivaldi.'

'Indeed?' I said hollowly. I've never dared tell Jenison how much I dislike Vivaldi; Jenison adores his music.

'You should have heard him, Patterson!' he said warmly. 'Quite astonishing! I've never heard anyone imitate the trumpet so well.'

'I've often said we should have trumpets in the band,' Mrs Jenison said.

This suggestion was easy to deal with; it had been raised before, and I had my answer ready. 'Unfortunately,' I pointed out, 'we'd have to bring in musicians from a military band.'

'Soldiers?' Mrs Annabella said, sitting up and clearly thinking of smart uniforms.

Her brother frowned. 'I think we all know how the military behave, Patterson; we don't want their sort in respectable company. But Mr Nightingale is an admirable solution. We can have our trumpets without the attendant unpleasantnesses!'

'Admirable,' I said. 'Excellent.' Vivaldi wrote a trumpet concerto, I recalled, and wondered if I could avert a very trying situation by claiming we were mere provincials and the shops didn't stock the music.

The door opened; the servant said with sonorous politeness, 'Mr Claudius Heron.'

Mrs Annabella sat up. Her hand went to her hair to pat it into place; she straightened her petticoats, pinned a gentle smile to her face. Good God, I thought, it's Heron she's after. A widower with extensive estates, coal mines aplenty, ships on the river and an elegant town house. The young son was a disadvantage, of course, but not an insuperable one.

Heron – my patron – lingered in the doorway, his gaze slipping from one to another of us. A slight fair-haired man in his forties; to use Mrs Annabella's phrase, he was not in the first flush of youth. But lean and handsome, and a man who had every confidence in himself and his position in the world. Just the sort to appeal to a maiden lady.

I wondered if Mrs Annabella had ever been on the wrong side of his cynical tongue.

Jenison was making the necessary polite noises of greeting; the footman was waiting his chance to continue his interrupted announcement. For there was someone else behind Heron, a nervous-looking young man who was wringing his hands together and reminding me uncannily of the Rev. Mr Orrick.

The footman took a deep breath. 'Mr Cuthbert Ridley.'

I caught my breath. *Cuthbert Ridley*. And I saw again a bag flung over a horse's back, and gold intertwined letters embossed into the leather.

CR.

Six

A gentleman should always be at ease, neither too forward nor too reticent.

[*A Gentleman's Companion*, October 1735]

I knew of Ridley, of course, as one knows of the younger sons of gentlemen one meets now and again. His father's a Director of the concerts – although he's travelling somewhere in the Baltic at this time – and two of his elder brothers occasionally turn up to yawn their way through concertos and symphonies, and ogle the young ladies in the interval. Cuthbert, I fancied, had been at Oxford, then somewhere in London, studying for the church, or the law, or something of the sort.

I scrutinized him as he bowed to the ladies. Tall, ungainly, possibly a few years younger than myself, twenty-three or twenty-four years old. His fresh raw skin and rash of freckles made him look younger. Under a fashionable tiny wig, which sat on his head like a feather on an egg, there was a stubble which suggested his own hair was probably red. He had a habit of fidgeting with his hands and when he sat down, he kept his gaze fixed on his knees, and mumbled and blushed.

Mrs Annabella was concentrating her attention on Claudius Heron. 'Your son is well, I hope?'

Heron hesitated, as if it took him a moment to remember he had a son. 'Very well, madam.'

'Such a charming boy.'

Heron paused. 'He promises well.' I silently applauded his phrasing; as the boy's harpsichord teacher, I knew he did indeed promise well but rarely kept his promises.

Jenison intervened. He wanted to pontificate on the price of coal; both he and Heron had mines on their property. Mrs Annabella smiled and nodded, and tried to give the impression of intelligently understanding what they said. Mrs Jenison was asking the servant to bring yet more hot water; I manoeuvred myself into a position next to Cuthbert Ridley.

He'd wrapped his hands round his tea-dish, and was staring fixedly into its depths. It was ridiculous to suspect a man of murder simply because of his initials, but Ridley was the only gentleman I knew with those initials, and I was certain the horse rider could only be a gentleman, from the cut of his clothes and the quality of his horse. Besides, what harm could it do to ask a few questions?

'You've been in London, I think?'

He started, stared at me like a hunted hare, mumbled.

'At the Inns of Court?' I suggested.

He nodded. So he'd been studying the law; I couldn't imagine how he'd ever bring himself to talk to any client.

'Have you come home to practise?'

He gulped tea, mumbled into the dish. In heaven's name, he was a full-grown man, not a shy child! I repressed my irritation. 'To see your family then. Have you been home long?'

Mrs Jenison smiled kindly at him. 'I saw your mother only yesterday. She said you were home. Thursday, was it not?'

The day before the child died. Ridley jerked his head.

'You rode, I suppose,' I said.

'It's much the best way,' Mrs Jenison agreed comfortably. 'The roads are so poor, the carriage jolts from side to side or gets caught in a quagmire. I find it intolerable! I trust you had no accident, sir.'

He shook his head. I was briefly distracted by realizing that Heron's gaze was on me. Did he want to say something? But he went back to his conversation with Jenison.

'I daresay you left your horse at the Fleece,' Mrs Annabella said comfortably, abandoning the gentlemen temporarily. 'Such an excellent hostelry. We dined there in the spring when we came back from London, while we were waiting for our chairs home. By far the best inn in town.'

'Nonsense,' Jenison said, catching this. 'They took an age to serve us. The George is the best. I've recommended it to our concert soloist and booked rooms for him there.'

'The Fleece *is* a warren of a place,' Mrs Annabella conceded, pliantly changing course. 'I got lost there. Twice! Ended up in the kitchens!'

'And the servants were not polite,' Jenison pursued, and went off into an anecdote about the insolence of a serving girl. I paid little attention, formulating my next question for Ridley, and, as I turned back to him, I caught him glancing at me out of the corner of his eye.

He looked hurriedly back into his tea.

'Have you been solving any more mysteries lately, Mr Patterson?' Mrs Annabella asked. She didn't allow me time for a reply but rushed on, smiling at Ridley who'd lifted his gaze from his tea an inch or two. 'Our Mr Patterson is very clever, you know. He catches murderers.'

That made me curse inwardly. If Ridley was indeed to blame for the child's death, Mrs Annabella's revelations would only make him wary of me.

'I wonder,' Jenison mused, having apparently changed tack while I was not listening, 'whether we should invite Mr Nightingale to dinner.'

Mrs Jenison looked astonished, but covered it up well. I couldn't imagine she was used to having entertainers at her dinner table. 'Whatever you wish, my dear.'

'To welcome him to the town,' Jenison said. 'He really is a most superior man.'

'Really?' Heron said dryly.

'You must meet him. Come to dinner too. And you, Patterson,' he said, warming to his subject. 'I'm sure he'll be of interest to you. As an example of a highly talented man. An example to emulate.'

I managed to avoid wincing.

'And Mrs Patterson must come too,' Mrs Jenison said, clearly hoping to give her dinner table some respectability. 'You *will* come, Mr Heron?'

'Of course,' Heron said.

'Such a gentleman,' Mrs Annabella said, almost swooning. I was unsure whether she was referring to Heron or Nightingale.

A little later Heron and I stood on Jenison's doorstep, watching the sun lower over the roofs of the houses on the other side of the street. A breeze lifted a strand of Heron's pale hair and wafted it across his forehead; like me, he prefers not to wear a wig. A cart struggled up the slope of the road; the carter climbed down to lead the horse. Inside the house, I could hear Mrs Annabella bidding a prolonged and verbose farewell to Ridley.

'This Nightingale must be special to tempt Jenison to invite him to dinner,' I said.

Heron's lips tightened. 'I have the greatest respect for Jenison's abilities as a businessman, but I have always found his taste highly suspect.'

'He heard the fellow in London in March. I hope he doesn't charge London prices.'

'We have had correspondence on the matter,' Heron said, dryly. He too is one of the Directors of the concerts. 'I suspect that if he brings his ladder with him, I shall find it remarkably difficult to get to concerts this season.'

'The prospect seems to be *encouraging* some people to buy tickets,' I said ruefully, and hesitated, watching the carter. I was reluctant to confide my suspicions to Heron – or to anyone for that matter – since they rested on such flimsy foundations, but he might have information which would help me, either to confirm Ridley was the villain, or to exonerate him. I said casually, 'I've not met Cuthbert Ridley before. He's been away from town some years, I understand?'

'Damn near ten,' Heron said, with surprising vehemence. 'He was sent to an uncle in London, then went on to Oxford from there. The last year or so he has been back in London practising the law with his uncle.'

'He's very shy.'

Heron was contemptuous. 'Affectation.'

I stared in surprise. 'He acts the part? But why?'

'I have long since ceased to make the effort to understand.' The carter had stopped to unload beer barrels two or three houses up the street; the breeze bowled his hat away and he ran after it. 'If it were possible,' Heron said, 'I would wash my hands of him completely. However, my late wife was his mother's closest friend and so I was appointed his godfather.'

'You're introducing him into local society?'

'I have promised his mother I will.' He grimaced. 'It is not likely to be an easy task. In the absence of his father, I am also supposed to find him a position, but since he clearly does not wish to exert himself in the slightest, that looks to be more difficult still. He seems to make it his business to defy his mother at every turn.'

'He's young,' I said. 'Sowing his wild oats.'

'I shudder to think how wild,' Heron said dryly. 'Some of his uncle's stories are, to say the least, disquieting.' He gave me a quick glance. 'I would advise you to stay out of his way.'

I was startled. 'You think—'

'I think he's a malicious fool,' he said.

A noise behind us. We both glanced back into the Jenisons' house. Ridley was saying something to the footman who was presenting him with his hat and cane; the footman looked faintly unsettled. Heron's hand started tapping a gentle tattoo against his thigh; he said, 'Do you have time to give me a violin lesson, Patterson? Tomorrow, perhaps?'

It was plainly impossible to talk further now and I wondered if Heron's request was intended to provide an opportunity to continue our conversation. I was relieved that he at least assumed I'd continue to teach despite my new-found wealth; Heron has a very fine sense of what is appropriate behaviour and what is not.

We parted; Heron bore Ridley off towards the centre of town, with brisk steps that oozed irritation. I paused to decide which house to visit next, then caught a glimpse of movement. I looked round to see Ridley staring back at me.

The look stopped me in my tracks. There was a kind of mockery in it. Did I fancy a challenge there?

But then Ridley turned away and I was left wondering if my imagination had got the better of me.

Seven

Every man and woman has a natural place in the world, and it should be the endeavour of every man and woman to be content with their lot, whether it be high or low.
[*A Gentleman's Companion*, June 1733]

I'd time for one last call on a potential concert subscriber. I turned my footsteps towards Westgate but I was preoccupied with thoughts of Ridley. It was difficult to judge − I'd seen the man on the horse so briefly − but I thought Ridley was roughly the same height. The horseman had seemed more stocky but his thick greatcoat might account for that.

I came out on to Westgate directly opposite the clockmaker's which stands almost as high as the West Gate itself. Above the clockmaker lives my friend, the dancing master Hugh Demsey, but he was not in town at present; immediately after our wedding, he set off on one of his regular visits to London to learn the latest dances. He would inevitably return full of amusing anecdotes. Hugh seems to enjoy London; my own single visit there was less than entertaining.

The sun was just sinking behind the houses on the other side of the street, plunging Westgate into gloom. I paused to let my eyes adjust— and heard a small sound. The scuff of hasty footsteps. I swung round, alarmed.

An alley. Empty.

'Round the corner,' an obliging spirit said high above me. It sounded as if it was stifling a bored yawn. 'Female, stinking clothes. Filthy face. Young, but old enough to know better.'

It sounded remarkably like the young girl I'd seen in the hovel. 'What's she doing?'

'Lurking,' the spirit said with relish.

'Why?'

'Ask her yourself,' the spirit said. 'She's still there. Round the corner.'

'Alone?'

'She'll charge,' the spirit said, jumping to conclusions. 'Some of 'em even charge a guinea, sir. And they're never clean. Leave her be, that's my advice.'

'I'm a happily married man,' I said dryly.

'Doesn't stop them asking, sir.' And the spirit added, with a touch of gloom, 'I was happily married once. For a day or two.'

I walked into the darkening alley, keeping a sharp lookout for danger. A twelve-year-old girl was unlikely to do me much harm, but she might have a weapon. The alley turned a corner and became a dead end, giving access only to a broken-down door into a yard. The girl was leaning against the end wall, one foot kicking back at the bricks.

I kept my distance. A stray patch of sunshine touched a grimy window high up, glinted brightly.

'You took your time,' the girl said.

'People who rush into alleys often end up robbed,' I said. 'Did you want to talk to me? About the baby?'

'Nah,' she said scornfully. 'Good riddance. Ma's always having kids. Too many. We don't have nothing to eat. She's real cut up, mind,' she added as an afterthought. 'She loves babies. Goes all soft over them. It's when we starts talking back she hates us.'

I thanked God for my own comfortable upbringing, even though my father had been cold and distant, especially after my mother's death. 'So why did you want to talk to me?'

'You're the fiddler, right?' She was still kicking the wall, rhythmically, regularly, more and more ferociously.

'I'm a musician, yes.'

'So's I. Here, listen to this.'

And she took a ridiculously large breath and launched into a popular ballad.

She was the girl I'd heard singing in the fog the night the child died, carolling bawdy songs far too old for her. Although, with the kind of upbringing she must have had, there were probably few of the more sordid aspects of life she hadn't seen. But her knowledge of the niceties of singing was annoyingly lacking.

'Don't breathe so deeply,' I said irritably, as she sucked in another breath. The glint of sunshine from the window was shining in my eyes. 'And don't bawl. You were singing far better than that on the Key.'

She scowled at me.

'Start again. Quieter. And don't breathe in the middle of a line.'

She stared, then surprised me by grinning. She heaved herself off the wall, stood up straight and began again. The childishly sweet voice was small and thin, and only of average quality, but she used it well, in an untutored kind of way, acting out the song with some relish, particularly the gory parts.

'So,' I said, when she was finished. 'What do you want now? A shilling for your trouble?'

'Nah,' she said. 'Anyone can give me that. I want to be your apprentice.'

The audacity of the request took me aback. She was filthy, wore rags, had a raucous speaking voice, and every bone of her was insolent; I tried to imagine her being polite to the ladies and gentlemen, and failed miserably. Besides, if I took on a girl as apprentice, the most unflattering of conclusions would be drawn; it's well known that female apprentices in the music world are frequently obliged to be 'friendly' to their masters.

And she'd no idea what she was asking from the financial point of view. 'Apprentices are required to pay their master for taking them on,' I said. I felt a pang of guilt mentioning this; I could now of course afford to forgo the premium. But it was a convenient excuse to discourage what was obviously a totally impossible suggestion.

'How much?' she said suspiciously.

'Ten guineas.'

'You're making that up!'

'No. And their parents pay the master for their board and lodgings.'

'Don't want that,' she said. 'I'll live with our ma.'

'Every penny they earn goes to their master.'

'That's unfair,' she said indignantly. 'You're fibbing.'

'You can check what I say with any apprentice you can find.

Besides, I'm a harpsichordist and violinist by trade. I'm not the best person to teach anyone how to sing.'

'I already know how to sing.'

'You do not,' I said forcibly.

'Anyhow.' She started kicking the wall again. 'Don't want to sing. Want to play the fiddle.'

Worse and worse. I sighed and squinted against the glint from the window. It was starting to give me a headache. 'The violin is not a suitable instrument for a young woman.'

'Why not?'

'A young lady should not make energetic movements. It's not polite.'

She grinned. 'I'm not a young lady.'

'No,' I agreed, fervently.

'So I can learn it?'

'No, you can't!'

We stared at each other. She said, 'You won't take me on, then?'

'It really would be impossible.'

Her expression changed. The foot kicked back one last vicious time. 'Then I'll tell,' she said. 'I'll tell everyone.'

'About what?' I said, bewildered.

'This!' And she darted forward and seized my hand.

The next moment I felt a violent shiver of cold, saw a flicker of darkness. A jolt as if I'd stumbled. Then I was standing under a midnight sky, with the full moon a brilliant shining orb overhead.

Eight

Those whom you see to be in danger of committing serious error should be reasoned with, but if they will not yield, it is better to withdraw for fear of being dragged down with them.

[*A Gentleman's Companion*, March 1730]

There is a secret world that runs alongside our own, next to it, yet separate, like pages in a book. I stumbled upon it a year or so ago, in company with a villain who was making use of it for nefarious purposes, and as far as I know – or as far as I have suspected until now – the only people who are aware of this world are those I have told.

It frightened me at first. To find myself thrown out of my own world, the *real* world, the *only* world, and to be inexplicably precipitated into some other universe, overthrew every idea I had ever taken for granted as true. The only 'other' world, we are taught, is that we hear about in church every Sunday; how can another world exist? And so similar to ours too. The streets look much the same, there are people walking and talking. My own counterpart lives there and the counterparts of many of the people I know. There are small differences: houses that have disappeared, people who have died who still live in our own world, events that happen at different times. The only substantial difference is that this secret world has no spirits and does not seem to know their lack. I have never been able to discover what happens here to the dead.

Over the months, I have *stepped through* to this world more and more, and have become increasingly at ease. Intrigued, even. At first I could not control what happened, now I can – at least to a certain extent. I never know exactly what to expect when I reach this other world, or quite when I will arrive back in my own world; time does not seem to run at the same rate. If I pass an hour in this world, I can find myself missing a day in my own world.

But I have never known anyone else who could *step through* except for the villain who first brought me here and who is now dead. To find the ability in a child . . .

Around us stretched silent fields, moonlit. Trees in the winter-bare hedges were silvered by the bright light; beyond the hedges stood the obscure hulks of houses. A distant church bell struck once, twice. There a was a chill of frost in the air. There's rarely any movement from place to place in stepping through. I was almost certainly still on the same spot in Westgate; the town could not be as extensive in this world. I stared around, feeling again the unnerving strangeness of it, the even more unsettling familiarity.

'Don't know how it happens,' the girl said. She flung her arms out, swung round and round. 'Just does. One moment I'm at home, next I'm here.' She was grinning like a child half her age, a child without a care in the world. 'You know what it's like.'

I said nothing.

'Saw you,' she said. 'Couple of months back. In that big square. Just took a step forward and disappeared. And no one noticed!' She grinned still wider. 'They never do!'

That came as a relief. I'd often wondered why no one noticed my disappearances. Perhaps you need to have the ability yourself to see it in others.

'I followed you,' she said, 'and you ended up in a big street, talking to a weedy fellow.'

I didn't recall the occasion but it could easily have happened. I regarded her thoughtfully. It's nearly a year now since I discovered my ability and in all that time I've carefully kept the secret, knowing the ignorant might fear it. But would this girl be as discreet?

She was grinning still, standing hands on hips. 'Nice here, ain't it?' she said. 'Quiet. I can walk and walk and no one ever yells at me.' She broke into song, her thin voice echoing in the still clear night. A simple love song of the naïve country sort, wistful and longing, seeping into the silence.

The echoes of the song died away and I heard the faint bleat of a sleepy sheep in the distance.

'I ain't going to be like ma,' the girl said passionately. 'I ain't going to go with every man as asks. I ain't going to end up with a dozen babies and nothing to eat. I want out.'

'I can understand that.'

'So,' she said. 'You take me on as apprentice and learn me to play the fiddle proper, then when I've learnt everything, you set me free and I get to keep all the money I earn. That's the way it works, ain't it?'

'Apprenticeships last seven years,' I pointed out.

'Lord,' she said. 'You gets your money's worth.'

'There's a lot to learn.'

She grinned. 'We're agreed, then?'

'We are not!'

She screwed up her face. 'I'll tell!' she shouted. 'I'll tell everyone!'

'You'll tell them there's another world running alongside our own, a near copy? They'll lock you up as a madwoman.'

'No smoke without fire, they'll say!'

Would they? I'd always been undecided. Hugh Demsey insisted I'd be had up by the Church as a heretic; Esther thought they'd call me a lunatic. It was undeniable that rumours, once started, take on a life of their own. People like Mrs Annabella, for instance, are quite capable of discarding things they dislike or can't understand, and substituting something more palatable. Within days, I'd probably be condemned for leading a double life with a wife in every town in the north-east; Sunderland and London are about as much of *another world* as most people can imagine.

I stared across the deserted field, feeling the nip of frost.

'Well?' the girl demanded.

'I'll think about it,' I said.

She recognized this for the sop it was. 'That ain't good enough.'

'It will have to do.'

'No,' she said obstinately.

I tried to stare her down. Her eyes met mine defiantly; her chin lifted.

'I will not be blackmailed,' I said. 'The only way you'll persuade me to help is by showing yourself amenable.'

She started to sneer. I said sharply, 'I don't mean in that way. If those are the depths to which you're prepared to sink then you may as well stay where you are. I want information.'

'What about?' she said sullenly.

I almost stopped myself. There was an element of callous cynicism in what I was about to do; she'd certainly believe that if she told me what I wanted to know, I'd reconsider taking her on, and that was not possible. But the image of that child's body, laid out on a table in the Old Man tavern for the inquest jury to gawp at, urged me on.

'Your mother,' I said. 'I take it she earns money by selling herself?'

She shrugged. 'They ain't choosy down our way.'

'Has anyone ever threatened her?'

She cackled with laughter. 'Never had to! She never said no to no one.'

'I was thinking of respectable gentlemen who might have been with her. She might think to get some extra money out of them by threatening to tell their nearest and dearest. And one of them might decide to try to silence her.'

'She never went with no one respectable in her life. Anyhow, it was the baby what died.'

I nodded. 'But that was purely chance. If the sailors hadn't been so quick, your mother might have died as well.'

She considered this. 'Nah. No one wants rid of her but me.'

Had it been a chance encounter, then? Had the woman simply been unlucky, in the wrong place as the horseman rode by? If that was the case, the child's death was even more tragic.

'You were there,' I said. 'I heard you singing. What did you see?'

'Nowt,' she said. 'Couldn't see my own hand.'

Thinking back to the fog, I believed her. But random chance – a death with neither rhyme nor reason behind it! How was I ever to prove anything?

'Do you know a man called Cuthbert Ridley?'

She was beginning to get bored. 'Nah. Don't tell you their names.' She smoothed down her petticoats as neatly as Mrs Annabella ever did. 'You thought enough yet?'

'Not yet, no.'

She grinned. 'Don't take too long. I'll be back.' And she danced off across the moonlit field.

Nine

A gentleman is always up to date in his accounts, and spends wisely.

[*A Gentleman's Companion*, December 1733]

I turned round, took one step, and found myself back in the dead end alley in my own world. Shivering, I walked briskly out on to Westgate, worrying about how much time might have passed. Then I heard St Nicholas's church clock strike and realized with relief I'd only lost half an hour or so.

What the devil was I to do about the girl? It was only a short walk, across Westgate and along a side street, to Caroline Square where Esther lives – where *I* live – but I managed to work myself into a fine frenzy of indecision. No one would actually believe the girl. Would they? Even the most ridiculous stories can gain credence, and I'd no wish to be thought a lunatic. But taking the girl on as an apprentice was out of the question. The assumptions that would be made! Besides, there's no railing against facts, and the fact is that a violin is simply not a suitable instrument for a woman.

I'd hardly opened the front door of the house when Tom, the manservant, appeared in the hall. He's barely twenty years old but proud of being the only male servant in the house, and assiduous in the performance of his duties. George was faster, however; Tom had hardly opened his mouth when the spirit slid down the banister, yelling. 'Notes for you, master! *Two* notes! On the table!'

I glanced at Tom. He straightened, put on a bland face. I'd caught his first reaction, however; he was furious.

'George,' I said, 'it's Tom's job to inform me of such things.'

'Just trying to help, master!'

'I can see that,' I conceded.

'You always used to tell me to keep busy!'

'Yes, but—'

'But, master?'

But you're dead, George, and there's nothing you can do except hang around for eighty years or so, getting in the way. 'Tom must earn his keep,' I pointed out, 'and it's not kind to trespass on his duties.'

'But I can do things much faster than he can!'

'It's not your job, George.'

'But master!' He dropped into the wheedling tone all boys of a certain age have, that they're fondly convinced will persuade you to do exactly what they want. If they use the tone long enough, they're usually right. I let him talk. If he'd been alive, I'd simply have snapped at him to bring him into line; now he was dead, things were more complicated. An angry spirit can cause havoc; if he chose, George could make the house impossible to live in.

I sneaked another look at Tom. He was patently very anxious. I managed to interrupt George. 'Is Mrs Patterson in, Tom?' *Mrs Patterson.* My heart missed a beat. Ridiculous!

'She's in the estate room, sir,' he murmured.

I dismissed them both; Tom went with dignified calm, George grumbled his way upstairs. I headed for the back of the house, glancing quickly at the notes as I went. One was from Hugh Demsey, detailing the fine time he was having in

London and promising to be back in a week at most (which certainly meant four or five weeks at least). The other was from Robert Jenison.

> *Patterson* [it said with imperious brevity], *Mr Richard Nightingale will be arriving at seven tomorrow morning by the mail coach. Pray meet him at the Golden Fleece and convey him to the George where he is to lodge.*

At the end of this peremptory missive, he had the audacity to describe himself as my 'obedient servant'.

The estate room is small and crammed with shelves and boxes and letter books and all the other paraphernalia necessary to the administration of Esther's estates in Northumberland and Norfolk. No doubt there are ten times as many documents sitting in various lawyers' offices about the country. It's the most daunting room I've ever been in. Esther – my *wife* – was sitting at the desk by the window, a bundle of correspondence in front of her. She was wearing a gown of pale green; the last of the sunlight glinted on the golden tendrils of hair curled against her gracefully bowed neck. I longed to run my fingers over that soft skin, that curve of neck, to take a strand of hair and—

No, this really would not do. Certainly not in the middle of the day. And at that moment, she looked up and I saw she was steeling herself for battle. But she merely smiled and said, 'You look tired. Let me ring for some brandy.'

Tom came and went again. George presumably had taken himself off to some dark corner of the house, or was tormenting the cook. I enjoyed looking at Esther while she murmured platitudes about the weather. The gown showed off her neat figure wonderfully. I loved the way she moved – elegantly but businesslike – the way she cast a sideways glance at me. She had a smudge of ink on one cheek that I longed to rub away . . .

'Have you solved the mystery?' she asked.

I dragged my thoughts back. 'I visited the mother.' I told her about my trip to the hovel where the woman lived, and about my encounter with the girl (though without mentioning the other world) and her desire to become my apprentice. Tom brought the brandy and disappeared again. To my surprise, Esther gave the girl some serious consideration. 'It is impossible, of course—'

'Of course.'

'But one has to admire the girl for her desire to better herself.' She sipped her brandy. 'Do you think Mr Orrick might be able to do something for her?'

I couldn't imagine the curate being effective in dealing with young women. 'I'll ask,' I said without conviction. The conversation had taken a serious turn so I regaled Esther with my adventures at the Jenisons. Esther shared my views of Mrs Jenison's feather pictures, chuckled at Jenison's raptures over the ladder dancer, and admitted, slightly ruefully, to pitying Mrs Annabella.

'I don't,' I retorted. 'She's the worst kind of elderly spinster.'

'I was a spinster too until three weeks ago,' she pointed out.

'Only in the sense of being unmarried,' I said. 'Nothing more. You could never be as coy and fawning as she.'

'She has to placate the people on whom she is dependent. She cannot afford to do otherwise. There was a time, not so long ago, I was in a similar situation.' She looked at me shrewdly. 'What else are you not telling me?'

She knew me too well. Ruefully, I told her about Cuthbert Ridley. She listened with a frown growing between her eyes. The sort of frown I longed to kiss away.

'You can't suspect a man simply because of his initials, Charles!'

'He's not a nice man,' I said, remembering that last look he'd cast me.

'Neither is the fishmonger but he is a man of appalling rectitude.' She pondered for a moment. 'I am acquainted with the family, of course. Ridley's, I mean, not the fishmonger's. The mother is a very good woman. The elder son is not well, I think, and the other is perfectly ordinary and dull. The father is away somewhere.'

'Narva, according to Heron. Negotiating with timber merchants, apparently. Who else do you know with the initials *CR*?'

She shook her head. 'No one. But that is nothing to the purpose. The horseman could have been a visitor to the town.'

'Heaven forbid!' I said. 'In that case, he'll be long gone and we'll never catch him.' I looked at her curiously. 'You believe me, don't you? About it being murder. What changed your mind? This morning you were accusing me of overreacting.'

She nodded. 'I have had time to think about it. I trust your judgement, Charles.'

I could find nothing to say. I caught my breath, looked into my brandy. It was a greater compliment than I'd been prepared for.

Esther started to say something, stopped. I sipped my brandy, pretended I hadn't heard. She said, with sudden vehemence, 'Charles, we cannot go on ignoring this problem.'

I fell from joy straight into anger. 'There's no problem. Give me the relevant papers and I'll sign them.'

'I believe you would find it more satisfactory if you were to understand the workings of the estates.'

'Alas,' I said lightly. 'I was never one for financial dealings.'

'Nonsense,' she retorted. 'Any man who can survive on no more than sixty pounds a year without falling into debt understands financial matters very well.'

I felt cornered. 'You'd hate to give up the management of your estates.'

'*Your* estates.'

'I'm quite happy to let you carry on dealing with them. You're so good at it.'

'That is not the point, Charles!'

'You mean you're going to insist on me dealing with them even if it means we go bankrupt within a year?'

'Now you are exaggerating,' she said impatiently. 'You can learn—'

'I do not want to learn!' I exploded. 'I am a musician, not a land agent!'

She visibly took a deep breath to steel herself before replying, which annoyed me even more. Was I so irritating to deal with? 'This is a matter of legalities, Charles. These estates do not belong to me any longer. They are yours.'

'Then I appoint you my steward,' I said. 'He would deal with all the routine matters, would he not, and merely ask for my signature? Very well, you are now my steward!'

'Oh, *really*, Charles!' she said, exasperated.

There was an uncomfortable silence. I prowled across the room, stared out of the window, gulped down my brandy. Esther said nothing, but sat at the desk with her hands clasped on its paper-cluttered surface. The reddening sunlight gleamed on her cheeks, her golden hair . . .

I could not bear it. To be at odds with her was unendurable.

'I ordered *two* coats,' I said. 'And a waistcoat. But without embroidery. Even though I was assured the latest thing in decoration is bumble bees, I couldn't do it. I've always hated honey.'

She burst out laughing. I watched the way her whole face lit up, the delicious crinkles at the side of her eyes, the elegant line of throat as her head tipped back. 'But you did not order new breeches?' she said in mock reproach.

'You're never satisfied.'

She held my gaze, smiled, said consideringly, 'We have just argued, Charles. For the first time.'

'Alas—' I caught her meaning, added more enthusiastically, 'Definitely, we have argued.'

'I do believe there is a popular saying—'

'About making up—'

'– being the best part of any argument.' She gave me a look as coy as any of Mrs Annabella's.

I gestured at the papers. 'Do you not need to finish your work?'

'Work!' she said, horrified. 'A lady never *works*, Charles!'

She stood and came across to me, took the brandy glass from my fingers. I didn't resist.

'Cook will have the beef already cooking,' I pointed out, teasingly. 'What will she say if we're late and it burns?'

She took my hand. 'Charles,' she said, 'I am not married to the cook! Now come on.'

Fortunately, we didn't see any of the servants on our way upstairs.

Ten

Outward appearance is always a true sign of inward nature.
[*A Gentleman's Companion*, September 1734]

A thin cold drizzle dampened the cobbles as I walked under the arch into the yard of the Golden Fleece. It was early, much too early for a newly married man; I began to wonder how fond Jenison was of his wife if he regarded getting up for the morning coach as a matter of indifference. One thing newly married couples are never warned about is the difficulty finding time to sleep.

A friendly spirit slid round the walls to keep me company. 'Off on your travels again, Mr Patterson?' The spirit had been an ostler in life, trampled to death by a frightened horse, an event he delights in narrating in unnerving detail.

'Meeting someone off the coach.'

The spirit sighed wistfully. 'I always wanted to travel but the furthest I ever got was Sunderland.'

'My condolences,' I murmured.

'Is he coming far, sir?'

'From London.'

'Now there's a man of good sense,' the spirit said. 'Why should anyone want to stay in that pit of iniquity?'

I shivered in the drizzle and contemplated a horse that was being led into the yard. It was a dark grey, and my mind slipped back to that other grey, that had ridden down the woman and child. If that was Ridley's horse, it would be stabled at his mother's house by now, a mile out of town on the Carlisle road. There was no possibility of getting a look at it; I'd no excuse to go there – Mrs Ridley is not musical.

There was a rattle of wheels. 'Here it is now, sir,' said the spirit. The coach appeared, slowing to take the arch into the inn, the coachman ducking low to avoid the roof. The horses blew gusts of rank breath into the cold air.

The Fleece's servants rushed forward; doors were pulled open, steps let down. Someone thrust a tankard of ale into the coachman's hands as he clambered to the ground; men began to untie parcels from the roof of the coach. I was relieved to see there was no ladder amongst them. Was that a good sign, or would Nightingale expect me to find a ladder for him? Jenison didn't want dancing in the concerts but Nightingale might have different ideas.

The first passenger down was a burly middle-aged man, tall and richly dressed in an astonishingly bright green, and an elaborate wig that made his head seem three times as big as normal. Imperiously, he brushed the servants out of the way, then turned to extend a hand to another passenger unseen.

Out tottered an immensely elderly lady, very tiny, muffled

up in a hundred cloaks and shawls. Her gratified simper was not hidden, however, as she allowed the gentleman to help her down. He bowed extravagantly, kissed the back of her gloved hand, murmured a compliment. She blushed.

There were five women in the coach, all well beyond their first youth and all immensely grateful to the gentleman for his assistance. They clustered round him, pressing thanks on him, showering him with appreciative gifts: an apple, a wrapped-up pie (*best London lamb*, the giver murmured seductively), a news-paper, a twist of tobacco. The gentleman kissed the hands of his adoring court. Behind the ladies, a young lad stood on the coach steps, ignored and sullen.

The lad seemed to be the only other male on the coach so this extravagantly dressed gentleman must be Richard Nightingale. I studied him as he paid out compliments by the score, told one elderly lady she must have a dozen beaux, told another he'd never seen such an elegant shawl on a 'young lady'. One thanked him for *such a wonderfully entertaining end to a long tedious journey*, another insisted he must visit her if he was ever in her part of the country.

The servants at last managed to usher the ladies away out of the drizzle to the warmth of a fire, a dish of tea and a comfort-able bed. The lad went off with a foul glance at Nightingale, suggesting he felt utterly eclipsed. Nightingale, deprived of an audience, yawned hugely and stretched.

I bowed. 'Mr Nightingale? I'm Charles Patterson, Mr Jenison's . . . *envoy*. Was the journey comfortable?'

He squinted as if not sure what to make of me. Then his gaze settled on my shabby coat and frayed cuffs, and he plainly decided he didn't have to honour me with any particular politeness. 'Damnable,' he said bluntly. 'I'm long past the days I could bear travelling day and night. Where the devil's the food? And the girls.'

Perhaps Esther was right about the coat giving the wrong impression. 'Mr Jenison's booked a room for you at the George Inn,' I said mildly. 'It has an excellent reputation. If you'd allow me to escort you there?'

He eyed me for a moment, then raised his head and looked round at the hustle and bustle of the Golden Fleece. 'Devil a bit of it. I'll stay here.'

'I believe—'

'Ostler!' he roared. 'Send my luggage in. Fast as you can.'
And he strode off into the inn.

I sighed, hurried to catch up with him. Jenison was not
going to be pleased at the oversettings of his plans; he was a
man accustomed to be obeyed. And the George was undoubt-
edly of better quality than the Fleece, quieter, more comfortable.
But it looked as if *quieter* at least was not to Nightingale's taste.
He ducked under a low lintel into a private parlour, issuing
orders to half a dozen servants. Bed, beef, beer: he wanted
everything instantly.

He dropped into a comfortable chair and swung his legs up
on to a scarred table that stood in the middle of the room. 'Is
there any decent entertainment this far north?'

'We're not in Scotland,' I said, needled by his tone. He
looked blank, and I realized he didn't recognize irony. 'What
kind of entertainment are you looking for?'

He threw his head back and laughed. 'You're an odd fellow,
Patterson! Do you never enjoy yourself? Women, I mean
women!'

'I was married three weeks ago.'

'Ah,' he said. 'On your best behaviour for a while, eh?
Pity. Never mind, point me in the right direction and I'll be
happy.'

The servants came back in, loaded with meat and bread and
a huge uncut cheese. Nightingale eased his feet off the table
to allow them to lay it.

'Mr Jenison's booked rooms for you at the George,' I began
again, but he waved a hand dismissively.

'I'll lay odds it's a stuffy place with no life in it! Just the sort
of place that fellow would like.'

'Mr Jenison is paying you,' I said, 'including all your expenses.'

He grinned. 'Think I should show a bit of respect, eh? I
always respect money. I'll make sure he gets plenty of expenses
to pay.' He pinched a serving girl on the bottom; she jumped,
scowled at him. He winked. 'First things first,' he said and tore
off a wedge of bread. 'Wants to see me, does he?'

'Today, at noon.'

'At his own home, his elegant mansion?' He waved a hand
in the air.

'At his agent's office on the Key.'

He was annoyed at this, clearly seeing it as an insult. I added,

'He didn't want to inconvenience you after such a long journey. The agent's office is next door to this inn.'

'Devil a bit of it,' he said, through a mouthful of bread. 'I could travel day and night for weeks without it bothering me!' It was plain he was mollified, however. I found myself oddly torn between annoyance at his manner and a reluctant liking for him. He behaved like a grossly overgrown boy out on a spree, and his very enthusiasm for the simple things of life was engaging. Even if his eating manners were appalling.

'I'm getting thirty guineas for the half-season,' he said, as the girl came in with a large jug of ale, giving him a wide berth.

I was tolerably sure Jenison had offered him thirty guineas for the *whole* season. 'You can of course discuss that with him this afternoon,' I said.

'True, true.' He cut himself a wedge of cheese, wrapped a slice of beef around it. 'Fine. You can go now.'

I hesitated, annoyed, then thought better of complaining. He didn't seem to me like a man who'd care what others felt. I nodded, said, 'Till this afternoon then,' and walked out.

In the damp yard, the spirit's gleam shot down to my eye level. 'A fine gentleman that.' Unlike Nightingale, I recognize irony when I hear it. 'The table inside the door,' the spirit said. 'Look at the table.'

I glanced round. And there, abandoned on the floor beneath the table, were the gifts bestowed by the ladies in the coach. Except for the meat pie, which was even now in the jaws of a terrier making off for a secret corner to enjoy its unexpectedly good fortune. No, Nightingale clearly didn't worry about other people's feelings.

I circumnavigated the hubbub in the yard. The tired horses had been unhitched and led off. Almost all the luggage was down and the coachman was sitting on a step in the thin drizzle, working his way through yet another tankard of ale.

There was a noise, a sudden flood of cold that made me shiver. In the gloom of the inn's arch, a figure came into exist- ence. One moment she was not there, the next she was. She looked dazed, confused. The ragged girl. Her gaze settled on me, and she brightened, as if I was exactly the person she'd been looking for. But she couldn't have known I'd be there; it's not possible to choose exactly where and when you will arrive after *stepping through*.

She straightened, sauntered across to me in that insolent way she had, a way far too adult for her years.

'You ought to be less obvious about what you're doing,' I said.

'Told you,' she said. 'No one ever notices.'

'No,' I said. 'All you can truthfully say is that no one has noticed *so far*.'

She scowled. 'I could mention it to them. Tell them what I've seen.'

'That would be blackmail,' I pointed out.

She grinned.

'But of course if you were to tell people, you'd lose the only weapon you have against me.'

I let the idea hang in the air. She bit her lip in annoyance. I smiled sweetly, made to walk past.

'I can help you find out who killed the baby,' she said quickly. 'I know someone as saw it all.'

I contemplated her for a moment. 'I see,' I said. 'You think that if you help me to find out who killed the baby, I'll help you by taking you on as apprentice.'

'You must,' she said, with sudden fierceness. 'I swear you must!'

I hesitated. To allow her to think I might change my mind was unfair, but at the same time I did indeed want to speak to anyone who'd seen the events on the Key. She waited, still chewing her lip, fists clenched at her side. I wondered if I could do her a better favour than she asked for herself, and find her a job as a servant in a good house.

I nodded.

Eleven

Charity should be dispensed judiciously; never give the poor money that will make them discontented with their lot— it is not kind.

[*A Gentleman's Companion*, August 1732]

We didn't go far. Walking out under the arch of the Fleece we came on to the Sandhill. Despite the similarity in names, the Sand*hill* and the Sand*gate* could not be more different. The Sandhill is the wide open expanse at the centre of the town; there are no slums here. The buildings are old and solid, and redolent of prosperity built on trade and commerce. The Fleece stands on one side of the Sandhill, amongst various shops and offices; across the other side is the tall Guildhall with its wide flights of steps. Some say the Guildhall is stylish and elegant; I think it's ugly.

The girl led me round the end of the Guildhall where the fish market is held, and on to the Key. Two fishing boats were unloading their catches there as the rain started to come down heavier, and a bevy of daughters and wives stood ready to gut the fish. There were whores too, eager to make off with as many of the single men as they could lay their hands on, once the unloading was done. One of these, a woman of about thirty, was sprawling on the Guildhall steps under the shelter of a porch but sat up straight when she saw me.

'Nah,' the girl said. 'He's not interested in you. He wants to know about Letty.'

'Oh, it's him,' the woman said. 'The mystery solver.'

She still managed to arrange herself so I was looking down her low-cut gown. I sighed and said again, 'I'm a newly married man.'

'There's room for more than one woman in every man's life,' she said. 'Well, get on with it! If you're not interested, there's those as are.' She nodded at a young sailor on one of the boats; he was looking at us in some annoyance. 'Kate says you want to know about the fellow as rode the horse.'

Kate was evidently the girl; she nodded enthusiastically, prodded me with her elbow. I eased myself into the shelter of the porch.

'Me and Letty were outside the Old Man when he came past,' the woman said.

The Old Man Inn is the most notorious haunt of whores on the Key; I nodded. The rain spat against my shoulder.

'He was in the devil of a temper,' she said. 'As if the whole world was against him. Thank God it was Letty he wanted.' She laughed raucously. 'Told me to hold his horse and he'd give me a penny. A penny! I don't work for pennies, love.' She grinned. 'Picked his pocket, didn't I?'

'Get much?' I asked sympathetically.

The smile broadened. 'A sovereign!'

Kate giggled. 'Serve him right.'

'So they went off into the alley. Didn't take long. Did I say he was drunk too? Letty said he couldn't do much. Didn't help his temper. Well,' she said philosophically, 'he paid her. That's what matters.'

I remembered the spirit at the lodging house had mentioned a man who'd been unable to perform. 'And then?'

She shrugged. 'Rode off. Hadn't been gone half a minute before we heard the screaming. Didn't think anything of it; you get a lot of that round here. Then we heard the sailors yelling.' She raised her voice. '*Man overboard!* Poor soul. By the time we got there, they had the lass out but took them a while to find the baby.' She stared at me. 'I know who you are. You were there. You sent for the constable.'

'That's right.'

'You telling me it wasn't an accident?'

'I'm not convinced,' I said evasively. 'Did you get a good look at this man?'

'Never once.' The young sailor was heaving boxes on to the quay and scowling ferociously at us; she gave him a friendly little wave. He scowled even more and slipped on the wet cobbles as he turned away; I heard him curse. 'He was all muffled up in greatcoat and hat. And it wasn't the weather for hanging around looking at people, not in that fog. Letty and me just wanted a nice friendly customer who'd treat us to a few beers in the warm. The horse was a nice one though. Grey. All his worldly wealth on the back.'

I said carefully, 'Did you get a good look at any of the bags?'

'There was one nice one,' she agreed. 'Had a picture on it in gold.'

'What kind of a picture?'

She shrugged. I realized, with resignation, that she probably couldn't read. 'What about his accent?'

She considered. 'Might have been local, but well taught.'

That could be a description of Ridley's voice. He'd lived in London then in Oxford for a good while; his north-east origins were occasionally proclaimed in his vowels, but only slightly.

'Tall?'

'Yeah.'

'Slim? Well-built?'

She thought. 'Couldn't tell. Not with that coat on him.' The young sailor had finished his unloading and was exchanging words with his friends. Rain slashed across the Key in a sudden flurry that sent everyone scurrying for shelter. The woman got up and dusted her petticoats. 'Got to go, love.'

'Where can I find Letty?'

She grinned at me. 'Halfway to London! The lads on the boat took a fancy to her and she went with them.'

'The boat?' I echoed incredulously. 'I thought sailors believe it unlucky to have women on board.'

'They count themselves even more unlucky *not* to have them!' she retorted.

The young sailor was walking towards us, oblivious to the downpour, talking himself into a fine belligerence, fists clenched, face set into what he clearly thought was intimidating anger. 'I got work to do,' the woman said. 'And you, sir, owe me a little re-mun-er-a-tion.'

The first coin I pulled out of my pocket was a shilling, and she looked at it with approval. Well, I could afford it now; I was a rich man. I gave it to her. 'I like generous gentlemen,' she said. 'I'll tell Letty to come see you when she's back.'

Which was what I'd hoped for.

The girl – Kate – fell into step beside me as I ducked into the shelter of the fish market under the Guildhall. It was crowded with women, shrieking, laughing, hands already slimy with blood and fish scales. The stink was overpowering. Kate had been remarkably quiet while I was questioning the whore; I'd known it wouldn't last. 'You owe me, too,' she said.

I took a deep breath. 'Not as much as an apprenticeship.'

She stopped dead. 'You promised!'

'I did not. But I did think—'

'I ain't giving up, you know,' she said glaring. 'Wait here.' And she darted away into the crowd of fishwives.

I considered walking off while she was gone. It was a tempting idea, but I knew it would solve nothing. The girl would find me again. Best to deal with her now. Seagulls squawked and darted at the piles of fish entrails, pecked pieces away, dropped them under attack, flew back for more. Women screeched with laughter. Fish flapped silver and pink on to ever increasing piles. A few more respectable women were already out shopping, haggling over choice specimens. The rain eased; drops splattered off the Fishmarket roof on to the cobbles of the Key. And then the girl was back, with an ancient battered fiddle in her hand and a bow so threadbare it looked unusable.

Without a word, she launched into a jig.

The fiddle was appallingly out of tune; the bow scraped and squealed. Her hold on the neck of the instrument was bad and if she played for long in that posture she'd end up with permanent pain in her back. But her speed of playing was amazing and she had the joy of the dance in her fingers. The fisherwomen started singing along with her (though the words they used weren't the respectable ones); children danced with excitement.

Kate threw herself into the playing. She couldn't stand still; she jerked about as if she wanted to join in the dance and when she finished, she flung up the bow and screeched in delight, as out of breath as if she'd run a race. And I suddenly thought of what I must do to make her into a violinist fit to play in a concert band: slow her down, keep her still, take that energy out of her fingers and make them controlled and disciplined and polite. I'd have to turn her into a violinist like any other. Even if the Directors allowed a woman to play in the band and not a word of gossip passed any old maid's lips, I couldn't do it. I didn't want to do it. It would ruin her.

'Well?' she asked, face glowing.

'No,' I said.

I went home to breakfast, hurrying through the drizzle before it turned into another downpour. In the breakfast room, Esther, coffee dish in hand, was browsing through a London newspaper that had evidently arrived from a correspondent. I loved the way her face lit up when she saw me; I bent to set a kiss on her cheek, trailed my fingers across her bare neck and saw her shiver with pleasure.

'Breakfast, Charles!' she said in a mock condemnatory tone.

I was ravenous. Getting up early always does that to me and seeing Nightingale wolfing down his victuals had only made the matter worse. I tucked into kidneys and eggs and bread. The room was warm and cosy as thin drops of rain sprinkled the window. I told Esther about Nightingale; looking back, the encounter had its humorous side, and I even brought myself to tell her about Nightingale's reaction to my coat.

She gave me a severe look. 'I told you so, Charles.'

I loved her honesty. 'I did order two new coats yesterday,' I reminded her.

'But no breeches.'

I scowled. 'Very well. I'll go and order breeches.'

'Today?'

'As soon as possible,' I temporized. 'I've promised Heron a violin lesson.' She frowned; I said, 'You know I don't particularly care about clothes.'

'I had noticed,' she said. 'It is because you have never been able to afford to do anything about the matter.' She forestalled me as I started to speak. 'However, I am grateful for small mercies, Charles. If you allow me to buy you a few handkerchiefs and shirts, oh, and a new pair of shoes, I shall be content. And a pair of boots.' She looked thoughtful. 'Though that greatcoat of yours is rather threadbare. And that hat!'

I looked at her; she giggled. I had now of course been privileged to see Esther's wardrobe and was horrified by its extent; what she was asking me to do was very little by comparison, but it still appalled me. All that money!

'Will you be teaching Heron's son this morning as well?' she asked brightly.

This was plainly an attempt to pass on to more congenial subjects. I expiated at length on the musical defects of Heron's son. 'And later I must go to Jenison's meeting with Nightingale. What are your plans for the day?'

I saw her withdraw at once. She put down her coffee dish. She said reluctantly, 'I have arranged to see lawyer Armstrong, about the dispute with the tenants in Norfolk.'

The eggs no longer seemed quite so appetizing; I forced myself to finish them. 'Then you'll have papers for me to sign tonight?'

'No doubt,' she agreed formally.

I could think of nothing else to say.

'Well,' she said, rising. 'I had better go, or I will be late. Pray give Mr Heron my compliments.'

'Of course.'

She hesitated, then nodded and composedly left the room.

Leaving me cursing. Myself, rather than her. Why the devil could I not simply give in gracefully and take the winning hand fate and my marriage had dealt me?

I would deal with it. I must. For Esther's sake if not my own.

After I'd sorted out this matter of the dead child.

Twelve

Entertainments of a suitable kind always ornament a town;
gentlemen should be at the forefront of providing elegant
and civilized amusements.
[*A Gentleman's Companion*, November 1735]

The lesson with Heron did not go particularly well. I was distracted by the argument with Esther, wishing it had never happened, wishing I could persuade myself to enjoy my new-found wealth. But that was the point. It did not seem like mine, it *was* not mine.

I looked around Heron's elegant home, the expensive mirrors, the fashionable Chinese wallpaper, the vases, a small Roman statue I could have sworn was the genuine article, not a reproduction (there was a small chip on the base and some discoloration as if it had at one time been buried in soil). I stared out of the windows at the rain-drenched gardens, immaculately kept, with their formal flower beds and statuary; a satyr adorning the fountain looked Roman too. This must seem natural to Heron, part of the estab-lished order of things, money and property passing down from father to son to grandson. To me, my own new-found wealth – *my* house, *my* gardens, *my* servants – seemed unreal, as if my imagination was creating wishful fantasies. I didn't want these things; I was half afraid of them. I merely wanted Esther.

Heron himself was businesslike as usual, tuning his violin and running through a few lines to warm up although I was certain he'd have been playing at least half an hour before I arrived to loosen up his muscles and let the instrument play in. But he disconcerted me by saying he needed music to calm him down.

'I have just seen lawyer Armstrong,' he said curtly, opening the music on his stand and looking for the right movement to play. 'Negotiating a place there for Ridley.'

I didn't want to think of Armstrong; it reminded me of Esther's planned visit there. I could hardly say so.

'Armstrong doesn't want help?'

'He wants help,' Heron said. 'He has more work than he can deal with and he is not getting any younger. He is, however, not certain he wants help from Ridley. He has heard stories from colleagues in London.' He glanced at me grimly. 'Why do you think Ridley was sent home? His behaviour began to threaten his uncle's good name; he considered he had no alternative.'

I wondered if I could ask what Ridley had done; it might throw light on what he was capable of. I reminded myself to be careful. I was convincing myself Ridley was the villain of the piece without any proof.

Heron was continuing. 'Armstrong is understandably torn between doing a favour for his old friend, the boy's father, and anxiety over the possible damage to his business.' He smoothed the music down as the pages threatened to drift closed. 'I met Mrs Patterson at Armstrong's.'

My heart sank but I kept my voice matter of fact. 'She's seeing him about the estates in Norfolk. Tenant problems.'

He raised an eyebrow. 'I was surprised not to see you there. Nothing can be done without your agreement.'

'It's an urgent matter,' I said, saying the first thing that came into my head, 'and I'm not yet fully conversant with the issues.'

He was still surprised. The eyebrow hovered; he looked for a moment longer before turning back to the music. 'Indeed?'

And he launched into the first movement of one of Geminiani's sonatas, leaving me embarrassed and depressed. I'd lied to him, if not explicitly, then by implication. But to admit the truth would be to forfeit his good opinion of me.

Damn it, what the devil was I to do?

After the lesson we walked down together to Jenison's agent's office. The long stretch of Northumberland Street, where Heron lives, was dark with the continuing drizzle; a tiny wind skittered leaves and fragments of straw towards us. Walking down the hill towards the Key, Heron was in an unusually talkative mood; he was, he said, planning a trip the following year to Italy. I knew exactly what his manservant thought of hot countries, and fancied he'd work on Heron to change his mind, but I let him tell me about the attractions and the perils of the Alps, and how the best way was to sail from Marseilles to Genoa, providing one took plenty of weapons to protect oneself against pirates. And then, just as we turned in the door to Jenison's agent, I realized why he was telling me all this.

'Of course,' he said, going ahead of me up the stairs, 'I can give you recommendations to several gentlemen in Rome who will help you make the necessary arrangements.'

Dear God, he thought Esther and I should make the trip! Worse than that – we could afford it!

We emerged into a dark room, full of books and clerks scribbling at desks. Jenison's agent is a spare man, who looks as if he never eats; he bowed very politely – too politely – to Heron and bestowed a much smaller bow on me. 'And how *is* Mrs Patterson?' he asked. There was a sneer in his voice.

'Mr Jenison is expecting us,' Heron snapped.

We were shown into an inner sanctum, where Jenison sat in splendour in a huge winged armchair, behind a desk overrun with papers. Jenison plainly didn't believe in shelves and books and boxes; he preferred piles on the desk. He frowned when he saw us. 'Is Mr Nightingale not here?'

In five years, I've never got a *Mr* to my name from Jenison.

'He wanted refreshment and rest before seeing you,' I said, and then, because I was tired and distracted, I foolishly added: 'I left him at the Fleece.'

Jenison frowned. 'You didn't take him to the George?'

I cursed my own carelessness. 'He bespoke a room at the Fleece. He said he likes somewhere busy and noisy.'

Heron shot me a look.

'But I recommended the George to him,' Jenison insisted, puzzled.

There was nothing I could say to this, so I kept quiet. Later, I'd point out that the Fleece was much cheaper than the George; Jenison would appreciate that.

A noise was heard downstairs. I said, with some relief, 'Here he is now.'

He was drunk. He reeled in, clipping the door jamb as he misjudged the opening, and staggered to a halt in front of Heron's fastidious – and condemnatory – gaze. I made the introductions.

'Damn fine town,' Nightingale said. 'Fine women.' He snagged his fingers in my coat sleeve. 'Shame you couldn't come.'

Jenison was a rotund ridiculous-looking man but he knew how to deal with his social inferiors. He said, 'Sit, sir,' in a certain tone of voice, and Nightingale sank into the nearest chair instantly. Jenison nodded at the clerk who'd brought Nightingale in. 'Coffee, and a great deal of it.' He looked back at Nightingale. 'Would you prefer this meeting postponed until tomorrow? When you are less . . . *indisposed*?'

Heron and I exchanged glances. I doubted Nightingale would be any less 'indisposed' tomorrow or any day of his stay. The clerk returned; Nightingale snatched up the dish with shaking hands, drank the coffee down in one draught. Two more dishes and he seemed sensible again. Sensible enough, at any rate.

'Thirty guineas, sir,' he said thickly. 'That was our bargain, was it not.'

'Indeed.'

'Per season,' I said, remembering our previous conversation.

'Half-season,' Nightingale said indignantly. 'And cheap at the price. You're getting the performance that startled London!'

I saw Heron's lips twitch.

'I cannot vary the terms,' Jenison said, every inch the shrewd businessman. 'At least, not without the consent of the other Directors. Our agreement, I believe, is that you'll give a concert for the subscribers. If everyone's amenable, we'll then decide on the final terms of the contract. If your performance is particularly impressive, there may indeed be room for increasing your fee.'

'Can't say any fairer than that,' Nightingale said, slapping the desk.

'And I'm sure,' Jenison added, slipping abruptly into the role of an admirer, 'that once everyone hears your admirable renderings of Vivaldi and Handel, they'll be only too eager to agree.'

Nightingale smiled beatifically. He caught my sleeve again; I staggered as he pulled me towards him. 'Here, Patterson,' he said, '*you* haven't heard me sing—'

'We'll need a rehearsal first,' I said hurriedly, fearing he was about to launch into song there and then. 'Tomorrow afternoon perhaps?'

Nightingale looked disappointed but Jenison brightened. 'Then we can have the concert on Thursday afternoon. That'll give me time to let everyone know about it.' He bowed his head to Nightingale. 'And of course you must come to dinner. I know my wife and sister are longing to see you again.'

Nightingale shook his head. 'Delighted of course but—' He swayed alarmingly and confided, 'Damnably tired!'

'Tomorrow night then,' Jenison said. 'Patterson and Heron have agreed to be there, and of course, *Mrs* Patterson. We're all looking forward to it immensely.'

'Indeed,' Heron said dryly.

I could not imagine for a moment that the evening would go smoothly, particularly when Nightingale leant towards me on our way down the stairs and murmured in my ear, 'They're devilishly straight-laced, Patterson.' Stale beer wafted in my face.

'Oh yes?'

'You should have seen them in London.' He belched, stumbled on the stair. I steadied him, grateful Heron had remained behind with Jenison. 'Will that fright be there too?'

I was pretty certain he was referring to Mrs Annabella, but could hardly assume that without appearing to endorse his opinion. 'Mr and Mrs Jenison and Mr Jenison's sister, Mrs Annabella Jenison, will make up the other guests,' I said diplomatically.

'That's her!' Nightingale groaned as we emerged into the bright sunshine. 'She's a silly old bat, Patterson. Gets funny notions in her head. I shall avoid her.' How he intended to do that in a small private dinner party, I couldn't imagine. He stumbled into the wall. 'Where the devil's the nearest tavern?'

'The Fleece is next door,' I reminded him, steering him in the right direction. 'I think you need a good sleep.'

He shook his head; as we came under the Fleece's arch, he took a handful of my coat in his fist. 'It's the devil of a job, Patterson, isn't it? Having to make up to frights like that? Take my advice, Patterson. Marry money!'

And he reeled across the yard, staggering into the wall on one side, then into the ostler on the other. If he made it to his room without falling flat on his face, I'd be astounded.

And his advice was well wide of the mark.

Thirteen

A gentleman should reward those who do him a service,
but it should be quietly done, without any great show.
[*A Gentleman's Companion*, May 1733]

I went home, tired and jaded. I could foresee the forthcoming
concert series being very trying. Nightingale's singing would
be a sensation for the first two or three concerts, then the
novelty would fade and the audiences, in all likelihood, drift
away. So now, while the attraction was still strong, was the
time to sell tickets; I'd four or five more calls I ought to pay,
and I couldn't summon up the enthusiasm for any of them.
They were a distraction from much more serious business.
What were Nightingale's idiosyncrasies compared to the death
of a child?

The moment I set foot inside the door, light flashed across
my sight. 'Note, master!' George said imperiously, clinging on
to a flower in a vase. 'You're getting a lot of notes these days!
You never used to.'

I looked around. Tom was standing by the drawing-room
door, patently seething with fury. His hands were behind his
back and I'd lay any odds his fists were clenched. He must
have been waiting for me, but no living man could move faster
than a spirit.

I really didn't want to have to deal with this, not now, not
at any time. It occurred to me that while he'd been alive,
George had been eager to placate me; now he was dead, I was
anxious to placate him. That annoyed me.

'Master!' he said. 'You're not looking at the note!'

'I'm in sore need of a brandy, Tom,' I said.

Out of the corner of my eye, I saw him snap upright. 'Yes,
sir!' he said, with a distinct note of triumph, and marched off.
There are things a spirit simply can't do, which is why I had
asked for a drink I didn't want. Tom understood that.

A pity George plainly did not. He said, 'You should get rid
of him, master. I don't like him.'

'That is apparent.' I unfolded the note.

It was written in the dashing, melodramatic hand of Solomon Strolger, the organist of All Hallows' Church, for whom I sometimes deputize. It said:

> *Devil take it, Patterson, it's this damned gout again. Take the services for me on Sunday, will you? And don't* [underlined three times] *play any of your dull tunes.*
> *Give 'em something cheerful.*

I heard movement and looked up to see Esther, halfway up the stairs, looking down on me in some concern. 'Was Heron that bad?'

She was holding a pile of linen in her arms; I fancied the top item was one of my old shirts that had a tear in it. I couldn't resist smiling at her. 'Heron was admirable as usual. I've just come from a meeting with Jenison and Nightingale. Nightingale was drunk and I very much fear it'll be up to me to keep him sober enough to sing. Do I really look so evil-tempered?'

She hung over the banister, a twinkle in her eye. 'Dreadful!' She cast a quick glance towards the servants' quarters, lowered her voice. 'I could help change that . . .'

I looked up into her mischievous gaze. 'I was going to visit the Ords,' I said feebly. 'And Dr Brown and Mr Wright—'

'I will come with you to the Ords,' she said, at once. 'I promised Lizzie a book of drawings. We can go together. *Later.*' And she reached down a hand.

'Master!' George said. 'I was talking about Tom! He says things you wouldn't like!'

'This is a *very* private conversation, George,' Esther said.

'But—'

'No buts, George.'

The spirit's gleam dimmed. 'Yes, mistress,' he said, unmistakeably subdued.

Tom came back with a salver on which reposed not one but two glasses of brandy; he looked smug at his foresight. I wondered if George had overheard him talking about me. Esther's servants were devoted to her. Did that loyalty extend to me? And wasn't I thinking just the way George must have hoped I would?

Devil take it. I didn't care. 'Thank you, Tom,' I said, and took the salver, and Esther, upstairs.

We did indeed make it to the Ords' house, some two hours later, in the late afternoon. Mrs Ord – formerly Lizzie Saint – is one of my pupils and she greeted us both with enthusiasm as the footman showed us into the drawing room.

'You must have tea, oh, and cook has some wonderful sweetmeats.' She'd done her dark curls in a very becoming fashion, one ringlet hanging over her shoulder; her dress was white spotted with tiny blue flowers: very suitable for a young lady. I discerned Esther's good influence at work; in the days after her marriage, Lizzie had dressed in much too severe a style. At only sixteen, she seemed far too young to have control over such a large house but I noticed she'd lost a great deal of her nervousness with servants. She poured tea for us and gossiped happily through the doings of our mutual acquaintances.

'Not everyone's back in town yet, you know,' she said and proceeded to give us an exhaustive list of those who were. 'Oh, and I saw a very odd young man this morning at the Barbers'. I couldn't get a word out of him!'

'Not one of the Ridleys?' Esther asked, glancing at me.

Lizzie made a face. 'The youngest. He's so shy!' She giggled. 'Maria Barber's much taken with him.'

Esther and I exchanged glances; Maria Barber, at seventeen years old, is not my epitome of good taste.

'I can't see why she likes him,' Lizzie confessed. 'I prefer someone much more decisive.'

As if on cue, the drawing-room door opened and her husband walked in. It was unlikely he'd heard us but Lizzie blushed fierily and looked becomingly confused.

Philip Ord is twenty years older than his wife, a fact which, to my knowledge, has never been commented on. But the way his gaze slid from myself to Esther suggested he was yet again noting Esther's seniority of twelve years with some distaste. Esther appeared oblivious to any undercurrent; she greeted him courteously and complimented him on the horse she'd seen him riding the previous day. He mellowed visibly and I seized the moment to offer the concert tickets.

Lizzie clapped her hands, and hung on his arm, eagerly entreating him to buy. He stared into my face, patted her hand, said calmly, 'Of course, my dear.' His lips widened into what might have been intended to pass for a smile. 'Will you accompany me to my study, sir?'

I accompanied him, but I didn't think concert tickets would be our topic of conversation.

The house had, I noted, been entirely redecorated recently; the matter would of course have been undertaken in the course of preparations for the Ords' marriage, and Ord would have deferred to Lizzie's wishes in the drawing room and the hallway and in her own private rooms. The result was a light airy look with the newest wallpaper and delicate chairs. This was how it was supposed to be: a husband redecorates his home for his bride, deferring to her choice, at least in the public areas of the house, which after all is where she entertains her friends and enhances his status. But in our case, I'd moved into Esther's home, already freshly decorated and done out in her own taste after she'd inherited it from her cousin a year ago.

In Ord's private rooms, his own tastes would naturally have ruled; his study was small, very masculine in style and a little old-fashioned, still with the dark wainscoting of an earlier age. Like Esther's estate room, it was full of books and papers that spoke of business; a document on the desk listed tonnages of coal carried down the river in a keel I knew belonged to Ord. I felt haunted by business, dragged my eyes away from it, watched as Ord unlocked a drawer and carefully counted out a guinea in small coins to pay for the two tickets. He slipped the rest of the money back in the drawer and locked it before standing, coins in hand, regarding me impassively. Finally, he held out the money, keeping it until I was forced to put out my own hand, palm upwards, for him to drop it into. Like a man bestowing charity on a beggar.

'A man cannot escape his history, Mr Patterson,' he said. 'Whatever good fortune comes his way, he cannot be other than he is and always was.'

A tradesman, he meant, one of the lower orders. Not one who could trace his ancestry back to the days of the Conqueror and probably earlier, like the Ords. 'I am, and always was,' I said, 'a musician.'

His lip curled. 'And this taste of yours for involving yourself in . . . *sordid* matters better suited to the petty constables and watchmen. I would advise you to put these things aside, sir.'

I looked at him steadily. Before his marriage, I'd rescued Ord from a very difficult situation which might have made him the ridicule of his peers and put an end to all hopes of marriage to Lizzie and her father's money. I thought he might have remembered that. But perhaps that was the problem: he did remember and would rather not.

He said finally, 'You put me in a very difficult situation, sir. I am supposed to pay you for these tickets and for the lessons you give my wife on the harpsichord, yet at the same time invite you to sit at my dinner table as if you were one of my intimates. I do not find this considerate, sir.'

'Then you have a simple solution to hand,' I returned. 'You can avoid inviting me to dinner.'

He nodded. 'But that would be to disadvantage your wife whom I have always believed to be a woman of breeding and education.'

'She is.' I was mollified, a little, by this evidence of consideration for Esther.

'Moreover, she is a good influence on my wife. An excellent friend and adviser. I choose my wife's confidantes very carefully, Mr Patterson, and scrutinize their *associates*.'

'You'll find nothing to object to in Mrs Patterson's *husband*,' I said, biting back anger. 'Except my birth.'

'Except, that is,' he retorted, 'that one thing that is above all essential. Good birth, good breeding. You are not a gentleman, sir, and never can be.'

I took a deep breath. It was not wise, not wise in the least, to talk about the birth and breeding of some of Ord's late *associates*— the 'lady' he'd once been intent upon marrying, for instance. Not wise to reveal the story I alone knew the truth of. And definitely not well-bred. But irresistible.

'I have one attribute of good breeding at least,' I said. 'As you well know. Discretion.'

He flushed. I laid the tickets on his desk, gave him a polite *thank you* and retreated.

I was furious; for Ord to presume to condemn me – particularly when he'd benefited from my activities in the past – was offensive in the extreme. But he couldn't be ignored; he had a great deal of influence. People would listen to him and they might not have his leavening of respect for Esther.

The rain was pattering down again as we stepped out into the street. Esther drew her cloak about her and I turned to ask if she wanted me to hire a chair to carry her home. She was just telling me, with some asperity, that she wasn't in her dotage yet, when I caught a glimpse of movement across the street.

The girl, Kate, hurriedly whisking herself out of sight into an alley.

'Charles,' Esther said as we turned into Westgate and walked up the hill. 'I was thinking that you will need a music room.'

I stared at her blankly, still thinking of the girl and her dead baby brother. 'The harpsichord's in the library.'

'Yes,' she agreed. 'But you have said yourself that it catches the sun too much there and goes out of tune. I was thinking: there is the boudoir my late cousin used to use; that would make an admirable music room. A little redecoration—'

'No,' I said.

There was a pause. Esther stared meditatively into the hedge of the Vicarage garden. The leaves dripped rain on to the cobbles. 'The Ords' redecoration brought it to mind.'

'I know it did!'

'I could send to London for wallpaper samples. And the harpsichord stool is very worn; we could do with new. Then shelves, of course, for your music.'

'I have no wish for a music room,' I said. 'The library's quite adequate.' First a breakfast room, now this!

More staring into the hedge; Esther said, 'Let me see if I have this right. You do not wish to take advantage of my money.'

'I do not.'

'You would much rather have nothing to do with it.'

'Exactly.'

'You would prefer me to continue to deal with it.'

'Precisely.'

'Very well.' She smiled beatifically at me. 'Then I think I will do the back parlour out as a music room. I will send to London for wallpaper samples and a new harpsichord stool.'

I opened my mouth, then shut it again.

'Exactly, Charles.' She smiled sweetly. 'You cannot have it both ways.'

I said nothing.

'You could of course refuse to use the room once it is done,' she mused.

'That would be petty.' I sighed. 'If I'd known you could run rings round me like this, I'd never have married you.'

'Really? Is that true?'

I grinned at her ruefully. 'No. Not in the least.'

She smiled and my heart turned over. No, I thought, not in the least.

Fourteen

A son should always reverence his father.
                [*A Gentleman's Companion*, August 1735]

I watched for Kate all the way home, to the extent that Esther started looking round too.

'Have you seen someone you know, Charles?'

'The girl,' I said. 'Kate. She seems to be following me.'

Esther smiled wryly. 'An admirer! Should I be jealous?'

'She still wants to be my apprentice.'

'I think I will have that talk with Mr Orrick,' Esther said thoughtfully. 'Persistence should be rewarded.'

'She's the sort of girl who won't ever be satisfied,' I warned her. 'Give her a little and she'll demand a lot more.'

'She sounds like a woman after my own heart!' She gave me a mischievous look.

'Esther,' I said, 'pray do not look at me like that in public.'

We turned into Caroline Square and started across to the house in the corner.

'We're nearly home,' Esther pointed out.

I got up very late on Wednesday morning; if only Ord knew, he'd have to admit I had at least one characteristic of the better-bred. Although my reason for rising late would never have been admitted to in polite society; relations between husband and wife should be cordial, but never warm. I suspected that Ord, contrary to all expectations, was in love with his wife, but would die before he said so.

Esther was lazy and sleepy at breakfast, daintily feeding herself fragments of bread. When I asked what she planned to do that day, she murmured something about letters, which made me think the wallpaper samples would not be long in arriving. I went out, annoyed at having been manoeuvred into spending more money but immensely admiring of how it had been done.

If I was to make a success of my career as a musician to counter the wealth I'd acquired from Esther, I had, perforce, to spend the morning selling subscription tickets. But during the polite nothings I murmured to the ladies and gentlemen, under the repeated reassurances that Mrs Patterson was very well, thank you, my mind was busy with the question of that poor baby, and with Cuthbert Ridley and how the devil I could find out more about him. I could ask Heron, but not without confiding my suspicions, and they were too nebulous even for my satisfaction.

And in the way of these things, as soon as I decided to put Ridley out of my mind and think about him later, I encountered him in Nellie's coffee-house when I went in for a bite to eat. The rooms were crowded with gentlemen sizing up their investments with the aid of the latest London papers; somewhere in those pages, I thought, were references to Esther's securities, accumulating interest pound by pound by pound. I looked round for somewhere to sit, and saw Ridley.

I stared in astonishment, for he was engaged in animated conversation with one of the serving girls. His face was lit up, his eyes aglow and one of his hands rested on the girl's back, very low down. She was, of course, encouraging him with all the sauce at her command, which was considerable; such girls depend on a shilling or two from fond customers. Claudius Heron had been right, I reflected; all the stuttering and wringing of hands had been mere pretence. There wasn't a trace of it now.

The girl winked at me as we came face to face, then hurried past. I sank into the empty seat opposite Ridley. He'd taken, with considerable rapidity, to twisting his fingers together nervously.

'And how do you like Charlotte?' I asked, borrowing her wink.

He stared at me for a long moment, then the slowest and

slyest of smiles started to curve his lips. 'I'm told,' he said, 'you're a newly married man. A rich woman. Related to a duke, they say.'

I wondered if he was one of those men who are only at ease with their social inferiors.

'She's related to an earl.' In fact, Esther doesn't recall ever seeing her noble relation; she was two years old at their last encounter. In addition to which, she is merely the daughter of a younger daughter of a younger daughter, which makes her particularly insignificant.

'And twenty years older than you,' he said, with an odd kind of triumph.

'Twelve years.'

'Pots of money, eh, Patterson? Don't know another one for me, do you?'

Fortunately Charlotte came back at that moment; if she'd been half a minute later, I'd probably have hit Ridley. It was not so much what he said, but the expression on his face as he said it. A knowing slyness combined with immense enjoyment.

Charlotte put an enormous slab of pie and a tankard of ale in front of Ridley. I'd lay any odds he'd already had several tankards elsewhere. She'd brought me coffee, which she knows I usually take at this time of day, and smiled prettily at me.

'Cold meats, Mr Patterson? We've a lovely apple preserve.' And, still smiling, she bent to whisper in my ear, as if making an assignation. 'Watch him, sir. I never met anyone I trusted less.'

She pranced away through the crowds, making sure we had a good view of her back. Ridley's eyes lingered, I noticed. Well, that was hardly to his discredit.

'Fifty would do it,' he said.

I frowned. 'Fifty what?'

'Guineas.' He held out his hand like a beggar. 'It's a real goer.'

'A horse?' I asked warily.

'A grey,' he said. I looked sharply at him but he was slicing up his pie with great dedication. 'Everyone knows greys always win. And it'll only cost you fifty guineas. Then we can run it. Start with the local races, work up to the big ones at York. It'll wipe the board. Grey Lightning.'

'That's its name, I take it.'

'Sired by Thunder.'

Miraculously, I'd actually heard of Thunder. It had won the big race at Newcastle only two months before. 'I don't want to own a horse.'

'Could make you a fortune.'

I sipped coffee, watched as he dug his fingers into the pie and levered out big chunks of meat; he stuffed his mouth, licked his fingers clean. A gentleman passing glanced down at me, a cynical smile curving his lips. 'But as you pointed out not a minute ago,' I said, 'I already have a fortune. Through my marriage.'

'You can never have too much money!'

I disagreed with that, fervently, but that was none of his business.

Charlotte brought me a plate with meats and bread and the promised apple preserve, and took herself off again with remarkable speed for a woman who regards a chat with a man as the best part of her working day. I was tempted to copy her example; Ridley was remarkably unpleasant. But then I'd never know what had happened last Friday when the child died.

'You like horses?' I asked.

'If they win!'

'You rode up from London, I take it.'

He grinned. 'Can you see me in a post chaise making polite conversation while the miles crawl by?'

'No,' I agreed. Charlotte was right; the apple preserve was delicious. I tried another tack. 'What made you come back at all? If I had a chance to settle in London . . .'

He made a face. 'Family.'

'I'd have thought they'd be pleased to see you well settled.'

'Want me under their eye.' He leant across the table grinning, and lowered his voice. 'Know my elder brother, do you?'

'Only by sight.'

He gave me a significant look. 'Coughing.'

'*Coughing*?'

'All the time.' He dug in his fingers again, waved a piece of pie crust at me. 'And blood in it. One of these days, there'll be a notice in the paper. *Died of a painful and lingering illness* . . .'

I stared at him. Not shocked, because illness and death is

part of the normal course of life, but surprised. 'I'd no idea. But you have another brother.'

'In Narva with my father. Nasty place, Narva. Like all these foreign places. Thieves and robbers everywhere. And then there's the ships. Ships can founder, go to the bottom in a flash.' He made a whooshing noise and gestured broadly with his hands, spraying gravy across the table. Heaven help any family, I thought, whose future depended on Cuthbert Ridley.

I sat back, and fragments of other conversations drifted to me. About the latest price of coal, returns on government stocks, the difficulties in Europe, the squabbles between Austria and France and the damage it was doing to trade. 'You must have come home the day the woman was knocked into the river,' I said casually.

He squinted at me. 'Oh?'

'And her child drowned.'

'Oh, *that*.' He grinned.

'It was your first night at home,' I said. 'Don't tell me you sat quietly in the house.'

He winked.

'Went out looking for fun?'

He gave me a smirk.

'In a brothel? Best brothels are on the Key.'

He was staring at me with some calculation now. Despite the drink, he'd clearly sensed something significant in my questioning. I said as lightly as I could, 'Did you see anything?'

'I was otherwise engaged,' he said, pronouncing his words carefully.

'But?'

He grinned at me over the top of his tankard. 'I may have.'

'Such as?'

He stared a moment longer, speared a chunk of meat on the end of his knife, looked as coy as Mrs Annabella ever did. He leered at another serving girl who walked past, followed her for a moment with his eyes. 'It was foggy.'

'So you saw nothing?'

'I heard her. She screamed.'

'The woman who fell in the river?'

'There was a pig.' He grinned broadly at me. 'Did you see the pig? Squealed like it was being stuck. *She* sounded just like a pig. And whoosh!' He threw up his hands again. 'Up went the baby and down again and such a splash.' He gulped down beer. I clenched my fists under the table.

'Were you alone?'

He roared with laughter. 'Me? At the Old Man? Never.'

'Who was she?'

'She? *They!*' He poked at my shoulder. 'Never take one when two are available!' He spoke rather too loudly and an elderly gentleman nearby leered at him with salacious interest.

'Who were they?' I asked. 'What were their names?'

He gave me a reproachful glance. 'Who worries about their names? Not making friends of them for life! A little financial transaction—' He mimed the passing of money, then grinned and made an obscene gesture. 'A little . . . *intimacy*. Don't want to live with 'em. Although,' he added on second thoughts, 'they'd be more fun than my mother.'

He roared at Charlotte for more beer; she was across the far side of the room, chatting to one of the other girls. 'You ask a devil of a lot of questions, Patterson.'

'So I've been told.'

'Had a good time with this woman, did you?' He sneered at me. 'The baby that died – had a personal interest there, did you?'

'I did not,' I snapped, then added more moderately, 'I merely want to catch the fellow responsible for its death.'

At least two gentlemen were glancing across at us, as if we were talking too loudly. Charlotte slapped down another tankard in front of Ridley and made off again with all speed. Ridley wagged a finger at me.

'Take my advice. Never meddle in other people's business. Not wise. You'll come a cropper, mark my words.'

'Is that a threat?' I asked, but he was deep into slurping the new beer. I wondered if he'd been drinking all night. Then he fixed on the remains of the pie and speared another lump of meat. He belched. 'Never go near water. Nasty stuff. Nor boats. They'll go down, you know.'

'Your father and brother?'

'Both of 'em. And then I'll have it all. That's worth coming back for, ain't it? I'll stand over the coffins, wringing my hands, supporting my mother . . . God, but she can weep! And then I'll sell the lot and be off to London again. There's nowhere better to live than London!' He gestured widely, still chewing.

'Take what you can get, Patterson. Sell all her lands and property, and come to London with me. I'll show you where the
best gaming can be had.'

'No, thank you,' I said, barely restraining my distaste.

'We can combine our worldly wealth and run a game
ourselves. I've done it before with a friend.'

'Then go back to that friend.'

'Turned respectable on me!' He waved his hand in the air.
'Well, all right, I admit there may have been disagreements.
But we can clean out. And there'll be dozens of women. Good
solid rumbustious women. Not like that wishy-washy spinster
of yours!'

I stared at him. He grinned. And it occurred to me he was
saying exactly what he knew would cause most offence. He
was playing games with me.

'I've business to do,' I said, pushing back my chair.

His laugh followed me out of the coffee house.

Fifteen

Do not be led astray by those governed by fashion and
frivolity.

[*A Gentleman's Companion*, March 1731]

I thought I'd conquered my anger by the time I got home but
Tom, hovering just inside the door, took one look at my
expression and straightened. 'There's a note for you, sir.'

'Another one!' I took it from him, turned it over. It looked
like Hugh's writing. 'Where's Mrs Patterson?'

Tom opened his mouth. A gleam sprang up on the bottom
of the banister. 'She's out shopping!' George yelled.

I fancied I could hear Tom grinding his teeth. 'This is going
to have to stop, George,' I said levelly. 'I told you to let Tom
do his job.'

'I was, master!' George said. The slyness in his voice was
close cousin to Ridley's, which only made me more annoyed.
'I let him tell you about the note. Then I told you about the
mistress. You know *I* always look after her!'

I regarded the gleam with misgiving. That note of jealousy again. 'George—'

The spirit's voice became more strident. 'I always keep an eye on what she's doing, master!'

He probably did. Spirits usually know all about the affairs of the living. But such scrutiny can easily become intolerable. I needed to talk to Esther, to reassure myself that George was not becoming intrusive. Something would have to be done. George would always remain a boy; for the next eighty or so years – almost certainly our entire lives – we'd have to live with him. If we didn't find a way to control him, our only escape would be to move.

It might yet come to that. 'Nevertheless,' I said, 'I was asking Tom a question. You interrupted a conversation, which is rude.'

'*He's* rude!' George retorted. 'He's always swearing at me.'

Tom reddened. 'I don't!' He looked briefly absurdly young. 'I don't, sir!'

'Do, do, do!' George shouted.

'That's enough!'

They both fell silent. The gleam on the banister shifted as if George was dying to say something more. Tom looked stonily into the distance.

'I want you both to understand,' I said, 'that I'm perfectly satisfied with Tom's performance of his duties. Thank you, Tom.'

'Sir,' he said, with a flush staining his cheeks.

'But I'm not prepared to put up with arguments and dissensions in this house. They must cease at once. Do I make myself plain?'

'Yes, sir,' Tom said, a little subdued.

'But master!'

'Do I make myself clear!'

'Yes, master,' George said sullenly.

'Good,' I said. 'Now, I came back for some music. And if there's any more argument, I'm going to be late for a rehearsal.'

'Sir,' Tom said again, and retreated to the back of the house. George lingered, muttering.

'I'm adamant, George,' I said. 'These arguments must end.'

'But master!'

I could hear the hostility in his voice. The spirit was turning more and more green; I sighed inwardly. 'I appreciate your concern for Mrs Patterson, George, more than I can say—'

'Really, master?' The green faded; he sounded gratified.

'But you must moderate your behaviour to Tom. After all, there are certain things you cannot—' This required some delicacy; no spirit likes to be reminded they're no longer as *active* as they once were. 'Tom's here to make Mrs Patterson's life comfortable, to bring her food and drink, and all the other trifles she needs. He can make her life so much easier.'

'Yes, master.' Dear God, now he sounded worryingly depressed, and I was getting later and later for my rehearsal with Nightingale.

'I rely upon you to make sure everything runs smoothly, George.'

'That's what I'm trying to do, master!'

'Yes, I understand that. But don't forget that other people can do their bit too.'

'Yes, master. But—'

'And you want Mrs Patterson to be happy, don't you?'

'Yes, master, but—'

'Exactly,' I said, and fled for the library.

My music sat in half a dozen piles on the floor behind the harpsichord. I thought I knew exactly the location of the copies I needed but I did not; after ten minutes of hunting, I finally conceded that Esther's idea of new bookcases had considerable merit. Only at the last minute, just as I was leaving, did I remember Hugh's note and retrieve it from my pocket. If it was another glowing encomium of London's virtues, I'd leave it until I was in a better temper.

It was not. The note was addressed from Westgate.

> *Charles* [Hugh had written] *For God's sake come round and console me. And bring some strong brandy.*

Hugh was back from London? But he'd only been gone three weeks; what was the point in braving the appalling roads for so short a visit? And why did he need consoling? It sounded very much like a disastrous love affair, and I wasn't in the mood for lovelorn descriptions of buxom beauties. For some reason, Hugh's always tempted by redheads, and the more vulgar the better.

He'd have to wait. The Assembly Rooms were only a few doors down from Hugh's lodgings; I could easily walk up there after the rehearsal. I heaved up the music, dashed out of the house – and ran straight into the girl, Kate.

She was lounging against the railings of the gardens at the centre of the square, apparently enjoying a patch of sunshine. She danced across to meet me. 'Here, did you know there's a drunken spirit in those gardens?'

'Yes,' I said shortly.

'I don't think he was respectable,' she said. 'You should have heard what he wanted me to do!'

I strode on, trying to outpace her. The sun was breaking through the clouds, drying the thin patina of dampness on the street. Midges bobbed around me. I batted them away irritably.

'Not going to get rid of me,' she sang. 'I ain't giving up.'

'And I'm not giving *in*,' I retorted.

I reached the Assembly Rooms only a minute or two late. The Steward of the Rooms was not there but he'd left the harpsichord key on its usual hook. I snatched it up and started up the long flights of stairs; the concert room is on the second floor. Kate was still at my heels.

'Here,' she said admiringly, looking at the decorations, 'this is canny. All this gold stuff.' She fingered velvet curtains at the landing windows. 'I like these. I'm going to have stuff like this in my house.'

'Oh yes?' I turned for the next flight of stairs.

'When I'm rich and famous,' she said, poking her tongue out at me. 'After you've learned me how to play the fiddle.'

I stopped in confusion on the topmost landing, sunlit through ornate windows. The most peculiar sounds were coming from the concert room. A succession of grunts and groans and rumbling and snorts. Kate made a face. Cautiously, I edged open the door. Kate peered under my arm.

Nightingale stood in the middle of the floor, a music stand in front of him. He had music on the stand, flinging over the pages with fiery abandon, as he wheezed and snorted. He broke into an unnerving falsetto, worse than any castrato. The truth dawned on me; he was working his way through one of Mr Handel's overtures.

'He's ill,' Kate said. 'He's eaten something bad.'

'No,' I said, sighing. 'He's singing the drum parts. And when he goes falsetto, that's the flute part.' I winced, as a nasal whine emerged. 'And that's supposed to be the violin.' I thought fleetingly that even the ladder dancing would have been preferable to this.

'False what?' Kate said.

'Falsetto. That very high-pitched voice.'

She giggled. 'I can do that. Here.' She let out such a piercing high screech I was surprised all the dogs in the neighbourhood didn't come running. Nightingale stopped in mid-phrase.

'Who's that? Come out at once!'

I made my appearance, followed by Kate. 'We were just admiring your performance.' I went straight to the harpsichord and unlocked it, unable to look Nightingale in the face with such an outrageous lie.

Kate stood grinning in the middle of the floor. 'I can do what you were doing.'

'No, you can't,' he said.

'Yes, I can!'

'No,' he corrected, drawing himself up. 'I assure you, young—' He gave her a derisory look, from the top of her tousled hair to the bottom of her frayed hem. 'Young *person*, you cannot.'

'I can, I can! Here, listen.' Kate took one of her ridiculously large breaths and repeated, faithfully, everything Nightingale had just sung. I paused in the middle of setting up the harpsichord lid. Her recall was amazing. She could never have heard the music before yet she reproduced not just every note, but also the exact manner in which Nightingale had sung it. If she'd been a boy, I'd have been signing her up as an apprentice on the spot.

Nightingale was not so pleased. He strode over, seized her by the arms and shook her, snarling. 'Get out, you little fiend!'

'Nightingale,' I said, starting towards them.

He took no notice, went on shaking as Kate struggled against him. 'Vermin! Filth! Get out!'

'Nightingale!'

He swung round on me, red-faced, veins standing out on his forehead, shouting wildly. 'I will not be mocked! Get the slut out of here! Get her out!'

'The girl was trying to flatter you. She was entranced by your performance!'

Behind Nightingale's back, Kate stuck her tongue out again. 'Here,' she said. 'I didn't mean to make you mad. I liked it. I really did.' Nightingale swung round on her; she put on an expression of angelic innocence. 'I like that high bit. The fiddle bit. I play the fiddle.'

He snorted in derision. 'You? Where did a slut like you learn to play the violin?'

'George Allen learned me.'

'Who?'

'He's a local fiddler,' I said.

'I can play you any tune you like,' she said proudly. 'Get me a fiddle and I'll show you.'

He stared at her for a long moment then swung round. 'Patterson. The concert band's instruments must be kept here?'

'You want her to play?' I asked, startled by his abrupt change of mood.

'Devil take it. A violin, man!'

I hesitated, but there seemed no point in arguing. Let Kate have her moment of triumph; Nightingale would forget her soon enough. I unlocked the cupboard and picked out a violin. I resined the bow, flicked fingers across the strings to make sure the instrument was in tune, and handed it to Kate. She smirked at me, put the violin against her shoulder, wriggled to get herself comfortable, and played, flawlessly, the tune Nightingale had been singing.

I itched to take hold of her and make her straighten her back, to show her how to hold the bow properly in order to produce a fuller, more pleasant tone. Nightingale just stared, watched her antics as she dipped and wove and bobbed about. And a slow knowing smile formed on his lips.

'She'll play in the concert,' he said.

'Yes, yes!' Kate shrieked. 'I'll play anything you like. I can play dance tunes too—'

Nightingale put his hand on her arm as she started to play again. Under his smiling gaze, she began to glow and blush, even to drop her gaze bashfully. God, but he knew how to handle women! 'We'll have to do something about those clothes.'

'I don't think this is wise,' I said.

Nightingale turned with a calculating look; behind his back, Kate smirked. Nightingale took me aside. 'My dear Patterson, there's nothing to worry about. The ladies and gentlemen adore novelties; they'll idolize her.'

'And what happens when the novelty wears off?'

'My dear fellow,' Nightingale said emolliently, 'trust me. I know how to handle these matters.' And he swung back to Kate. '*Now* we'll see what else you can play.'

He started sorting through a huge pile of music on the harpsichord stool.

'See.' Kate poked me in the ribs with her bow. 'Told you I'd get to play the fiddle. And,' she added, 'it's none of *your* doing. Which means you'll get no more help from me over the baby.'

Sixteen

Amity is one of the pleasures of life, if conducted in a restrained manner.

[*A Gentleman's Companion*, April 1734]

I was in a rage as I went up the street the few yards to Hugh's lodgings above the clockmaker's. Down the alley to the side entrance that gives directly on to a flight of stairs. Up past the door to Hugh's dancing school, up again, past the lodgings of the snobbish widow who always frowns on me. Up another flight, to Hugh's lodgings in the attic.

I was a yard from the door when I heard the sneezing. I knocked cautiously. A voice full of cold called, 'Cub in.'

Hugh was lying on his bed under the slope of the roof, a blanket tucked around him, although he was plainly fully dressed apart from his coat and shoes. His nose was extraordinarily red, his black hair down around his shoulders and his eyes dark-circled.

His left arm was in a sling.

'Hugh!' I stopped aghast. 'What the devil happened to you?'

'Fell,' he said thickly. 'Into a lake.' His gaze settled on what I held in my hands. 'Oh, thank God. Brandy!'

I'd called in at a tavern on my way up Westgate and bought the best they had to offer. Looking at Hugh's face, I wished I'd done more.

'When did you last eat?'

He groaned. 'Don't mention food. Just pour a glass of that stuff. A large glass.'

He dragged himself into a sitting position against the pillows, sneezed again. He wiped his nose with the back of his hand, and took the brandy from me. I sat down on the only chair in the room, as far from him as I could get. He gulped down the brandy, sneezed. 'Never agree to musical parties on barges, Charles.'

I broke out laughing. 'You were never dancing on a barge!'

'No, playing the fiddle. Damn it, Charles! It rained every last moment from beginning to end. And the boards got sodden and someone bumped into me, and I went flying, fiddle and all. Smashed the fiddle but don't worry, it was borrowed. Hit my arm.' Another sneeze. 'Heard it crack.'

'You got it set properly?' I said alarmed.

'Fellow who owned the barge was some sort of society physician. Set it for free. Said he felt guilty. Only good thing about it.'

I poured him more brandy as he pulled the blankets around him. He said plaintively, 'I was never so glad to get home.' He gave me a sly look and sniffed mightily. 'How's Mrs Patterson?'

'Very hale and hearty.'

'And married life?' He winked.

'Very happy, thank you,' I said primly. 'In fact, everything's fine except—'

He raised an eyebrow.

I gritted my teeth, but it was a relief to speak to someone about it. 'The money,' I admitted.

Hugh frowned. 'You're wealthy. What's the problem?'

'I didn't earn it.'

He sighed melodramatically. 'Charles! Why is nothing ever simple for you? Nothing wrong with marrying money; it's not illegal.'

I said glumly, 'I don't have the least idea what to do with it.'

Hugh grinned. 'You *save* it, Charles! Invest it with some coal-owner: Heron or Ord or Jenison. They give you four and a half per cent interest and you have a nest egg for when your fingers are too stiff to play the harpsichord and you forget every tune you ever knew.'

'I never earnt above sixty pounds in any year,' I said, 'and now the accounts are for never less than two or three hundred. Hugh, you've no idea how much income we have a year!'

'I can guess. Six hundred? Eight hundred?'

'More like a thousand,' I said gloomily.

Hugh whistled.

'Armstrong keeps presenting us with bills for huge amounts to be spent on draining land in Norfolk or building a barn in Northumberland. How am I to know whether that's money well spent or not?'

'Ask your wife.'

I hesitated. 'I'm not interested,' I confessed.

He grinned and sneezed again, tried to wipe his nose with the back of the hand that held the brandy. 'Let her get on with it, Charles. Just sign the papers and get back to your compositions.'

'I haven't set pen to paper for months. And now I'm tangled with the arrangements for the winter concerts.' Which reminded me of the disastrous rehearsal from which I'd just come. 'I've just been at the Assembly Rooms with the new soloist.'

'Who is it? Anyone I know?'

'Richard Nightingale.'

'Who?'

'He's a ladder dancer.'

'Charles, no! Not the fellow who imitates violins and flageolets!'

'That's the one.'

'I saw him in London two years back. Charles, he's dreadful!' Hugh groaned. 'I'm all for a little novelty but the man has no taste!'

'You don't need to tell me,' I agreed. 'I've just heard him.'

'And,' he prompted.

'And?'

'What else, Charles?' He said patiently, 'I know when you're keeping something from me.'

'You're as bad as Esther.'

'Sensible woman your wife.'

I sighed. 'I've been wondering if I should take on another apprentice. Well,' I corrected myself, 'it's been suggested I take on another apprentice.'

'Do it,' he recommended. 'It'll give you more money. Match

your wife's income with your own. Not that you need to, but
if it makes you feel better—'

'Her name,' I said, 'is Kate.'

'Whose name?'

'The girl who wants to become my apprentice.'

He stared. 'A *girl*! What do her parents say?'

'Her father is notable by his absence. Her "ma" is usually
so drunk on gin I don't believe she knows what any of her
children are doing.'

He squinted at me, shook his head. 'You're not making sense.'
He held up a hand as I started again. 'Don't bother. My head's
so thick with cold I can't deal with anything more complicated
than a piss. You can't take her on, though.'

'No.'

'You know what people will think.'

'Yes.'

'And your wife wouldn't like it one bit.'

'I do know all this, Hugh.'

'And she couldn't perform in public anyway. Not a woman.
Not the thing at all. Not modest.'

'No.'

'Only one kind of woman performs in public.'

'Yes.'

'The available kind.'

'I know.'

'So you wouldn't get any money from her anyway.'

'Hugh,' I said wearily. 'Drink your brandy.'

He squinted at me. 'There's something else, isn't there?'
His face lit up. He struggled to pull himself up against
the pillows, sneezed. 'Not another murder, Charles! Damn
it, I knew a visit from you would cheer me up. What
happened?'

'This is serious, Hugh!'

'Of course it is.' He briefly assumed a pious look then broke
out in smiles again. 'Charles, I've spent four days in a coach being
bounced about in utter agony and then twelve hours in my own
bed with only my own company. Tell me about the murder,
damn it!'

I told him what I'd seen on the Key: the drunken woman
and the baby, the horseman, the sailors valiantly rescuing the
woman, and the child being lost. Hugh questioned me minutely

on the rider, what he was wearing, the quality of his clothes, of the horse.

'He was a gentleman, Hugh; that was no livery stable horse.' Then I thought of myself and the new coats under construction at the tailors. 'Or at least a man with the money to dress and ride as a gentleman.'

Hugh was silent, considering the facts, tugging one-handedly at the blankets that threatened to slip to the floor. '*CR*,' he said, thoughtfully.

'On a bag thrown over his saddle.'

'Pretentious.'

'Some people are.'

He turned his head to look at me. 'You've someone in mind. Tell me, Charles.'

'Cuthbert Ridley.'

He frowned. 'Isn't that the youngest boy? I thought he'd been sent in disgrace to London.'

'In disgrace?'

He grinned. 'I used to teach the daughters before they married. Got all the gossip from the kitchen maid.'

Which was precisely what I'd have expected of Hugh. 'Which was?'

'He did nasty things to the cats.'

'I like cats,' I said.

'But when he transferred his attentions to the expensive hunting dogs, that's when the trouble really began. Particularly when he blamed it on the stable boys.'

'They believed the stable boys before him?'

'The steward saw it all. The old steward, who's been fifty years with the family man and boy, and never uttered a harsh word against anyone.' He stifled a sneeze. 'But you can't *prove* this was murder, Charles.'

'I know what I saw.'

'And especially you can't prove Cuthbert Ridley is the only man in town with the initials *CR*.'

'He admits to being there.'

'The devil he does!'

I related my conversation with Ridley; Hugh's lips curled with distaste. But at the end of it all, he still shook his head.

'It's not proof, Charles. Nowhere near proof. He could have been doing exactly as he said.' He sighed. 'And it's not always the nasty people who do nasty things. What are you going to do?'

'Brood.'

'And then?'

'We're dining at the Jenisons' tonight. With Richard Nightingale.'

'I mean, what are you going to do about Ridley?'

'Heron will be at the dinner. I'll try and manage a few private words. See if he knows more than he's said. Other than that—' I looked up at his red face, tensed for another sneeze. 'It was foggy, Hugh. Visibility was erratic and most people were keeping to the safety of the buildings, not wanting to fall into the river. Only the sailors and I were in any real position to see what happened and the sailors were busy with work on board. There can be no other witnesses; all I have is that bag with the initials, and the grey horse.'

'You could try the livery stables, see if you can find the horse there. Or the inns.'

'It'll be at his mother's home, well out of my reach.'

Hugh frowned. 'There's something not quite right here. He galloped off across the bridge? Heading south?'

'As far as I can tell.'

'But if he was heading for his mother's house, he would have turned west.'

'He may simply have wanted to get away as fast as he could.' I got up, put the remains of the brandy on the table next to his bed, within easy reach. 'I must go. Esther will be fretting we'll be late for dinner. I have an uncomfortable feeling, Hugh, this is one death that'll go unpunished.'

Seventeen

The intercourse of friends, and a few hours spent in sober conversation, is highly beneficial to society.
[*A Gentleman's Companion*, February 1734]

I told Esther about Nightingale's adoption of Kate as we walked up to the Jenisons' house in the thickening dusk. The hem of

Esther's gown rustled gently against the ground; I'd offered to send for a chair to convey her without dirtying her petticoats, but she'd refused and I was glad. I loved quiet moments like this, just the two of us, arm in arm, close enough to feel each other's warmth.

Esther was horrified. 'One cannot blame the girl,' she said. 'Of course she will seize any opportunity that comes her way. But Nightingale's behaviour is reprehensible!'

'I don't think he has any nefarious intent towards her,' I said. 'He sees her as a novelty to attract audiences.'

'Perhaps,' she said grimly. 'But I hardly think that will deter him from taking advantage of her in the worst way!'

I'd been right – taking on a girl as an apprentice *always* gives rise to talk.

It was clear from the start that the dinner party was going to be a trial. Heron was in a bad mood – when we arrived, he was standing against the mantelshelf above the unlit fire, glowering at anyone who dared come near him. And I felt horribly shabby. Heron was immaculately dressed as always, wearing clothes that had patently cost a fortune; Jenison had dignified the occasion with his best coat of chocolate brown, and the ladies were very fine, Mrs Jenison in plum-coloured satin, Mrs Annabella in a white gown more suited to a young girl. At least I didn't cut such a ridiculous figure as she did, with an amazingly elaborate hairstyle and inexpertly applied rouge.

It was plain that having a private word with Heron would be well-nigh impossible; indeed, if he was in a bad mood it would probably not be advisable. Moreover, his temper worsened by the minute as Mrs Annabella simpered and smiled and flattered him outrageously.

Nightingale was late. *Very* late. Jenison began to fidget and look at the clock. 'Dinner will be ready before he arrives.'

'Do you think he's quite all right?' Mrs Annabella said to Heron as if he should know. 'Perhaps he's ill. Perhaps he was dreadfully incommoded by the journey.'

'Not by the journey, no,' I said. Heron's lips tightened.

'Perhaps he's got lost?' Mrs Annabella pressed her lace handkerchief to her bosom. 'He doesn't know the town.' She turned an accusing eye on me. 'You should have called for him on the way in your carriage.'

'We walked,' Esther said, and smiled into the horrified silence. 'It is only two short streets.'

'But the town can be dangerous at this time of night,' Mrs Jenison protested.

'He's been robbed!' Mrs Annabella said faintly. 'Even now, he could be lying in a gutter!'

'He has probably taken a chair and the bearers are fleecing him by carrying him the long way round,' Heron said curtly, tapping his foot.

Jenison was staring out of the window into the street. 'The beef will be overdone. I *detest* overdone beef.'

Nightingale made an appearance at last and it was spectacular. He was dressed from head to foot in yellow, the colour of buttercups. Jet-black buttons winked on his coat, and tiny but distinct ladders were embroidered in silver on his waistcoat. He paused in the doorway so we could all admire the effect, and seemed gratified by Mrs Annabella's gasp of amazement.

And behind him was Kate. Resplendent in matching yellow with hoops so large as to almost weigh her down. She wasn't able to moderate her usual stride so the hoops bounced from side to side, making her stumble. The dress must have cost a fortune, I thought, not merely because of the quality of the material but because some lucky dressmaker must have had a dozen girls working all day on it to finish in time.

It made her look like a whore.

Jenison, caught in the act of inclining his head graciously to his guest, stopped, head tilted like a puzzled sparrow. 'Er . . . um . . .'

Nightingale made a large gesture to the room. 'How gracious of you all to welcome me. *Such* a friendly town.'

Jenison thawed, a little, though his gaze lingered on Kate; both Mrs Jenison and Mrs Annabella were staring at her with something akin to horror. Esther whispered in my ear. 'Is that the girl? What in heaven's name does he think he's doing, bringing her into this company? This is unfair!'

Nightingale was enlarging on the virtues of his quarters at the Golden Fleece, ignoring Jenison's protests that he'd engaged rooms for him at the George. Mrs Annabella said, loudly, 'And pray who is this?'

Nightingale swooped on her. 'My dear lady, has anyone told you how wonderful you look in white? It's *so* becoming to you. Can I say how much, how very much, I've been counting the hours until I saw you – and your family – again. I've such fond memories of our acquaintance in London.'

Mrs Annabella was plainly torn. She tilted towards Nightingale's tempting bulk but her eyes flitted irresistibly towards Kate. Mrs Jenison was apparently lost for words, rigid with disapproval.

'Dinner must be almost ready,' Jenison said anxiously. 'I'll ring for a servant to escort the – er – *young person* to the kitchens.'

'But my dear sir,' Nightingale said, wide-eyed with innocence. 'My apprentice is to eat with us.'

'This is cruel,' Esther said passionately. 'The girl cannot feel anything but out of place!'

Nightingale and Jenison argued in the politest of fashions. Nightingale protested he thought the invitation had included Kate; Jenison said he hardly thought there'd be enough food. Nightingale protested the girl ate like a bird; Kate looked mutinous. Jenison thought she'd be more comfortable downstairs. Mrs Annabella continued to scrutinize Kate with distinct hostility; Mrs Jenison had become every inch the woman of gentility, whose well-bred expression gave nothing away.

In the end, Nightingale won the day, by saying comfortably how he remembered Jenison's lavish hospitality in London and how he'd often spoken of it to friends, recommending the warm northern spirit to its colder London counterpart. Jenison thawed under this blatant flattery; Mrs Jenison said wearily that at least one more would even up the numbers.

We went into dinner, Nightingale oozing triumph. Jenison followed the new fashion of alternating men and women; I found myself with Mrs Annabella on one side and Mrs Jenison on the other. Almost directly opposite me, Kate sat between Heron and Nightingale, who, of course, proceeded to ignore her now he'd got his own way. Jenison sat Esther next to himself and devoted himself to her needs as if she was the only female in the room, which, I saw, annoyed Mrs Jenison.

Kate glowered at the array of silver as if it had personally offended her. She glanced across at me, and for a moment I saw a lost little girl thinking about crying. I smiled at her; she put her nose in the air and straightened her back.

The servants brought in the soup. Nightingale devoted himself to Esther; I heard him explaining the many measures he was taking for Kate's welfare; plainly he'd noticed Esther's

hostility and was trying to disarm it. Mrs Jenison undertook
to entertain me with tales of the iniquities of her servants, and
asked if I was satisfied with mine. Mrs Annabella, opposite
Nightingale, looked put out at the lack of attention paid to
her by the gentlemen and attacked her soup with angry stabs
of her spoon, creating little waves in the bowl.

Kate, I was glad to see, was more sensible than I'd given her
credit for, sitting in prim stillness until she'd seen what other
people did. She was an extraordinarily good mimic; by the
time the overdone beef had appeared, she was dabbing at her
lips with her napkin as delicately as Mrs Annabella. Her success
evidently gave her confidence; she turned to Heron beside her
and said, 'You like music too, eh?'

He said, shortly, 'Yes.'

'Fiddle music? Here, do you know the tune *Buttered Peas*?'
And she started humming.

Heron glanced at me. 'I fancy that's called *The Devil to Pay*.'

Kate didn't recognize irony either. 'Nah, that's different.' But
fortunately at that point a servant offered her potatoes.

Nightingale took charge of the table. He enlarged on his
performances in London, and the wonderful reviews he'd
received. I suspected he'd probably written them himself. But
Jenison plainly took them as genuine, and quizzed Nightingale
on every one, a lengthy process in which he was ably abetted
by Mrs Annabella, eager for attention. There was one awkward
moment when Nightingale recounted a tale about half a dozen
adoring young ladies, but he then saved the day by leaning
forward and twinkling at Mrs Annabella. 'But none of them,
dear madam, was as beautiful as you.'

Heron's contemptuous gaze met mine. Mrs Annabella
simpered.

Throughout the meat and the fish and the jugged hare and
the quails and into the desserts, Nightingale held court. Jenison
gave him the benefit of homage, Nightingale scattered compliments in Mrs Annabella's direction, and the rest of us confined
ourselves to murmurs connected with the food. Kate said hardly
anything, but I noticed her gaze was darting here and there,
watching, patently learning. She did indeed peck at her food,
though I suspected she was probably eating ten times as much
as she ever had at home, and of much richer fare.

At last, the ladies rose to go to the drawing room. Esther took charge of Kate, drawing the girl's arm through hers and saying she must see Mrs Jenison's new curtains. Kate looked dubious. Mrs Annabella sailed off ahead, barging Kate out of the way as they happened to get to the door together.

We were left, the four of us, and Nightingale seemed to wither. Heron was a slender man of only just above middle height, and Jenison was rotund and an inch or two shorter still. Nightingale should have looked larger and more vivid in his yellow glory. But he sank down a little in his chair and a false note sounded in his conversation. He was a man plainly more at ease with the ladies.

My hopes of speaking privately to Heron were dashed straight away; Jenison engaged him in business talk almost as soon as the ladies were out of the door. Nightingale, obviously bored, stared into his glass. His yellow coat had gravy stains along one cuff, as if he'd leant on something spilled on the table. He must have sensed me watching, for he looked up. 'Devil take it, Patterson,' he muttered, with a quick glance to be sure Jenison and Heron were not listening. 'I know what you're thinking. I don't mean the girl any harm. My tastes run to a woman with a bit of meat on her.'

'You may find it difficult to convince other people of that.'

He seemed to take what I said to heart for when we repaired, not long afterwards, to the drawing room, he went straight to Mrs Jenison and Mrs Annabella and began to talk to them. The ladies were all subdued, I thought. Kate looked bored and stared morosely at the huge arrangement of feathers on the far door; Esther, beside her, had an air of exasperation. Mrs Jenison was looking weary and harassed. But Mrs Annabella glowed as Nightingale's gaze settled on her; I heard him murmur he was bored by young people – their conversation so tedious, their opinions and taste so unformed.

Esther moved slightly so I could sit down beside her. 'I have told Kate she will sleep in our house tonight. There is a spare bed in the housemaid's room. They are much of an age so may get on well.'

'I ain't a servant,' Kate said sullenly. 'Mr N's promised me a room at the Fleece.'

'You are not staying with that man,' Esther said. 'I do not trust him.'

'I can look after myself,' Kate said defiantly.

'You should not need to. You will stay with us.'

'No, I won't.'

I intervened as Esther's expression hardened. 'If you come with us, I'll give you a violin lesson tomorrow.'

Kate gave me a sour look. 'You won't. You'll say you've changed your mind. Anyhow, Mr N's going to take me to London.'

I opened my mouth to urge caution, then saw how she glowed with pleasure. Kate must have had very little in her life to please her; I decided to let her have her dreams a little while longer.

'We can sort all that out later,' I said. 'When we're less distracted by conversation.'

Kate smirked. 'Do you always talk and talk *and talk* like this?'

'It is called civilized conversation,' Esther said and turned to return a comment of Jenison's. Kate made a face at me.

'It's called dull,' she said. 'I nearly went off you know where and came back at the end of the evening when you'd all talked yourselves out.'

I hoped she was only joking.

At the end of the evening, as Nightingale bid everyone a magnificent melodramatic farewell, I at last found a moment for a private word with Heron. He spoke before I could, saying curtly, 'Ridley. His mother sent me a message this afternoon. He is insisting on having lodgings in town – at the Old Man Inn.'

The ladies were fussing over Esther; a maid brought her cloak. Kate stood to one side, ignored and patently very tired. Jenison was complimenting Nightingale yet again on his rendition of Handel; I'd never seen him so admiring before.

I winced. 'Ridley couldn't have picked a more unsavoury resort.'

'I am assuming the whores there are the attraction,' Heron said dryly. 'But it distresses and worries his mother, which is unacceptable. She is not well. Moreover, lawyer Armstrong has sent word the boy did not visit him as arranged. He is not pleased. He says that if he does not see Ridley tomorrow, he will no longer consider taking him on.'

I couldn't imagine Ridley would mourn the lost opportunity.

'And now he has completely disappeared.' Heron's exasperation was evident in his voice. 'I visited the Old Man Inn this after-noon but he was not there. Out carousing, apparently. I am off there again now in search of better luck.'

'Would you like me to—'

But Jenison interrupted us. 'Mr Patterson, the concert tomorrow is arranged for two o'clock. I trust that is a convenient time?'

Jenison was asking for my opinion? That was new. 'There will of course be no band,' I warned him. 'Just myself accompanying Mr Nightingale on the harpsichord.'

'Of course, of course.' Jenison returned to Nightingale's side.

'And now,' Heron resumed forcefully, 'it transpires he has stolen money from his mother. No less than fifty pounds! Taken from the drawer in her bedroom. He rifled the room for it, left it all in a turmoil.'

I pondered on the thought of leaving so much money casu-ally in a drawer.

'Well—'

A sharp blow landed in the middle of my back.

Eighteen

Drink should be taken in strict moderation.
[*A Gentleman's Companion*, May 1730]

I stumbled. Heron caught my arm, steadied me. Cuthbert Ridley staggered drunkenly past, plainly oblivious to the fact he'd just nearly knocked me over. He was singing a bawdy song – a *very* bawdy song – and waving his arms wildly.

Mrs Jenison and the maid scattered in alarm. Esther stepped back smartly out of the way. Mrs Annabella shrieked and edged behind the nearest man – Nightingale; he put out an arm as if to defend her, looking rather pompous but obviously well-intentioned. Kate, caught isolated, took a step towards Jenison but he was retreating too.

Only Heron, as ever, seemed unalarmed. 'You want to see me, Ridley?' he asked dryly.

It was plain Ridley didn't know what he wanted. He stumbled

to a halt, stopped in mid-note and squinted about as if he wasn't sure who'd spoken. 'What the devil—' His gaze missed Heron and me altogether, and the footman behind us, leered at the ladies, then settled on Nightingale. He lunged forwards, arms opened wide, face alight with pleasure. 'It's the crow himself! My dear fellow. I haven't seen you since—' He cast Nightingale a sly glance and a wink. 'Well, never mind. Ladies present, eh?'

Nightingale drew himself up proudly. 'You are drunk, sir!' he said with considerable dignity. 'I do not know you. Go away.'

'But my dear old songster!'

Nightingale withdrew with a contemptuous gaze; Ridley went after him.

'This is intolerable,' Heron said shortly. He took a brisk step forward, grasped Ridley's arm. Ridley tried to shake him off.

'Time to leave,' Heron said. 'Patterson, will you oblige me by checking if my carriage is at the door?'

The footman forestalled me, hurrying out to the street. Ridley pulled free. 'Night's young! Plenty to do.' He saw Kate and went straight for her. 'Now, here's a pretty young lady.'

She ran, hoops bouncing, for the stairs, snatched up a candlestick, and swung round, ready to brain him with it. Hot wax globules sprayed across the wooden banister. I suspected Ridley was not the first man Kate had had to fight off, and I wouldn't have bet on him to win.

'Servants!' Jenison called imperiously. The maid fled to the rear of the house for help; the footman came dashing back in from the street.

Ridley had seen Mrs Annabella now, with her rouge and ridiculous hairstyle, and her low décolletage. He ignored Kate's defiance, peered at Mrs Annabella. 'Devil take it!' He grinned salaciously. 'Here's another of 'em!'

Mrs Annabella shrieked. The footman made purposefully for Ridley but Nightingale was there first. He was shaking, I noticed, but drew himself up, and stared down his nose at Ridley in an imperious manner. 'Leave the lady be.'

Mrs Annabella swooned into the arms of the onrushing footman, who plainly didn't know what to do with her. Abruptly, Ridley started shouting, rantings so obscene they startled us all. Spittle sprayed into Nightingale's face; as he flinched away, Ridley struck out. One fist caught Nightingale a glancing blow on the shoulder; he howled in outrage, lifted his own fists. Then Ridley brought up his knee and caught him in the groin.

Nightingale shrieked and went down to his knees.

'This is not an edifying spectacle,' Esther said. She strode across to Kate and thrust her unceremoniously towards the drawing room. Kate went, grinning. Mrs Jenison hurried after, red-faced and shocked, dragging with her a reluctant, even excited, Mrs Annabella. Jenison looked ready to follow.

Heron and I both went for Ridley, aided by the footman freed from the burden of Mrs Annabella. None of us could get near him. His arms and legs windmilled. One hand caught the footman in the stomach; he grunted, fell back, staggered forward again. I tried to grab one of the flailing arms and had to duck away from a wild punch. Then servants in shirtsleeves came running from the rear of the house, seized Ridley *en masse* from behind. A burly groom put out a foot and neatly took Ridley's ankles out from under him. Ridley hit the floor with a thump that made him gasp. I heard Jenison mutter in satisfaction.

Heron strolled forward, put a foot in the middle of Ridley's chest and pressed down hard. Ridley yelped. Heron said, 'Now you will apologize to Mr Jenison, and to his family and household, for your boorish behaviour.'

Ridley made a gurgling noise. Heron pressed harder. 'Now!'

'I . . . I apologize,' Ridley yelled.

'And now to Mr Nightingale.'

Ridley mumbled. '*And* to Mr Patterson.'

Ridley got out, 'Yes, yes!'

'Properly,' Heron said inexorably.

'I apologize!'

'Very well,' Heron said. 'Now we will put you in my carriage and convey you home to your mother.' He bent over Ridley's squirming body, smiling grimly into his red face. 'And let me tell you, sir, if you cause her any more distress, I will personally throw you in the Tyne and leave you to get yourself out.'

He nodded to the servants. The footman and groom hauled Ridley to his feet and hustled him out into the street. They did not treat him gently.

'Do you need my help?' I asked. Heron shook his head, took his coat and cane from a maid, and sauntered out to his carriage, as cool as if nothing had happened.

Nightingale had crawled to the stairs and was trying to haul himself on to the bottom step. I reached to help him and, after a moment, he struggled to his feet with my aid, clinging on to the banister. Tears streamed down his face. The butler, unprompted, brought him a glass of brandy which he tossed back in one gulp.

'Get him a chair,' I said to the butler. 'He needs to get back to his lodgings.'

'A chair,' Nightingale repeated, breathing deeply. He straightened. 'Yes, a chair. But first I must reassure the ladies!' And he staggered across to the drawing room, flung open the doors and called out: 'Ladies! The danger is over. I have vanquished the villain!'

'What an evening!' Esther sighed and blew out the nightlight on the bedside table. The room was plunged into darkness. Beyond the bed curtains, one side of which was still undrawn, I could see the faint rectangle of the window with pale moonlight shining through.

Esther plumped up the pillows behind her, shuffled closer to me and laid her head against my shoulder. 'What a thoroughly unpleasant man!'

'Ridley?' I nodded.

'I am so glad you are nothing like him.' She laughed softly. 'Or Mr Nightingale. One must feel sorry for him, of course, but he is pompous and preposterously conceited.'

'He did his best to protect the ladies,' I pointed out. 'He must have some credit for that.'

'True.' Her hair tickled my skin above the collar of my nightshirt.

'Would you prefer me to be like Heron?'

'No, no,' she protested. 'Much too cold for my tastes.'

A moment's silence. I was comfortable and at ease; at moments like this, I knew I was glad we were married. 'I'm pleased you're not like Mrs Annabella,' I said.

She laughed outright at that. 'You know I'm not one for needlework.'

'Is Mrs Annabella? Beyond the normal mending that all ladies undertake, I mean.'

'Did you not see the covers to the chairs?'

'Not the tapestry owls?' I said, horrified. 'And the purple roses!'

'I think the roses were Mrs Jenison's,' she said. 'Or did one of her daughters sew those? I think Mrs Jenison does the feather pictures. But I confess I am not sure. The purple roses are certainly to her taste.'

'I prefer your sketches.'

'I must sketch you,' she said. 'Perhaps even paint a portrait.'

'Heaven forbid!' I had a sudden appalling vision of seeing myself staring down at me every breakfast.

We lay in the near darkness, Esther's head heavy on my shoulder, her hand warm on my chest through the thin material of my nightshirt.

'Kate did not like the room,' she murmured.

I laughed. 'She's probably climbed out of the window by now and is halfway to Nightingale in the Golden Fleece.' Or, I thought with sudden appalled horror, she'd *stepped through* to the other world. Ought I to tell Esther about that? She was already wary about my own abilities.

'No,' Esther said. 'She is full of the violin lesson you promised her tomorrow.'

I sighed. 'I'm regretting that impulse. I simply wanted her to behave.'

'And I am taking her off to the dressmakers to order clothes more suitable for a girl of her age. Did you know she cannot even read? Although she could be taught, of course.'

I stared uneasily at her in the dim room. 'We're not adopting her, Esther. And she's not becoming my apprentice.'

'No, of course not. That would be totally inappropriate. In any case, she tells me Nightingale is going to draw up articles for her.'

'You can't believe that! He'll exploit her as long as she's useful then cast her off.'

She poked me lovingly in the shoulder. 'You should not associate with Claudius Heron so much; you are catching his cynicism. Do you really think I will abandon the girl to Nightingale? I never saw anyone more selfish. He does not care for her welfare in the least.'

There was silence. Outside, in the garden, a fox barked. I didn't want to think of Kate and her problems. Or Nightingale. Or Ridley and the baby. It all seemed too much effort. Lying here in the darkness with Esther in my arms was better. Much better.

'Charles,' Esther said.

'Yes?'

'Are you tired?'

I thought about this. 'Yes.'

'Oh,' she said, plainly disappointed.

'But not *too* tired.'

She giggled.

Nineteen

When dealing with the lower orders, a firm manner always
earns respect and obedience.

[*A Gentleman's Companion*, June 1734]

I awoke invigorated and refreshed, and breakfasted heartily.
Esther entertained me with the most ludicrous portions of her
London newspaper and sighed over her list of chores for the
day. 'Consult with Cook over the menus, get the gardener a
new boy to help him.' She fixed me with a severe gaze. 'This
is a sign of the excitement I shall be indulging in today, Charles.
Doing an inventory of the pots and pans!'

I laughed. 'I shall think of you as I flatter the ladies and
gentlemen into buying tickets. Two or three people actually
came up to me in the street yesterday, *asking* for tickets.'

'They'd heard of Nightingale?'

'Alas, yes. And talking of Nightingale, have you seen Kate
this morning?'

'I sent my maid in to check on her. She is still asleep.
Snoring, apparently. You had better enquire at the Jenisons'
today too. To ensure the ladies have not taken harm from last
night.' She looked at me severely when I made a derisory noise.
'Really, Charles, I do know neither of them was in the slightest
danger! It is a matter of politeness.'

'We'll see them at the concert this afternoon.'

She frowned. 'True, I'd forgotten. I will send a note instead.'
She folded up the newspaper. 'I suppose we needn't concern
ourselves about Ridley today. Heron will probably have him
in chains!'

'It would be no less than he deserves.' I could not forget the baby's body in its sodden rags. 'I begin to think nothing but death will reform him.' And probably not even that; not so long ago, I'd tangled with a very unpleasant spirit who'd carried grudges beyond the grave.

It had rained overnight; there were damp patches on the ground still and the bushes in the gardens in the middle of Caroline Square dripped moisture on the skirts of my coat as I brushed past. I'd planned to start the morning with a visit to Hugh to see how he was, and to regale him with the events of the previous evening which I knew he'd enjoy, but when I reached his lodgings he wasn't in. He must be feeling better and gone out for a bite to eat.

I stood for a moment in the street, debating whether to try and find him. If he was better he might well be at the concert this afternoon; was it worth wandering around town after him? I was on the verge of finding a spirit to enquire for me where he was, when I wondered if he'd gone up to the stables where he kept his horse – and that put me in mind of Ridley's horse and the events of *that* evening.

What exactly must have happened? Ridley – the horseman – had ridden into town, found two whores, paid one to hold the horse while he tried his luck with the other. He was in a bad temper and his unsuccessful drunken fumblings with the girl made him more angry. Then he'd ridden off, accidentally or deliberately cannoning into the woman.

There were a number of problems with this version of events, I realized. As Hugh had said, why should Ridley ride south? It was in quite the wrong direction for his mother's house. And why had he come to Newcastle at all? Surely not just to spend a few minutes with a whore?

He must have had other business here. The business had gone badly, he was angry, sought out the whore, grew even more angry. But in that case, what had he done with his horse while transacting his original business? He couldn't leave the horse to wander round the streets. He must have left it at stables.

I had tickets to sell. I could hardly complain about Esther's money when I did nothing to earn my own. I didn't have time to chase after a mystery that would never be solved.

I went up to the stables Hugh used.

The grooms listened politely but said they'd seen no horse like the grey; the only grey they had was much lighter. They let me look at it and it was almost white. Well, there were plenty of other stables in town; I'd work my way round them in the course of the next day or two. Meanwhile, I really must get back to selling tickets.

I traipsed down towards the Key in hope of seeing Lizzie Ord's father, Thomas Saint the printer, who usually buys two or three tickets. Inns stable horses too, I thought; someone who didn't know the town particularly well – and Ridley had been away since he was a child – might find an inn more easily than livery stables. Which inns might he have tried? The Fleece was the most obvious, being nearest the bridge from the south. The Old Man of course, but that was a mere tavern. Then there was the George, easily the most reputable inn in town.

The George lies just up from St Nicholas's Church, and I was only a street or two away. It wouldn't take long to get there and ask a few questions; I turned down an alley, across a street and into the inn yard.

The inn is a rickety old place, whose haphazard beams and homely whitewash disguise excellent service and a hearty welcome. A maid directed me to the stable lad who was, she said, breakfasting; I found him sitting on a bench outside the kitchen, in a patch of sunshine, enjoying a very large tankard of ale and a wedge of freshly baked bread. He was two or three years older than Kate, maybe fifteen, and stank of the stables. Dried horse-shit lined one boot and a streak of mud his right cheek; he had a nervous habit of scratching at his leg.

I described the grey horse to him. He screwed up his eyes in thought. 'Oh, aye. Fine horse that was. Left it here two or three hours.'

'That's not long. Did he say why he wanted to leave it?'

The lad stared. 'He wanted it looked after.'

I rephrased the question. 'Did he say where he was going?'

He thought, shook his head, drank ale, scratched his leg. 'Didn't ask.' He grinned. 'Didn't like him. Rude.'

'Insulted you, did he?'

'Had a filthy temper on him. Said he'd been told the George was good and it better had be. Like I'd not look after the horse right!'

He expiated on the horse's good points at length, growing more and more enthusiastic. It had obviously been a well-bred, expensive animal.

'What did he look like?' I intervened. 'The man, I mean, not the horse.'

He shrugged and immediately lost all inclination to talk. 'Dunno.' Another scratch.

'You must have been close to him, if you took the horse out of his hands.'

'Had a hat,' he said, at last. 'And a big coat.' He shrugged. 'It were foggy. He were just some fellow.' Light seemed to dawn. 'I remember the bag. Chinked as he took it down. Money, lots of it.'

That puzzled me. Ridley had had money? Why then did he need to steal from his mother? Unless he'd lost the money, gambling perhaps. Was that why he'd come to Newcastle in the first place? But somehow I couldn't imagine Ridley getting annoyed over losing money. He'd regard it as just another amusing incident.

'Was it a bag with letters on it?'

'Dunno.' Another one who couldn't read. 'Had gold on it. All swirls.'

I scratched the monogram on the stone bench, using the sharp end of a pebble. He looked at it dubiously. 'Mebbe.'

I sighed. 'Was he still in a bad temper when he came back for the horse?'

The lad grinned. 'And how!'

'But he didn't say why?'

'Just took the horse and went off. No,' he corrected himself, 'I forgot. He asked which way for the bridge.'

'He was riding south then?'

'I told him, and then he goes off in the wrong direction!' The lad grinned. 'Well, I weren't running after him to say. Not after him being so rude.'

He scratched at the leg, stared reflectively into the bottom of the empty tankard. I fished a sixpence out of my pocket. He stared at it with growing appreciation.

'I can tell you more,' he said, adding, just as I was getting hopeful again, 'Dunno any more but I could easy make something up.'

I gave him the sixpence and retreated.

I thought of going to the Old Man Inn to question the girls there, and see if Ridley had been telling me the truth about what he'd been doing on the night the child had died. But it would be well-nigh impossible to find two girls whose names I didn't know and who might not be connected with the inn at all, so I went back home to give Kate her promised violin lesson. Having sold not a single concert ticket.

She was in the estate room with Esther, wearing a neat, rather drab dress I fancied Esther must have borrowed from a servant, and her brown hair was down (and washed) as befitted her age. Apparently, she was demonstrating she could write her name; this, I saw over her shoulder, consisted of writing a large ungainly K.

I took her into the library. She scampered after me with a child's eagerness and hung over the painted images of nymphs and shepherds on the harpsichord lid. 'What are they doing? Are they dancing? Why are they doing it in the middle of a field?'

I took my violin out of its case. It's not a valuable instrument but one with sentimental value for me; I'd seen enough to know Kate would handle it carefully. She ran her fingers over the age-smoothed wood, clearly appreciating the feel. I gave her the bow and was just telling her to play me something she liked, when a sparkle of light caught my attention and the spirit George shot along the raised edge of the harpsichord lid. 'Master! You can't teach her. You know you can't!'

Kate stared. 'Who's he?'

'My former apprentice,' I said, sighing.

'I'm *still* your apprentice, master,' George said indignantly. 'You can't teach her. Girls can't play the violin.'

'Who says?' Kate demanded.

'It isn't proper!'

'George—'

'Besides, girls aren't any good at music.'

Kate spluttered in indignation. 'Don't suppose you ever talked to a girl in your life!'

'Girls are silly!'

'I bet you never got a look in,' Kate said. 'Bet you had spots.'

That was an unluckily accurate guess; George's skin had been horribly scabbed. The gleam of light throbbed. 'I bet *you* got the pox!'

Kate shrieked. 'I do not!'

'Kate—'

'Well,' she said, ignoring me, 'at least I ain't dead!'

'Master!' George protested. But the rest of what he had to say was lost as Kate launched into a very fast, very loud jig.

Kate played; the spirit skittered about the harpsichord lid, yelling. Its high-pitched indignation cut into my head like a saw; I had a raging headache in seconds. I tried to stop Kate but she pretended not to hear me, said, 'Eh? What?' a couple of times. George yelled, 'Stop her, master, stop her!'

I took a deep breath and bellowed. 'Be quiet!'

Kate stopped in mid-phrase, with such a look of dread on her face I was startled. She took a step backwards, said, 'I didn't mean— I wasn't going to— honest, I wasn't . . .'

'She shouldn't be playing, master!' George said with an edge of triumph.

'George.' Esther's quiet voice came from the doorway. 'Come with me.'

The gleam of the spirit jittered about uneasily. 'But mistress . . .'

'Now, George.' And Esther turned on her heels.

'Master!' George wailed. I said nothing. The gleam hesitated, then shot off across the floor after Esther.

There was silence for a moment after they'd left. Kate stood hugging the violin, looking fearful. She could fight off a drunken man with no hesitation but someone shouting at her made her tremble. I realized I hadn't the slightest idea what her life must have been like in that slum.

'I apologize for shouting at you,' I said formally. 'But if you and the spirit are going to yell each other down all the time, living in this house is going to be intolerable.' Inwardly, I was groaning; first George took a dislike to Tom, now to Kate. Perhaps Esther could talk him round; I was beginning to think I could not. 'Now,' I said to Kate. 'You're not standing properly.'

Criticism, as ever, worked its magic. The tension melted out of her. 'I am!' she said indignantly. 'I'm on my two feet. How else do you stand?'

'Straighten up,' I said. 'Rest the violin on your shoulder and keep your palm away from the neck.'

She held the violin out. 'Show me.'

I took the instrument and stood in the correct position. Kate walked round me, peering under my raised bow arm, ducking under the violin, standing on tiptoe to see over my shoulder. Then, with a look of complete smugness, she took the violin from my grasp and held it perfectly.

The lesson was a new experience for me. Kate did not respond well to being told what to do, but *show* her and she copied it, well-nigh perfectly. And if it wasn't perfect, she was willing to do it again and again, and if need be, again, until it was. I was impressed; most pupils want to play just well enough to bumble through the piece and then move on to the next. Not Kate. She even submitted to playing her favourite tunes as slowly as possible, to make sure the bowing was even and the notes perfectly in tune.

The only thing she couldn't do was read the notes on the page. She couldn't even see the sense of being able to do it.

'Look,' she said, pointing at the score on the music stand. 'That little dot there.'

'That represents the note C.'

'Why?'

'Because it does.'

'Why can't it be K?' For Kate presumably.

'Because it isn't.'

'And why not apple?'

'Apple!'

'And why are there five lines on that little ladder thing they sit on and not four?'

She didn't know her letters but she could count.

'Kate,' I said, 'you're doing excellently. But if you play that violin in public . . .'

'I'm going to,' she said, firing up at once. 'This afternoon. In the old fellow's concert.'

'You'll be branded as no better than your mother,' I warned.

'That's unfair!'

'That's the way it is. Women who appear in public are not respectable.'

'Your wife plays the harpsichord.'

'Only in private. And even then, only the harpsichord and harp are suitable instruments for women.'

'Anyhow,' she said, changing tack skilfully. 'Don't matter. I ain't respectable.'

'You'll be made the butt of all sorts of offers, which you'll not like in the least.'

'I'll say no,' she said. 'If you won't let me play, how can I ever earn any money without selling myself?'

She had a point. 'You could take up a position as a servant, in a respectable household—'

She shrieked with derisive laughter. 'How do you think my ma ended up where she is? I ain't doing that.'

'An apprentice is a servant of sorts,' I pointed out.

'Right,' she said, thrusting the violin back into my hands. 'You don't want me, I'll go to the old fellow.'

'Nightingale simply wants to make money out of you.'

'Well, that's all right,' she said, 'because that's what I want too. Lots and lots and *lots* of money!'

I nearly said she could have mine.

Twenty

No gentleman ever raises his voice.
[*A Gentleman's Companion*, July 1732]

The first person Esther and I set eyes on when we entered the crowded Assembly Rooms that afternoon was Claudius Heron, standing by one of the tall windows. If by keeping to the shadows, he was hoping not to draw attention to the large bruise disfiguring his left cheek, he was mistaken. It gave him a raffish air totally at odds with his character.

'Ridley was not quite as pacified as I anticipated,' he said dryly. 'He was perfectly well-behaved until we drew up outside his parents' home, at which point he apparently realized where he was and started flailing about. It took three footmen to subdue him.'

I grimaced. 'His behaviour to Nightingale last night was unforgivable. In a private house – in front of ladies!'

'I am beginning to think him insane.'

Esther said tartly, 'He needs a firm hand, and work to keep him occupied.'

'I agree entirely,' Heron said, 'but only so much can be done by force. If he will not discipline himself, there seems little others can do.'

'He's not seen Armstrong yet?' I asked.

'He has been given until the end of the day to do so.'

Jenison was talking to Nightingale on the other side of the room; he signalled to me and I excused myself to Esther and Heron. A surprisingly large number of people had already arrived for the concert and as I made my way through the company, I received some hard stares; I heard someone murmur, '. . . rich woman. All the same, these fellows . . .' I gritted my teeth, prevented myself – just – from turning to give them a hard stare. That's what Heron would have done; I don't have the confidence to carry it off.

Nightingale was in pink, with the usual silver ladders climbing all over his ample stomach. All that embroidery must have cost a fortune. Jenison was saying, 'Just a little demonstration, not a full concert. A few airs to entertain us.'

'Of course,' Nightingale said. I smelt a faint aroma of beer; he'd plainly been indulging but not, I hoped, *over*-indulging.

It was almost impossible to get him to the harpsichord; every lady wanted to greet him and he wasn't in the least averse to returning the greetings fivefold; old or young, he treated them all with the same flattering flirtation. When he arrived at the harpsichord at last, he was breathless and glowing.

'The Vivaldi,' he said. 'Slow movement, just to warm us both up, eh? Then the Handel. The overture to *Giulio Cesare*.'

'All of it?'

He had a pile of music on the harpsichord stool and handed it to me as I was trying to unlock the instrument. I put it back on the stool again.

'Then the last movement of the Vivaldi. Do you know *The Lass of Patie's Mill*?'

'Of course.'

'We'll do that then. All five verses. I'll do verse one as a violin, verse two as a trumpet, verse three—'

'Alpenhorn?' I suggested.

'And I'll sing the rest of them. Then the trumpet march by Purcell . . .'

'Jenison asked for a *few* airs,' I reminded him.

'And the witches' song from *Macbeth*.'

I gave up trying to persuade him to exercise restraint and

concentrated instead on tuning the harpsichord. There was a flurry of satin and a breathless voice said, '*Dear* Mr Nightingale.' I glanced up to see Mrs Annabella, in the most amazingly elaborate white dress with an exceedingly low neckline, simpering at Nightingale. He bowed deeply, took her hand and bestowed the breath of a kiss on it. Then he drew himself up to his full height, standing just a fraction too close in a protective manner. 'My dear lady, it is *so* crowded in here. Allow me to find you a seat.'

She fluttered and simpered and disclaimed, but finally agreed to put her hand on his arm, and sailed off with a flushed face and a triumphant look at the other ladies who were hovering hopefully.

The harpsichord keeps in tune well in the Assembly Rooms; I put down the tuning key and glanced round before opening the music. And there at the back was Hugh, sauntering in, dressed in his favourite dark blue, attracting as large a cluster of ladies as Nightingale. With his arm in a sling, he contrived to look as romantic a figure as any lady could wish for.

And behind Hugh came Cuthbert Ridley.

I looked to the windows for Heron, but he was already pushing through the crowds. Ridley was staring round the assembled company with a look of amused contempt. Then a young lady nearby glanced round, and Ridley was instantly diffident, twisting his hands together and staring at his feet.

I glanced about for Nightingale. He was well out of Ridley's way. He and Mrs Annabella had been caught in a cluster of ladies, all eager to be introduced. Mrs Annabella still had her hand on Nightingale's arm but was looking a little put out by his attentions to the others, particularly as he interrupted her in the middle of a sentence. Mrs Jenison too hovered, looking uncertain. Nightingale bowed to one middle-aged lady, then another, had them all smiling and laughing at his *bons mots*. A few husbands looked disgruntled.

Then an even bigger attraction presented itself. Nightingale straightened. His mouth stretched into a gracious smile, his eyes fixed on a young lady coming towards him. Mrs Annabella pouted; Mrs Jenison seemed disapproving. The other ladies looked annoyed.

One of the matrons made the introduction. Nightingale bowed deeply over the hand of young Lizzie Ord. He must have said something complimentary for she blushed and gave him her fingers, but then couldn't extricate them again and stood helplessly protesting as Nightingale acclaimed her beauty. She plainly felt trapped; she cast an appealing look over his shoulder, as if for help. I started up, but her husband was at her side at once.

Philip Ord is a jealous man. I didn't hear what he said, but Nightingale let go of Lizzie's hand and moved smoothly on to two others coming up behind her – a lady with her daughter, younger but not as pretty as Lizzie. 'Heavens above!' he cried. 'I never saw a town so full of beauties!'

Lizzie gave me a mischievous look and went off to sit demurely by her husband on a sofa in a window embrasure. I laid out my music in the order Nightingale had mentioned – not that I expected him to do anything as simple as keep to what he'd said. Jenison came to collect his wife and sister. Heron, I noted, had taken a seat directly behind Ridley; Hugh and his adoring little court had settled into a cluster of chairs under one of the chandeliers, the ladies competing to find a cushion soft enough to place behind his injured arm. And – heavens above! – there was Kate in her yellow dress and a grin that she clearly imagined was gracious, making her way imperiously through the crowds.

Nightingale sauntered over to her. I watched them together. His attitude to her, I thought, was overfamiliar, but nothing suggested he had untoward designs on her; he was treating her like an amusing little pet who would entertain the company with its tricks. He went off again to be gracious to an elderly matron.

Esther stopped by the harpsichord for a moment. 'It is agreeably busy,' she said. 'And Nightingale is making a distinct success with the ladies.' She gave me an impish smile. 'He has ignored me entirely. Walked straight past me. I was ready to take offence!'

I laughed. 'He plainly has too great an opinion of your good sense; he knows he can't twist you round his little finger.'

'Nonsense,' she murmured. 'He clearly believes no lady can resist his charms.'

I nodded towards the other side of the room. 'Mrs Jenison's not particularly entranced. She doesn't look well.'

The lady in question was sitting on a hard chair, listening to Mrs Annabella's eager chatter with an air of great weariness.

Esther nodded. 'She has a headache. I have already promised her one of my cordials. Well,' she said sighing, 'I had better greet one or two of my acquaintance or they will think I am snubbing them.'

She went off to talk to her friends, plainly not having seen Kate. The girl was looking a little lost; I smiled at her and she started across the room towards me. But Nightingale was striding up imperiously, bending across the harpsichord. 'Devil take it! Why are you looking so sour? Smile, man, smile!'

He was on edge, I realized; the incident with Ord must have upset him more than he liked to show. I hesitated, but the matter could not be ignored. 'Do you still intend the girl to perform?'

'Damn it!' he said. He glanced round, saw Philip Ord staring at him, and lowered his voice. 'Don't get so disapproving, man, I'm only humouring the girl. I'm not carrying her off to London or Edinburgh! God knows what they'd make of her there,' he added contemptuously.

Kate, just behind him, stood stock still, face set hard.

I said, 'It's hardly kind to raise her expectations, then dash them.'

'She's a novelty, man! Novelties never last. Two or three concerts and that's it.'

Considering Nightingale could himself be regarded in the light of a novelty, I thought his words remarkably imperceptive. But then, I'd come to realize, he was a man who saw what he wanted to see.

'I still don't —'

His short temper snapped. 'It's none of your business!' And he strode off, finding his smiles again with difficulty.

Kate sauntered up to me, defiance in every line. 'I'll show him. He'll not throw me off so easily. I want the fiddle.'

'Kate—'

'I want the fiddle!'

'Fiddle?' Philip Ord said sharply behind me. 'The girl is not going to play, surely?'

I met his gaze, saw another hostile gentleman behind him. They could be the answer to my problem, I thought; armed with their opposition, both Kate and Nightingale might be easier to withstand. 'I regret,' I said, steeling myself for Kate's fury, 'that I've left the key of the instrument cupboard at home.'

Kate glared. 'Go and get it, then.'

'Young woman,' Ord said frigidly. 'Pray go back to your—' He cast an eye down her gaudy dress, remembered he was amongst ladies and said, 'To wherever you come from.'

Nightingale came sailing up again. 'Katherine, my dear! No violin?'

'I don't have the key to the instrument cupboard,' I repeated.

And to my astonishment, without further provocation, he flew into a huge rage, shrieking at me. 'You thwart me! You want to ruin my performance? Jealousy, that's what it is! Just because I have more talent than you can ever imagine—'

Kate jerked back, plainly forced herself to stand still. Esther came up behind her and put her hand reassuringly on her shoulder. The room was disturbingly quiet; I heard Mrs Jenison say faintly, 'Oh dear.' Ord's face had turned purple with outrage.

'Call yourself a harpsichord player? I've heard better playing from a pet monkey! *You* thwart *me*! Get that damned cupboard open and get the girl a fiddle. Who do you think you are, sir, to countermand me? How dare you? A provincial scraper and squaller . . .'

'At least *he* is a gentleman,' Ord said loudly.

Not a sound in the entire room. Over Nightingale's shoulder, I saw Hugh staring and Ridley grinning. Heron stood up and walked towards us, hand on sword, footsteps echoing in the silence.

Everyone was looking at me expectantly. I had the feeling this was the crucial moment, the moment the ladies and gentlemen decided whether I was worthy of being accepted into their midst, or whether I remained forever an upstart who'd married above his station. What the devil was I to do? I knew what I *wanted* to do; I wanted to knock Nightingale flat on the floor. What would a *gentleman* do? I had a panicky feeling that swords at dawn were expected.

I said calmly, 'Do you wish to continue the concert, sir?'

Nightingale stared, caught in the middle of another rant. He snarled, teeth bared. 'I do not!'

'Then there's nothing more to be said.' And I stood up, put the harpsichord lid down and locked it.

Nightingale glared at me. Then he drew himself up, and swung round to face the audience. 'I will continue alone.'

Silence.

'Vivaldi,' he said loudly.

Hugh stood up, bowed elegantly to the ladies and turned for the door. He was the first but not the last. Several of the ladies rose with him; one said something about vulgar upstarts with no manners. Ord extended a hand to his wife; Lizzie, biting her lip, cast me a sympathetic look as she was led away. More than one lady ushered an excited young daughter to the door. Jenison watched horrified, as one by one the audience marched out.

As I made my own way down the side of the room, a lone figure at the back of the room stood up and started, in slow ironical fashion, to applaud loudly.

Cuthbert Ridley.

Twenty-One

The end of hubris is always disaster.
[*A Gentleman's Companion*, December 1730]

The minute we were in the house Esther told Kate to go upstairs and change into 'something more suitable'. Kate stood defiantly in the hallway in her gaudy yellow satin and glowered at us all. Heron strode straight into the drawing room, plainly in a foul temper.

'Brandy, Tom,' Esther said, handing her cloak to a maid. 'And make up a tray for Kate to have in her room. Lemonade and something to eat.'

Tom retreated with ill-concealed relief. The gleam that was George lingered on the bottom of the banister. 'I said girls aren't any good, master.'

'Not now, George.'

'She'll only be trouble!'

'Go, George!'

'You always tell me off, master!' he said sullenly. 'I don't like you any more.' And he shot off up the stairs.

We followed Heron into the drawing room. Esther sank down as if the afternoon had exhausted her. I tossed the music books on to one of the delicate chairs, gripped its back and hoped Tom would bring the brandy quickly. Damn Nightingale. He must have had experience of the humiliations musicians can suffer and to inflict that on a fellow performer was intolerable. And to involve a child like Kate!

Kate had come in with us and was standing with her arms folded around her as if she was cold. 'It ain't my fault,' she said defiantly.

'No one ever said it was,' I agreed.

'Quite entertaining, actually.' Hugh lowered himself into one of the more comfortable armchairs, and tried unsuccessfully to suppress a grin.

'I never asked him to argue over me.'

'I think this is a matter for the morning,' Esther said. 'When we are all less tired and irritable.'

'I ain't tired and I ain't irritable! He's ruined everything! Now I won't get to play in the concert.'

Hugh cast me a warning glance but I was too tired even to think of placating Kate. 'I wouldn't have let you play anyway.'

'It ain't fair!'

'It would not be proper,' Esther said repressively. 'There is only one opinion of women who play in public: their morals are loose, they have no virtue at all, and they are fair game for any man who wishes to try his luck!'

Kate glared and swung on her heels. 'I'm off to find the old fellow.'

'You are not.'

'He's the only one as wants me.'

'And ask yourself why!' Esther said in exasperation.

'He'll be drunk by now,' Hugh pointed out. 'Probably started drinking the moment he walked out of the Assembly Rooms.'

'Hugh's right,' I said. 'He won't be capable of knowing what he's doing. I'll have a word with him in the morning.'

'You're only saying that!'

She was right; I'd merely been trying to placate her. I took a deep breath and considered more calmly. 'No, I'll go down to the Fleece first thing and sort everything out.' It would hardly be a pleasant experience but quite apart from anything else I'd have to come to an accommodation with Nightingale or the series could never go ahead.

Kate stared. 'Promise?'

'Promise. Now go to your room and change.'

She glared, then turned and went up the stairs with ferocious dignity.

Heron was staring out of the window at the gardens, lit by the red glow of early evening sunshine. 'Nightingale's behaviour was unforgivable,' he said curtly.

Esther nodded, plumped up one of the cushions with more force than was strictly necessary. 'You can't play for him again, Charles. After such insults, it would be unthinkable!'

I shifted the music to the floor and sat down on the worryingly delicate chair. I was weary out of all proportion to the time of day and the amount of physical exercise I'd had. Somehow, emotional upsets are always more tiring. That was plainly what had happened to Nightingale; the confrontation with Ord had unsettled him, affected his judgement. And we'd already clashed over Kate; he'd have been feeling defensive about that. Still, his behaviour had been unacceptable.

Tom brought the brandy and we all lapsed into silence until he bowed himself out again. Hugh was plainly seeing the humorous side of the affair, grinning as he sipped the brandy. 'That's the second vocal soloist you've seen off in two months, Charles! You'll be getting yourself a reputation. There won't be a singer in England who'll come to the town.'

'I cannot imagine what Jenison was thinking of to invite him in the first place,' Heron said.

'A ladder dancer,' Esther said contemptuously.

'The *master* ladder dancer.' Hugh eased his arm, a little frown of pain between his eyes.

'I have no doubt his act is entertaining,' Esther said. 'In its own way. However, it is not what I am looking for when I go to one of the subscription concerts.'

'But you're a newly married woman,' Hugh said. 'Nightingale's exactly what most of the other ladies are looking for – you saw that for yourself. Mrs Jenison, Mrs Annabella, half a dozen others.'

'And most of the audience is female,' Heron said, as if it was something slightly discreditable.

'Jenison admires him,' I pointed out.

'I will talk to Jenison tomorrow.' Heron turned. The anger on his face took me aback. 'He cannot relish the idea of more incidents like this afternoon. And as for Nightingale—'

Hugh, out of Heron's view, mimed swordplay. I searched for a way to defuse the situation.

'I don't stand on my dignity,' I said. 'I've suffered worse.'
Though, admittedly, not usually so publicly. Given a choice
between a glamorous London performer he admired and a
musical director who was merely workaday, I wondered how
Jenison would choose. I was much cheaper than Nightingale,
of course, which must count in my favour, but Jenison was
plainly not comfortable with my newly ambiguous social
position.

'You should not have to put up with such indignities!' Heron
put his head back, threw the brandy down his throat in one
draught. The bruise on his left cheek was vivid.

'It's not so unusual,' Hugh said.

I intervened hurriedly; at any moment he'd point out that
most ladies and gentlemen regarded musicians with contempt,
which would be true but hardly uncomplimentary in present
company. 'I suspect the argument will simply add to the attractions of the series. Even before this, people were coming up
to me in the street and asking for tickets. The remaining
subscriptions will no doubt sell quickly now and the concert
series will, financially at least, be a great success.'

Esther and Heron were staring at me as if I was a complete
stranger.

'*Money*?' Esther said, with a touch of incredulity. 'Money is
not important, Charles!' I couldn't believe she could say such
a thing, considering the circumstances we found ourselves in.
'This is a matter of principle!'

'A matter of honour,' Heron said curtly. Hugh mimed swordplay again.

'He insulted you, Charles!'

'The matter cannot be allowed to rest,' Heron ground out.

'I wonder,' I said cautiously, 'if some compromise—'

'No,' Esther and Heron said together.

The doors were pushed open. We all turned to stare; Tom
was hesitating in the doorway. He opened his mouth to speak—
and George rushed past him so quickly I almost felt the breeze
from his movement. He hung from one of the branches of
unlit candles, and his glee was audible in his voice. 'She's gone,
master! She's gone!'

We looked at Tom. He started, 'I regret to say—'

'Ran off!' George crowed.

'The young lady has indeed—'

'I told you she would! Never trust a girl, master.'

'Have you searched the house?' Esther asked.

'Everywhere, mistress, everywhere!'

'I was speaking to Tom,' she said, barely restraining her annoyance.

'The maids have searched the rooms upstairs, madam. And we know she couldn't have come into the kitchen or slipped out the back door without us seeing her. But there is a window open in the library—'

'She must have slipped out into the garden,' Hugh said. 'Is the gate into the street open?'

Esther sent Tom off to check the gate and search the gardens. George shot off after him to add his mite of provocation. I stared past Heron into the garden and knew Kate could not have gone that way. She couldn't have slipped out unseen while Heron was staring out of the window and when he'd turned back into the room, I would have seen Kate behind him.

There was only one way she could have gone. She'd *stepped through* into that other world. She must be planning to step back and go down to the Fleece to confront Nightingale. That in itself didn't worry me greatly; Kate was amply capable of looking after herself. They would argue and shout, and Nightingale would throw her out, or Kate would storm out, vowing vengeance.

What worried me was Kate's apparent ability to step through and back again so precisely. I knew only too well the difficulties of stepping from one world to another; it was impossible to say how much time would pass or choose when to return to our own world. If Kate did intend to step into that other world then come back again, and was able to calculate where and when she would find herself, her abilities must be greater than I'd suspected.

I felt a distinct pang of envy.

We searched the house, but of course we didn't find her. I wasn't in the mood to care very much; in the morning we'd no doubt find her in her bed, and at breakfast she'd rant over Nightingale's perfidy and make another attempt to persuade me to take her on as an apprentice.

Nothing to worry about.

★　★　★

In the middle of the night, I woke from a deep sleep to find Esther shaking my shoulder. 'Charles . . . Charles!'

Blearily, I stared at her. 'What time is it?'

'Nearly three.'

'In the morning!'

'George has just had a message from a spirit at the Fleece.'

I propped myself on my elbows, rubbed at my eyes. I should have known. I'd been too cavalier about Kate. She was a child, no matter how independent-minded. She needed looking after.

'It is Nightingale,' Esther said. 'He has been attacked.'

Twenty-Two

There are times when we must simply accept the dictates of Divine Providence with humility.

[*A Gentleman's Companion*, November 1730]

Joseph, the lad who kept night watch at the Fleece, was wandering about the yard; he dashed over to me as soon as I trudged under the Fleece's arch. 'Mr Patterson. Thank goodness! He's in a real temper.'

He nodded back at the inn. The landlord, in shirtsleeves and waistcoat, was pacing up and down in front of the door to the kitchen passageway, being snappy with a maid who poked out her dishevelled head to see what was going on. He was snappy with me too, saying, 'Oh, it's you,' in the tone of one who knows a nuisance when he sees it. I wasn't looking at my best; I'd thrown on the first clothes that had come to hand, and I was unshaven and grubby. And tired. And tempted to snap back.

'Thank you for taking care of Mr Nightingale,' I said, and saw his broad red face soften somewhat. 'Yes, well,' he said, and led the way into the kitchen passageway.

'Is he dead?'

'Not yet.'

That didn't sound very good.

'Gale the surgeon's with him,' he said.

Well, that was something.

'He's up in his room.' He nodded at a narrow staircase opposite the door to the beer cellar. 'Go up if you want.'

'I wouldn't mind some refreshment,' I said, allowing coins in my pocket to chink.

He melted at once. 'I'll send the girl up with some beer.'

A wooden stair led up from the kitchen passageway, four or five steps only, but musty and trapping the scent of beer so strongly as to make my senses reel. Five or six spirits came flocking towards me as I climbed, firing questions: *What happened? Do you know who did it?* Well, at least I'd not have to question them − they clearly had no useful information. Which meant that *no* spirits knew anything about it; they have such an efficient message system that if one spirit had seen anything, every spirit in town would know about it by now.

On a tiny landing with warped floorboards, a door stood open into a substantial room. It was dim, the curtains had been drawn and the room was lit only by three candles in a gleaming new holder that stood amongst a clutter of personal possessions on a table. But it was light enough to see Nightingale in bed.

He was propped up against pillows, his face almost as pale as the sheets in which he lay, as if he'd lost all his blood. His eyes were closed, his arms on the sheets limp and unresponsive. The room stank of blood; Nightingale's bright pink clothes, stained and stiff, lay on a chair.

From the side of the bed, Gale the surgeon, a thin spare man with a round sombre face, nodded at me.

'How is he?' I asked.

'Very bad.' Gale was rarely so direct; such forthrightness could mean only one thing: Nightingale was at death's door.

'I was told he'd been attacked.'

Gale nodded. 'Stabbed. At least four times, maybe five. And there are some small scratches that suggest other attempts.'

'Attacked from behind or in front?'

'Both.' Gale considered, said at last, with judicious caution, 'It's hard to be certain but I think he was attacked first from behind; there's one wound high on his right shoulder at the back. That wound's not particularly deep or severe. Then I think he must have turned, for he was stabbed three times from the front. There are scratches on his hands which suggest he tried to defend himself.'

'You're sure there were not two attackers? One behind, one in front?'

'I think not. If there were two, why did the one behind stab only once?' He began to pack his instruments away.

'And the wounds in front were more deep, more dangerous?'

He nodded. 'One was in the left shoulder, the others in the belly.'

'Can you tell what the weapon was like?'

'I can tell you it wasn't sharp,' he said dryly. 'There was a great deal of tearing and bruising around the wounds – always a sign of something blunt.'

'And would there have been a lot of blood? Would the attacker not have been drenched in it?'

He shrugged. 'There could have been a great deal. But if the attacker was wearing a dark coat, it could have gone unnoticed.'

I looked down at Nightingale's pale face. It had been red with anger when I last saw it. 'What are his chances?'

'None at all,' Gale said bluntly. 'Even if he'd been found earlier, and hadn't lost so much blood, the belly wounds would be fatal. I suspect he'll not last the night.'

I looked on Nightingale's pale face, listened to the breath that whispered through his bloodless lips. If he'd turned to face his attacker, he would have seen the man's face, might be able to identify him. 'Is he likely to wake? To talk?'

Gale shook his head.

A serving girl pushed open the door. She bore a tankard of ale for me and a glass of the sweet wine Gale prefers. He took the glass and downed the wine in one draught. I went across to the window. Nightingale's travelling trunk was directly under the casement; I leant across it to lift the curtain. Outside there was a wall, scarcely three feet away on the other side of a narrow alley. It was pitch black, unlit; I could see nothing.

'Who should I send the bill to?' Gale put the glass down on the bedside table.

'Jenison,' I said, unhesitatingly, letting the curtain drop. When hiring Nightingale, he'd agreed to cover all the gentleman's expenses. I doubted he'd envisaged something of this sort.

'Good,' Gale said shortly and nodded to the girl. 'I want someone with him constantly.'

I took my beer downstairs, said goodbye to Gale at the

door to the kitchen passageway and watched him cross the cobbled yard to the arch. The night was dark, lit only by a few stars, a sliver of moon. Behind me, I could hear talking in the scullery; the Fleece was a warren of extensions and additions and it was difficult to be sure of anything, but Nightingale's room was probably directly above the kitchens. It would be noisy, but I fancied he would rather have liked that.

The landlord materialized at my shoulder. Before he could speak, I dropped a coin into his hand to pay for the beer. Mollified, he said, 'There's the cost of his room . . .'

'Jenison,' I said.

'And his food and drink. He could drink the Tyne dry. My cellars—'

'Jenison will pay,' I said again, curbing my impatience.

'And I had to give the two fellows who carried him back a penny each.'

'Add it to the bill.' I frowned. 'Did they say where they found him?'

'In the alley round the side.' He jerked his head. 'Between us and the mercers.'

'When?'

'Brought back maybe an hour ago. Surgeon said he must have been lying there a good while.'

The hall clock had said three a.m. when I let myself out of the house; Nightingale had been found at around two, perhaps attacked around midnight . . .

'Who found him?'

'Couple of sailors. Didn't recognize them – visitors, I daresay.'

Useless to try and find a pair of unidentifiable sailors and ask if they'd seen anything or anyone suspicious. In any case, the attacker had probably been gone long before they'd come on the scene. 'No weapon near him?'

He shrugged.

'And money?'

'None on him. But I don't reckon it'd been stolen – he still had his watch.'

I vaguely remembered having seen a watch on the bedside table.

'He'd probably spent all his money,' the landlord said, chuckling. 'He was a fine one for women and drink.'

An owl, white as snow, swooped over the yard, floated in to land on the peak of the inn roof.

'Had anyone threatened him, do you know?'

He grinned. 'More than a few. Couldn't keep his hands off the ladies, married or no. There were a couple of lads objected. The ostler's walking out with one of the maids and got uppity.' He realized what he was saying, beat a hasty retreat. 'But the lad'd never do anyone any harm.'

I tried to sound as casual as possible. 'Have you seen Mr Cuthbert Ridley here at all?'

'Oh, aye.' He laughed. 'Last night. Drunk as a lord.' He added, almost admiringly, 'Has a fine turn of phrase on him. Comes of being a lawyer, I daresay.'

'Did he and Mr Nightingale meet?'

'Never came near each other. Never saw Mr Nightingale at all last night.'

'He didn't come back from the afternoon concert?'

'Not till they carried him back.'

I finished the beer and contemplated the owl, still as a statue on the roof. 'Are there any spirits in the alley?'

'One or two in the house that go there. But none as saw anything. We were all asleep and even the spirits tend to keep quiet in the small hours.' He added tartly, 'They know I'll make it difficult for them if they don't.'

I handed him back the tankard. 'I'll go and take a look, see if there's anything left there.'

'Leave it till morning,' he advised. 'I don't want you carried in here as well.'

'I'll be careful.'

My footsteps were loud in the still night; I came out of the Fleece's yard on to the Sandhill and stood contemplating the Guildhall across the other side of the open expanse. The owl swooped over my head and was lost in the night. The landlord was right; if the attacker still lingered, I'd be putting myself in danger. And I'd see more in daylight. Yet there was a chance the knife might remain there, overlooked, and I didn't want to risk a thief coming along and making off with it.

A torch on the façade of the mercer's shop still burned. I lifted it down and hesitated at the mouth of the alley. The torch cast a bright light, but only over the first few yards.

There was no reason an attacker should have lingered here

but I went in cautiously, just in case. The flaring light showed a narrow alley sloping steeply upwards, then turning into a flight of steps climbing the Castle Mound. There was the usual litter – rotten fruit, abandoned fragments of wood, even a rat that skittered away into a blocked-up doorway as I approached.

A small window showed a faint blurring of light, low down, two feet or so from the ground. I bent to peer in. There were curtains, but they didn't quite meet in the centre, and I saw the flicker of candlelight. Pink clothes on a chair. Nightingale's room. The Fleece was built into the slope of the Castle Mound; a room that was up a few steps from the level of the inn yard was partially below ground here.

I straightened, walked, torch guttering, to the steps. There was a large dark patch on the cobbles at the foot of the stairs, irregularly shaped. I bent to touch the stain; it was still sticky in places. This looked like the place Nightingale had fallen.

It could have been an ideal place for an ambush, I thought, looking about, particularly at night when there were few people around. The attacker could have hidden in the blocked-up doorway; it was too shallow to be ideal but in the dark it might have served. I wondered what Nightingale had been doing here. He could have been returning to the Fleece, but this was not an obvious way to come, particularly for a stranger to the town.

I searched but there was no knife either in the alley or on the lower reaches of the steps. I went back out on to the street and returned the torch to its holder. Nightingale might have been attacked by thieves, of course. But why should a robber stab four times? That seemed a personal attack. Unless of course Nightingale had struggled and panicked him.

Was I being over-cautious? Was there any doubt about who'd done this? Ridley had attacked Nightingale at the Jenisons'; he'd been sarcastic with his applause at the concert and he'd been at the Fleece early in the evening looking for Nightingale. I'd good reason to believe Ridley had been instrumental in the death of the child on the Key, and I knew him to be capable of violence. His motive for arguing with Nightingale was mysterious but the two men had plainly known each other in London; Nightingale's refusal to acknowledge Ridley might suggest a previous association that was not entirely respectable. But would

Ridley have been foolish enough to attack Nightingale so soon after their public quarrel?

I thought he was stupid enough for any folly.

My eyes were aching. I rubbed them.

And caught, just at the edge of my vision, a flutter. Something bright reflecting the torchlight. A small figure in yellow, darting back into hiding.

Kate.

Twenty-Three

The coffee house should be a place for quiet contempla-
tion and perusal of the day's news. All too often, however,
it is merely a gossip shop.
[*A Gentleman's Companion*, July 1734]

I snatched a few hours' uneasy sleep and was already awake when Esther brought me a dish of hot chocolate. She perched on the edge of the bed, in a distractingly thin nightgown, her blonde hair in one long braid over her shoulder.

'Is he dead?'

I shook my head. 'Not when I left him at any rate. But Gale doesn't think he'll last long.'

'Robbers?'

'Unlikely. And unfortunately no one seems to have seen anything.'

'Have you sent a message to Jenison?'

I yawned. The chocolate was soothing and rich and bitter, and I was sitting in bed with a beautiful woman – *my wife* – dressed in hardly anything at all, smiling at me, resting her hand on my arm, warm and gentle. There was little more, I thought – well, only a *little* more – required to make me feel Paradise really existed.

I dragged my attention back to the matter in hand. 'I thought it was better to give Jenison the news face to face rather than send a message by the spirits, and I didn't want to wake him in the middle of the night. I'll go down to the Fleece to see if Nightingale's still alive and then go on to Jenison.'

'I will carry the message,' she offered. 'I am going up there now to take Mrs Jenison her cordial. And it will lessen the risk of them finding out by chance before you can reach them. You can join me there.' She hesitated. 'There is still no sign of Kate, by the way.'

That glimpse of yellow the previous night, outside the Fleece. Kate had had an argument with Nightingale, had reason to be angry with him. 'She'll turn up again,' I said.

'I hope so. She needs help, Charles.'

I went out without breakfast. It was late morning when I walked into the Fleece again. The first person I saw was Joseph, the lad who watched overnight, sitting on a chair at the entrance from the yard into the kitchen passageway. He was yawning hugely and rubbing his tousled hair. 'He's not dead yet,' he said and jerked his head at the stairs.

Nightingale was much as I'd seen him the previous night. Propped against the pillows, unnaturally still, unnaturally white. The only change was in his breathing, which sounded even more raw and hoarse. The girl by the bed was mending a petticoat and never looked at Nightingale once in all the time I was there. In a way, I didn't blame her. What was there for her to do? She was waiting simply for the moment when that husky breathing stopped.

The sound followed me out of the room.

I'd hardly stepped into the street again when a hand took my arm. Heron's voice said in my ear, 'We need to talk. Have you eaten?'

We went into Nellie's coffee house; for once it was relatively quiet. We sat in the window where we could see the fish market across the other side of the Sandhill; I ordered bread and cold meats; Heron declined food but took a dish of coffee.

'The servants are saying Nightingale has been attacked. Killed.'

'Attacked, yes. But he's not dead yet, though Gale thinks it's just a matter of time.'

'Do you know what's happened?'

I told him as much as I knew, excepting my glimpse of Kate. I needed to think more about that. I did tell him I suspected Ridley of some involvement. Heron listened in silence, lean fingers playing with his coffee dish. When I'd finished, he was silent for a moment, then said abruptly, 'Ridley has disappeared.'

I was not surprised. I cut a chunk of bread and laid meat on top. 'Do you take that as an admission of guilt?'

He considered. 'Some people will think so. But he is quite capable of disappearing simply in order to annoy his mother and me.'

'He's not at the Old Man?'

'I sent my manservant to enquire. Ridley was there early last evening and has not been seen since.' He added dryly, 'They are eager to find him – he has not paid his bill.'

'The real problem,' I said, 'is that the attack seems to be on the wrong person. Obviously Ridley and Nightingale weren't on good terms after that incident at the Jenisons', and Ridley's behaviour at the concert yesterday hardly improved matters. But surely that would give Nightingale a reason to attack Ridley, not the other way round?'

'I think Ridley is capable of picking an argument just for the fun of it,' Heron said.

'But this was a determined assault, with intent to severely injure, if not to kill.'

'Nothing would surprise me with Ridley. Does Jenison know of the attack?'

'Esther's gone up to tell them, and I promised to follow once I'd established how he is.'

'There'll be the devil to pay with the ladies,' Heron said. 'They'll be inconsolable.' He drank a little, a very little, of his coffee and got up. 'I have business meetings today – I may have to ride out of town for an hour or two. I have set my servants to look for Ridley but in truth I am growing very tired of his antics. I am more than inclined to let him take his chances.'

I watched him out of the room, pondering on the likelihood of Ridley being the attacker. But as I finished my coffee, my thoughts were on that small figure I'd seen in the darkness of the early morning. Ridley was not the only person who'd disappeared. And not long before Kate had gone, she'd been angry with Nightingale, and determined to confront him.

Someone was tapping on the window. A face peered at me from the street. Hugh. He waved and hurried off. A moment or two later he was banging the coffee house door and calling to one of the girls to bring him ale. He dropped into the chair opposite me with a sigh.

'Quiet in here, ain't it? I've just seen Heron – he said you were here. Who killed Nightingale?'

I sighed. 'No one. He's not dead yet.' Briefly, I outlined yet again what had happened.

'Poor devil,' Hugh said. He was out of breath but otherwise looked fit and healthy. Immaculately dressed as always, that sling giving him a dashing air that made the serving girls glow at him. And, given the paucity of customers, there were four girls occupying their time ogling him.

'What happened to the cold?'

'Disappeared,' he said happily. 'Woke up this morning, clear nose, no headache. Fit as a fiddle. Must have been all that excitement yesterday.' Charlotte put a plate of bread and pie in front of him; he grinned at her, shifted the plate awkwardly with his good hand. 'So who did it?'

I hesitated. 'It could have been a thief.'

'Come on, Charles! This isn't up to your usual standard! You usually have everything sorted out by now. Was he robbed?'

'No, but that's not to say it mightn't have been an *attempted* robbery. The villains could have been disturbed before they got anything.'

He speared a piece of pie with his knife. 'But you don't believe so?'

I glanced round to make sure we couldn't be overheard; the other customers all looked half-asleep. I lowered my voice. 'Cuthbert Ridley's disappeared.'

Hugh chewed. 'Now there's an unpleasant piece of work. Think he did it?'

'If Nightingale had been hit over the head with a bottle in a tavern, I'd say yes straight away. But it seems someone lay in wait for him. That's too calculating for Ridley.'

Hugh gestured with his knife. 'And?'

We paused while Charlotte brought me more coffee and gave Hugh another admiring glance. He winked at her. 'And what?' I said, after she was gone.

'And what else are you not telling me? Come on, Charles, you have someone else in mind as our possible assassin.'

I sighed, sipped at my fresh dish of coffee. 'Kate.'

He frowned. 'Did she not come back to the house then?'

'No.'

'But what motive would she have?' he protested. 'He was

going to take her to London – he was her only chance of leaving her wretched life behind.'

'No such thing,' I said. 'Yesterday, at the concert, he told me he'd no intention of taking her on permanently – she was just a novelty to enliven a concert or two. And she heard what he said, Hugh. That's why she was so angry afterwards.'

'But why attack him? Surely she would have tried to change his mind?'

'Suppose she did, but he wouldn't listen? She might lash out, do more damage than she anticipated. She's not a genteelly reared child, Hugh, she's lived on the streets since she was old enough to walk, and she's seen a lot more, and is capable of a lot more, than the average child.'

'Charles,' Hugh said patiently, waving his knife, 'Nightingale's a grown man, taller than you, about my height. Big and burly. The girl's twelve years old and small for her age. Where were his injuries?'

'Shoulder and belly.'

'How would she stab someone twice her height in the shoulder?'

I drained my coffee. 'What's behind the Fleece, Hugh?'

'What's this – the catechism? There's nothing behind it except the Castle Mound.' He stopped, staring.

'Exactly,' I said. 'The alley where Nightingale was stabbed runs alongside the Fleece then climbs up the mound in a series of steps up to the castle yard itself. Suppose Nightingale was coming down those steps. Kate comes down after him, and when he gets to the bottom she darts forward and from the vantage point of three or four steps up, she strikes. The steps are very steep, Hugh – it might have been a stretch, but I doubt it was impossible.'

He was silent for a moment. 'He'd have heard her come up behind him.'

'Not if he was drunk – and I suspect he would have been *very* drunk.'

'But still!'

I sighed. 'She can step through, Hugh.'

He shivered as if he was cold. 'Charles, you know how much—'

'You hate the idea? Yes, I do know.' It puzzled me, that dislike – was Hugh not even curious about how the process worked?

'Kate could have stepped through from that *other* place and attacked Nightingale from behind.'

'Could she do that?' he asked incredulously. 'I thought it was all very imprecise, that you can't govern where you go or when.'

'It is with me,' I admitted. 'I'm beginning to think Kate has abilities I don't.'

'Oh God,' he said. 'A girl like that! Who knows what might happen?'

'I am trying to keep my eye on her,' I said dryly. 'I'm not saying Kate *did* attack Nightingale, just that it isn't physically impossible.'

Hugh drank down a long draught of ale. 'Well,' he said, at last. 'There's one obvious thing to do, isn't there? If either Kate or Ridley — or anyone else for that matter — did see Nightingale again that evening and argued with him, someone might have witnessed it. You're going to have to find out where Nightingale was that night, Charles.'

'I agree.'

'I'll come with you.'

'You don't have to,' I said. 'You need to take it easy with that arm.'

He grinned. 'Charles, how long have you known me? There's nothing more guaranteed to make me feel better than a bit of excitement! Where do we start?'

Twenty-Four

Adversity should be met with quiet courage and endurance.

[*A Gentleman's Companion*, November 1731]

I left Hugh to learn what he could of Nightingale's movements from the spirits; they can pass messages from one side of the town to the other in an instant, and ferret out every scrap of news. Meanwhile, I bore the latest news to the Jenisons; I'd join him as soon as I could. But when the footman threw open the doors of the Jenisons' drawing room and I heard the noise, I fervently wished I'd gone with him straight away. Mrs Annabella was in full wail, sobbing, crying, lamenting, repeating Nightingale's name again and again in broken accents. The footman couldn't resist giving me a speaking look as he retreated.

Mrs Jenison rose to meet me. She looked strained, as if she hadn't slept. Behind her, Esther was sitting beside Mrs Annabella, patting her hand in barely concealed exasperation. Mrs Annabella, drooping on the elegant new sofa, had her handkerchief – a frivolous scrap of lace – to her eyes.

But none of them had a chance to say anything before the doors burst open again. Jenison came hurrying in. 'Patterson!' He looked haggard, drawn. 'Is he dead?'

Mrs Annabella swooned back. Esther murmured something consoling and, unseen by the others, rolled her eyes at me.

'He's much the same,' I said diplomatically, wanting to avoid distressing the ladies further.

'Thank God,' Mrs Jenison said, sinking back in her chair. She cast a glance at her sister-in-law. 'All may yet be well.'

'Is there any news of who did it?' Jenison demanded.

'I'm afraid not.'

'But who would shoot him?' Mrs Annabella wailed, clutching the handkerchief. 'Such a gentleman . . .'

'Really, Annabella,' Jenison said irritably. 'You know we were told he was stabbed.'

Mrs Annabella gasped and fell back again; Esther, looking grim, seized the smelling salts from the table by the workbox and waved them under Mrs Annabella's nose, perhaps more enthusiastically than was strictly necessary. Mrs Annabella coughed, spluttered and sat up, tears running from her eyes. Mrs Jenison looked helplessly on.

'Look, Patterson.' Jenison took my arm. 'This is not a suitable subject for the ladies. We'll go into the library.'

'No!' Mrs Annabella sat up very straight; her grey hair was in girlish ringlets, complete with trailing pink ribbons. 'I need to know what happened! The devil that did this must be brought to justice!'

'Of course, of course,' Jenison snapped.

'You've seen him?' Mrs Annabella fixed me with her watery gaze. 'He's being well looked after?'

I thought of the bored girl at his bedside. 'Everything that can be done is being done.' That is, *nothing*. 'He's in a very comfortable bed . . .'

'The best bedroom, I hope!'

Jenison frowned. 'That would be very expensive, even at the Fleece.'

'But nothing else will do!'

'Annabella.' Mrs Jenison quietly put a hand on her sister-in-law's arm to restrain her. 'This is not becoming.'

'He's in a small room,' I said, trying to pacify both Jenison and his sister at the same time. 'But very comfortable and convenient in many respects. Just off the kitchen passageway.'

Mrs Annabella was shocked. 'He has to put up with the servants coming and going?'

'It makes it easy for them to look after him.'

'It doesn't sound suitable.' She glared at her brother. 'Robert, you must have him moved to the best bedroom.'

'Not at all,' Jenison said loudly, then muttered *sotto voce* to me, 'Ridiculous expense.'

'I cannot think it would be wise to move him,' Esther said soothingly. 'What if the wounds were to reopen?'

Mrs Annabella's handkerchief flew to her lips. She said, in a more subdued fashion, 'Yes, yes, I'm sure you're right. Leave him where he is then. Yes, yes. Mr Patterson, you will ensure he's not moved?'

'I will indeed, madam.'

Jenison ushered me out of the drawing room.

His library had shelves full of books, clearly bought by the yard, all the same size and colour, and apparently unopened. Jenison always refers to himself as 'a plain man' which I take to mean he never reads more than the newspaper. That doesn't stop him being one of the shrewdest businessmen I know, and business was what he wanted to talk to me about.

'Look, Patterson,' he said, as soon as he'd shut the door behind us. 'We're in severe difficulties here. Where are we going to get a new soloist so late in the day? The concerts start in a month's time; anyone of quality will already be engaged.'

I should have known he'd not be concerned too long with Nightingale himself, despite his admiration for the man's abilities. 'The theatre company will be back by then. We can hire an actress.'

He clicked his tongue. 'Things will be said. The ladies will talk about morals and setting good examples to their daughters. These actresses are no better than they should be, you know.' He looked as if he was having trouble getting the next words out. 'And . . . you were quite right. That child could not have performed. It would have been totally unacceptable. It is very clear what kind of young person she is!'

I found myself annoyed. 'She has of course been very badly brought up and her origins are, to say the least, unfortunate—'

'Disgraceful,' Jenison murmured.

'—but she herself is of good character and very anxious to better herself.' Well, the latter part of that sentence was true, at any rate.

Jenison frowned. 'Then she should get herself a position as a maid, not intrude on her elders and betters. Now, about the vocal soloist.'

'One of the singing men from the Cathedral in Durham?'

'The last one we had was a drunkard and sang bawdy words to the songs,' Jenison said tartly. 'No, we'll have to do better than that. Write to London, Patterson, find us someone suitable. And quickly.' He started leafing through papers on the desk. 'I leave the matter in your hands.'

Well, there was a surprise.

I went back to the drawing room to collect Esther and found her already taking her leave. Mrs Annabella was more subdued although she was still squeezing tears from under her eyelids; Mrs Jenison was gripping a book of sermons.

Mrs Annabella caught hold of my hand as I bowed to take my leave. 'Mr Patterson, you're so clever when it comes to these things. Do you know who did it? Do you know the dastardly villain who stabbed him?'

'I have some ideas,' I murmured.

'No one in particular?'

'Not as yet.'

'There was someone on the coach,' she said. 'He told me. A great hulking brute with a club. He was insulting the ladies as they came into town and Mr Nightingale had to speak to him about it. The fellow was very threatening – and he was always worried that he might meet him again in the street.'

I smiled and said nothing. There'd only been one other man

on the coach and that had been a boy. It sounded very much that Nightingale had been trying to impress the ladies with his courage and intrepidity.

Mrs Annabella looked at me expectantly. 'I'll see if I can find him,' I said.

She smiled feebly.

At long last we managed to escape, and stood in the street for a moment to catch our breath. A few spots of rain splattered out of a blue sunny sky. Esther put her hand on my arm and we turned for home. The streets were busy; someone shouted that a cart had overturned and half a dozen boys went running off in high excitement.

'Some people are extraordinarily trying,' Esther said with a sigh. 'Mrs Annabella has been fainting off and on all morning.'

'She likes being the centre of attention.'

'She has evidently been weeping all night too. No one in the household got any sleep.' She looked at me sombrely. 'Is Nightingale done for?'

I nodded. 'I'd like to think it a good sign he's survived the night. But the way he's breathing—' I shook my head. 'I expect to hear of his death at any time.'

'Well, he was a vain man,' Esther said, 'and it will be a long time before I can forgive him that outburst at the concert, but he did not deserve to be killed.'

'At least his outburst prompted Philip Ord to call me a gentleman.'

She laughed, looked at me with mischievous grey eyes. My heart turned over. 'It has not been so very bad, has it, Charles? Our marriage, I mean – the way it has been received by society.'

I stared at a passing horseman, who was dawdling along and ogling the ladies in the street. 'For the most part, no. Nothing worse than some intrusive questions. A few ladies like Mrs Annabella thinking it a great romance.'

She squeezed my arm, and smiled up at me. 'So it is.'

Really, if she looked at me like that again, I'd disgrace myself by kissing her in public. I looked resolutely away. For some reason, a man in a baker's apron was hauling a big bucket of water up the street. 'I suspect Claudius Heron of some hand in the matter,' I mused.

'That goes without saying, I should think.' Esther pulled her cloak about her as the rain splattered harder. 'He has probably been suggesting you have some distant connection with nobility, four or five generations back.'

'Nonsense. My ancestors were all wandering ballad singers and fiddlers.'

'Oh, no, Charles,' she said reprovingly. 'That would be *very* low. You should try for a cheesemonger, at least.'

I laughed with her and we strolled on. The rain eased and the sun came out again and warmed us. Esther proposed to visit Barber's bookshop; I volunteered to accompany her. She nodded at an acquaintance who passed in a carriage. 'In all seriousness, Charles – do you regret marrying me?'

'I regret your money,' I said, not looking at her.

'If you administer the estates,' she pointed out, 'then you would indeed earn every penny.'

Reluctantly, I had to admit she had a point. 'But it would drive you mad,' I said. 'You'd hate it if you couldn't deal with matters yourself.'

She winced. 'I could get used to it.'

'Why trouble yourself? Why not leave things as they are?'

We walked in silence for a moment.

'We'll talk about it again later,' Esther said at last. 'You have a lot on your mind at the moment. With Nightingale, and the baby's death.'

Dear God, I'd almost forgotten about the baby. I said ruefully, 'We'll never get anywhere if you keep offering me excuses!'

She laughed; encouraged, I said, 'There's no help for it – I'll have to become a rich and famous performer and composer.'

'You could always take up ladder-dancing,' she murmured.

We'd come to Barber's bookshop, and stopped by the over-hanging sign. A woman came out with a parcel of books; a gaggle of young girls crooned over ribbons in the shop next door. 'So what will you do now?' Esther asked.

I sighed. 'Jenison wants me to find a new vocal soloist for the winter series. I need to write to my contacts in London, ask if they can name me an up-and-coming young lady who'll charge reasonably in return for an engagement of three months and a good set of references at the end of it. Then Hugh and I are going to see if we can find out what Nightingale did last night, before he was attacked.'

'You were being polite with Mrs Annabella, I take it. You do have a firm suspect in mind.'

'I wish I did. No, Ridley must be in the picture, and,' I added reluctantly, 'Kate.'

I expected her to tell me I was talking nonsense; instead she considered the idea seriously, while the girls giggled in a huddle over some silly tale or other. 'She would have the audacity to do it if she had the inclination. She's a feral creature, Charles. And she disappeared before the attack. Though I cannot for the life of me understand how she got out of the house.'

'I'm afraid I do.' I glanced round but there was no one close enough to overhear us. 'She can *step through*.'

Esther started to say something, stopped. I glanced down at her face. She was looking her coolest. But she merely said, 'Then surely she will be unreachable.'

'She must return at some time.'

'I cannot see why. If she did injure Nightingale, she will surely stay away.'

'She'll come back,' I said. I was convinced of it. Poor though it was, Kate's home was in this world.

Esther was abruptly businesslike. 'Then it is all the more important we look out for her. I will make some enquiries with the spirits to see if they can locate her in the town. If they can not, then we must assume she is still in the other world.'

I hesitated. 'I know you don't like this ability—'

'Really, Charles,' she said with a small rueful smile, 'it is hardly to the purpose whether I like it or not. It exists, and therefore has to be taken into account.'

Like Esther's money, I thought uneasily.

'I will discover her,' she promised. 'Though I don't know what I will do if I find her – locking her up will hardly answer if she can disappear at will!'

'I'm sure you'll find a way.' I bent to kiss her hand.

'Really, Charles,' she said teasingly. 'A gentleman showing gallantry to his wife in public? Not proper at all!'

'But I'm merely a tradesman,' I said. 'Descended from a long line of cheesemongers.'

I left Esther at the bookshop and wandered off to find a spirit. One hung on the corner of the Post Office, a gentleman whose daughter I used to teach. I had to endure a long digression on all the friends he'd seen in the past week, but at last he told me

Hugh was in the Bigg Market. I asked him to send a message telling Hugh to stay where he was and I'd come to him. Then I set off through the narrow streets around St Nicholas's church, cut through an alley heading for the Clothmarket—

And found my way barred by Cuthbert Ridley.

Twenty-Five

Disputes should be settled in a quiet civilized manner.
                    [*A Gentleman's Companion*, August 1730]

'Looking for me?' He slouched against the wall of the alley, dishevelled, his hair tousled, his clothes creased and dirty. They were the same clothes he'd worn to the concert yesterday so he must have slept in them, if he'd slept at all. He looked befuddled, as if he didn't quite know how he'd got here; his eyes flickered from side to side as if he wasn't sure where 'here' was. I was willing to bet he had a devilish headache. 'What time is it?' he said.

'I was indeed looking for you,' I said grimly. 'Where were you last night? Or, to be more precise, at around one this morning?'

He was recovering fast. 'Oh dear,' he said mockingly. 'You want me to have attacked poor old Crow.'

'Crow?'

'The gentleman who sings his tunes like a broken-down duck.' He chuckled. 'Mr Duck. Mr Quack-quack-quack.'

'Richard Nightingale is dying.'

He pulled a face. 'So sad.'

I changed direction abruptly to try and throw him off-balance. 'Why did you leave London?'

He straightened. 'Devil take it, none of your business!'

'Trouble, was there?'

'I said, none of your business!' He took a step forward, fists clenched, then stopped, looked at me slyly. He folded his hands, refolded them, smirked, lowered his head. 'Sir— what do you— I'm sure I don't—'

'Very convincing,' I said, dryly. '*Exactly* like the Rev Mr Orrick.'

He grinned. 'Very well, if you want it outright, *did* you attack Nightingale last night?'

His smile broadened. 'Yes.'

The frank admission took me aback. I stared. He smirked at me. I took a grip on myself. It wasn't wise to take anything Ridley said at face value; as Heron suggested, he was a man capable of saying anything, simply for the fun of it. I remembered, and used, Mrs Annabella's mistake. 'You shot him?'

'Stabbed,' he said smugly, negotiating the trap. He mimed the action, raising his right hand, jerking it backwards and forwards in a stabbing motion. He accidentally scraped his hand along the wall of the alley, looked at the wall as if it had personally offended him.

'How many times?'

He thought, obviously trying to remember. Or was he trying to remember what he'd been told? 'Four?'

'Wasn't that overenthusiastic?'

He threw up his hands melodramatically. 'I was carried away. I must admit, I'm disappointed he isn't dead.'

'You won't have to wait long,' I said. 'Where did this attack take place?'

'In the alley beside the Golden Fleece.'

'*Why* did you attack him?'

He thrust his hands in his pockets, struck an attitude. 'Because I wanted to. Because he needed attacking. Because I couldn't stand that damn tweeting of his.'

'You knew him in London?' I remembered the advertisement Esther had been sent. 'At Covent Garden theatre?' I couldn't resist a little dig at him. 'I suppose you enjoy the attractions there all the time.' I was referring, of course, to the ladies of easy virtue that frequent the London theatres.

'Devil a bit of it,' he said. Someone came to the mouth of the alley behind him, took one look at us and walked off again. 'I went to a concert. A proper concert. Held by Lady This or Lady That. My uncle was trying to educate me.' He smirked again. 'Not that it was necessary. I've got all the education I need.'

'So you'd argued with Nightingale before? In London?'

He drew back, considered me, plainly deciding which answer best to give. 'I might have,' he said, grinning.

This was getting me nowhere. I said, 'So what's to stop me

calling the watchman and having you conveyed to prison on a charge of attacking Richard Nightingale?'

He brought his hand out of his pocket. Between his fingers jutted a blade.

It took me a moment to recognize it – one blade of a pair of scissors, folded open. A brand new pair of kitchen scissors, with the price label still attached.

'Scissors?' I asked surprised, trying to envisage Nightingale's wounds and what Gale had said of them. Could scissors have inflicted them? 'Not a knife?'

He smirked. 'They're sharp enough. Want to test them?' He made a mock stab in the air. Oddly, I felt no fear. The way he was swaying, first against one wall of the alley, then against the other, suggested he'd probably not be able to hit a church door.

'So what now?' I asked. 'Am I supposed just to let you walk away – perhaps to attack someone else?'

He shrugged. 'Who knows? Who cares?'

'Someone ought to have tipped you into the Tyne when you were a baby,' I retorted.

'Too late,' he said grinning. 'Much too late. Well, come on, Patterson. Aren't you going to try to take me prisoner?' He jabbed the scissors in the air again.

I shook my head. 'Not today.'

'You won't catch me unarmed, you know. Not ever.'

'Thanks for warning me. I'll bring a troop of militia with me next time.'

Then without the slightest warning, he jabbed at me in earnest. The scissors whisked dangerously close to my arm. I took a step backwards, stumbled on an uneven cobble, and fell. The scissors scraped the wall above my head.

He loomed over me, grinning, holding the scissors like a knife, clenched in his fist. He was probably just trying to frighten me but I wasn't going to stake my life on that. I kicked out a foot, caught him on the ankle and knocked him sideways. He fell, yelping and swearing. The scissors clattered to the cobbles. I crawled across to pick them up.

Ridley grabbed at me, caught my ankle. I tugged free, got to my feet. He dragged himself up the wall, ran at me. Straight towards the scissors I was holding. Alarmed, I threw them to one side, tried to duck out of the way.

A hand reached between us and caught Ridley's cravat. He jerked to a halt, choking, pawing at his throat.

'Good afternoon,' Hugh said. 'You know I always thought it the mark of a gentleman to be armed with a sword. Are scissors *de rigeur* nowadays? Of course, it could just be that you're not a gentleman.'

Ridley glared at him.

'I admit I'm hampered by being one-handed just at the moment.' Hugh twisted the cravat still further. Ridley gasped, went up on tiptoe to ease the pressure on his neck. 'But in my experience a little use of the wits usually triumphs over mere impulse. And you're *very* impulsive, aren't you?' He tut-tutted. 'Not a good idea.'

Tears were pouring down Ridley's cheeks. He batted ineffectually at Hugh's hand, then tried to twist and bring up his knee. Hugh was more prepared and quicker-witted than Nightingale had been; he shifted, exerted more pressure, and Ridley's face, which had been bright red, started to whiten and turn blue around the lips.

'Let him go, Hugh,' I said. 'We don't want another death on our hands.' I dipped for the scissors, to keep them safely out of Ridley's reach. Hugh released his grip; Ridley fell back against the wall, coughing and spluttering.

'Don't stay on my account,' Hugh said, giving him a little wave of farewell. 'I'm sure you have lots to do.'

Ridley took a step sideways along the alley wall, scuttling away like a crab. Then with a wordless snarl, he turned his back and strolled insolently away.

'Well done, Hugh!' I said, watching him go. 'You've talked him into submission.'

Hugh grinned. He jerked his head after Ridley. 'So he's our man, then.'

'He says he did it,' I agreed. 'And he knows things he shouldn't. But he didn't do it with these scissors. He's just bought them – they still have the price attached.'

Hugh gave me a speaking look. 'Answer the question, Charles! *Did* he do it?'

I stared after the figure strolling away into Amen Corner. 'I don't have the slightest idea.'

Twenty-Six

Good wine and good conversation is the mark of a civilized man; drunkenness is the mark of a ruffian.
[*A Gentleman's Companion*, February 1731]

A spirit had told Hugh that Nightingale had been seen the previous night at Mrs Hill's tavern in the Fleshmarket; as soon as we walked into the inn, we spotted the lady herself on the far side of the crowded taproom; she saw us approaching and folded her arms belligerently. Hugh bowed, with a touch of mockery.

'It's always trouble when you two turn up,' she said. She's a fine woman on the far side of fifty, and shrewd, a widow who knew better than to remarry and have the business taken out of her hands.

'Not a bit of it,' Hugh said audaciously. 'We've spent a good few shillings in here over the years.'

She allowed, begrudgingly, that this was true. 'But I hold to the general point,' she said sternly. 'Musicians are always trouble!'

As if to prove her point, someone started singing raucously in one corner and soon had every spirit in the house singing with him.

'And my girls have to listen to that filth,' Mrs Hill said in disgust. A serving girl, walking past, gave me a wink.

'I'm told there was a London musician in here last night,' I said, raising my voice to be heard over the singing. 'He's pretty unmistakeable. Tall, burly and raucous.'

'Dressed in pink,' Hugh added.

'The songs *he* knew!' Mrs Hill said, grimacing. 'Is he the one killed?'

'He's not dead yet,' I said, yet again. 'How long was he here?'

She considered. 'No more than an hour. Early on, maybe around seven.' She nodded at a customer who walked past.

'Alone?'

'Until he started offering free beer, yes.' She added, with reluctant fairness, 'He did pay his bill.'

So Nightingale had started the evening with money and set about getting rid of it fast. Maybe that was why he'd none on him when he was attacked. 'Anyone in particular seem friendly with him?' A burst of a bawdy chorus drowned my words; I repeated them, more loudly.

Mrs Hill shrugged. 'Everyone who wanted free ale.'

'Did you see him go?'

'I did. Full of beer but he looked and talked sober. I thought at the time he could take his drink.'

'Did he say where he was going?'

She shook her head. 'But I'll warrant he wasn't finished for the evening.'

The girl who'd winked at me came past again, bearing a platter of bread and cheese. She said, 'He was looking for a woman. Asked where he was likely to find one. No sooner he was out the door than he picked up a girl. Twelve, no more.'

'Wearing a yellow dress?'

'Yellow as a dandelion.' She nudged a drunken admirer away. 'Went up to him the minute he was out the door. They talked a bit – arguing over the girl's charge, I dare say. Then they went off.'

'Did you see which way?'

'Down towards St Nicholas.'

We went outside again, relieved to be out of the heat and noise. The blue sky was clouding over; rain spotted the cobbles.

'I didn't think you were serious about the girl.' Hugh eased his sling and brushed dust from the shoulder of his coat.

'I agree it's unlikely,' I said. 'But if she's perfectly innocent, where is she? Why hasn't she come back to the house?'

'Maybe she saw something? Maybe she's just gone off in a temper, back to that hovel she was brought up in. Have you looked there?'

'No. She wouldn't go back, Hugh – she's set her mind on getting out of there and she'll not give up on that. And remember, she can step between worlds.'

He bit his lip, scowled, waited until a man with a terrier strolled past. 'Look, if you think she's *there*, can't you just go and get her?'

I shook my head. 'No. The time difference is the very devil. She's been gone several hours; I might find myself several *days* behind her. And I daren't linger there too long in case I'm mistaken for my counterpart – or even meet him.'

'So what then?'

'Did your friendly spirits not give you another clue?'

'Not one.'

'Which suggests,' I said, 'that he went where the spirits are less cooperative.'

Hugh frowned. 'The Key?'

'Or one of the chares off it.'

Hugh glared. 'Oh, no, Charles, I'm not going down there again! We had some very nasty experiences there, remember.'

'You can go home,' I pointed out. 'I'll go on my own.'

'And leave you defenceless in the midst of ruffians? Thank you, Charles, but I'm not a fair weather friend!'

We spent the afternoon making our way down to the Key by the most obvious route, thinking that Nightingale, as a stranger to the town, wouldn't have known the byways. Finding news of him was not difficult; he'd stopped at almost all of the taverns, drank there until he gave offence and then tottered out. Kate had also been seen once or twice, hovering outside, or sitting on a shop doorstep, waiting for him. We asked after Cuthbert Ridley too but drew a blank. And no one else had apparently taken much interest in Nightingale.

Eventually, we came down on to the Key by the Old Man Inn. The doors of the inn were open, and half a dozen ruffians and sailors were staggering about outside, in a drunken attempt to dance a hornpipe.

'I keep coming back to this inn,' I said, standing in the doorway.

'Ridley keeps coming back to this inn,' Hugh said.

I went inside cautiously, with Hugh on my heels watching my back. The taproom stank of beer and smoke and worse things I didn't pause to identify. I saw no one I recognized and was so busy looking about, I didn't realize for a moment that everyone had fallen silent, staring at us.

'I'm looking for Cuthbert Ridley,' I said into the silence. 'I'm told he was in here last night.'

'He's always in here,' said one man sourly. 'Never a moment's peace. *And* that other one. You'd think we'd be able to get away from you gentry here.'

'Which other one?'

'Started tweeting like a bird,' another man said. 'Then asked for a ladder.'

'He dances on it,' Hugh said.

'Sure he does,' said the man in good-humoured disbelief. He lit a pipe.

I was almost choking on the smell of smoke. 'Was he on his own? No girl with him?'

'Tried to sweetheart Meg.'

A dark-haired girl straightened from wiping a table at the back of the room. 'I know what he was after!'

'Make sure you charge him high!' pipe man said to general laughter. He puffed out a huge acrid cloud. 'Plenty of money, that one.'

'But you weren't interested?' I asked.

She cocked her head. 'He looked rich enough. But he was angry – looked mad enough to slap a girl round a bit. I wasn't going to take that. And he already had a lass waiting outside.'

'In a yellow dress? No more than twelve?'

'Some like them young,' she said philosophically.

The customers were eyeing us thoughtfully and it wasn't our conversation they were interested in. There was all too much concentration on our clothes and presumably on how much they'd fetch if they could be sold. 'You know Cuthbert Ridley too?' I asked the girl.

'Aye,' she said coyly. 'I know Cuddy. Many a time. In the Biblical sense.'

I smiled politely as everyone laughed again. '*Was* he in here last night?'

'He was.'

'Were Ridley and Nightingale in at the same time?'

'Nah,' she said. 'I don't do nothing like that.'

I winced as she grinned and the laughter echoed. 'I meant, were they in the tavern at the same time?'

'Nah. I'd sent the singing gent on up to the Castle. To the Black Gate. A man can find anything he likes up there. Plenty of obliging girls.' She frowned. 'Cuddy came in later. But he asked for the singing gent, mind. And went out again, soon after.'

'Did you tell him where the – er – *singing gent* had gone?'

She shrugged. 'Why not?'

I gave her sixpence, knowing full well it was a lot more than she expected, and she said saucily that I could come in any time I liked.

We beat a quick retreat to the street. Hugh breathed in the fresh air with a satisfied sigh. 'If Nightingale ended up at the Castle, it would have been natural for him to come back to the Fleece down that Stair.'

I contemplated the possibilities, looking around at the bustle of everyday life, the sailors, the whores, the respectable house-wives, the carrier bustling to and from the Printing Office with bundles of newspapers. Seagulls wheeling and squawking overhead.

And saw a flash of bright yellow.

I took off after her.

Twenty-Seven

Women of the lower orders have frequently been the downfall of many a promising youth; sons, therefore, should be watched carefully and their associates chosen with the utmost care.

[*A Gentleman's Companion*, September 1735]

I raced across the road, darting in front of a cart that turned suddenly out of a side street. The driver yelled after me, swearing. I was certain I knew the road Kate had turned down but when I got there it stretched before me, long and straight and empty. I glanced down a side street. Nothing.

I ran on. Street after street. Chances were she'd stepped through to the other world again. I ought to follow her at once. But there were too many people around – I needed somewhere quiet to step through. And she *might* still be here.

A spirit hovered on a doorknocker.

'Have you seen a young girl—'

'No, I haven't,' she said stridently. 'And if I had, I wouldn't tell you. You ought to be ashamed of yourself!'

Damn. I started off again. The spirit called after me, 'I know your type – give her fine clothes, bribe her to do as you want.'

So the spirit had seen Kate, in all her yellow finery. I glanced into an alley – and caught a glimpse of a bright petticoat whisking round a corner at the far end. I darted after her.

Spirits danced high up under the eaves. 'Villain!' cried one. 'Ravisher!' shrieked another. I spun round a corner. Another empty alley. A spirit on a windowsill said sleepily, 'What's going on? What's all the noise about?'

I'd lost Kate.

I looked about. In my mad dash, I'd worked my way westwards across town; I wasn't far from my own house in Caroline Square. I checked one or two side streets, called Kate's name, was stared at by suspicious passers-by. No trace of her.

There was only one place she could have gone, and one thing to do – follow her. I ducked into an alley, glanced around to make sure I was alone, and took a deep breath. Footsteps behind me, a woman called out to a friend. Hurriedly, I took one step forward, felt a sudden chill. Blackness.

Then I put my foot down on to grass and a brilliant sunset was dazzling me.

I ducked instinctively, turned my back on the huge bright low sun. Purple spots scattered across my sight. I was in someone's garden, on a neatly scythed lawn. Close by a clump of trees; I drew back into their shelter and peered through the foliage.

Three children were playing on a terrace in front of a house; a woman, stylish in pale petticoats, came out on to the terrace to laugh and joke with them. Behind her, a nurserymaid cradled a baby. Were these people I knew in my own world? But now was clearly not the time to indulge curiosity. Cautiously I retreated – and came up against a wall. Six feet of it, adorned on the top with broken glass.

Damn. I peered through the tree branches, trying to spot a gate out of the garden. If all else failed, I could step back to my own world, then back again, but that would make finding Kate almost impossible.

There *was* a gate, across the far side of the garden; I'd have to work my way round the wall to it. At least this world had no spirits in it, to spot me and give warning of my presence.

It didn't need them. It had sharp-eyed nurserymaids instead. I heard a shriek, glanced round, saw her pointing at me. I started running for the gate. A child leapt up from the terrace, a boy of ten or so, quick, lithe and fast.

I jerked to a halt. Damn, damn, damn. There was a dog too, one of those ridiculous lapdogs, a white ball of fur, yapping as it bounced over the neat lawn.

I turned, took a step, felt the cold, and found myself back in the alley.

Where a fat woman was squatting and relieving herself.

I pulled back into a corner, squeezed my eyes shut. She was singing beneath her breath, occasionally grunting with effort. Resigned, I stepped back again—

And found myself in a street, just outside the garden gate, in pitch-black night.

Facing a tearful Kate.

Twenty-Eight

Children should obey their elders, and be firmly disciplined when they do not.

[*A Gentleman's Companion*, May 1735]

She lifted her chin. Tears had traced grimy marks down her cheeks; her yellow dress was grubby and torn around the hem. She said in a voice full of wavering defiance, 'Don't want to talk to you.'

I glanced round to orientate myself. We were on Westgate and it looked much the same as it did in our own world, although I glimpsed open ground in gaps between houses, where I'd have expected to see more buildings. A full moon rose high above us; the street was deserted except for a fox slinking across the cobbles a hundred yards away. I moved to the nearest doorway and sat down on the step, patting the stone beside me.

'Well, come and not talk here.'

She burst into tears.

She sobbed and sniffled, and wiped her nose on the grubby dress then, scowling to make sure I knew she did it unwillingly, came and sat down beside me. 'I'm hungry.'

I patted my pockets but found nothing edible. 'How long have you been here? In this world?'

'Weeks!' she said despairingly, then, 'maybe two or three days.' She sniffed. 'I went home. Well, not *my* home. I mean, my home's back there. In the real world.'

'What happened?'

'I was there already.' Tears coursed down her cheeks again; she wiped them away angrily. 'With a sailor.' She glared at me. 'I was just like ma. Don't you understand? Here, I'm just another whore and— and—' Her voice nearly failed her. 'With child. Big. Huge! And *still* going with men!'

I sat silent. The fox pattered up the other side of the dark street, casting us wary glances, occasionally pausing, one foot lifted, to scent the air.

'I ain't going to be like that,' Kate insisted. 'I ain't!' She must have known how desperate she sounded.

'You came back to our world,' I said. 'I saw you. Why didn't you come and talk to me?'

She twisted the yellow satin between her fingers; she was shivering in the chill night air. 'I hate this dress. Makes me look like a whore.'

'Why avoid me?' I insisted.

'Scared,' she said, in a muffled voice.

'Of me?'

'You'll send me back to ma.'

The fox had seen prey, was creeping forward.

'I don't want to be stuck on street corners, singing ballads for pennies,' she said passionately. 'I want proper gowns like your wife has, I want somewhere nice to live. I want money. And I want to earn it proper.'

I winced. Her words struck a chord. 'Kate.' I hesitated. 'About Mr Nightingale.'

'Yeah, I know,' she said. 'He only wants one thing. That's what all men want.'

'I don't,' I said mildly. Certainly not from her.

'Anyway.' The tears were dry now; she stared belligerently at the fox which was nosing in the dark holes under the hedge of the Vicarage gardens. 'It ain't going to happen now, is it? He's dead.'

I stared. 'You know?'

She nodded, said in a small voice, 'I saw him.'

I waited for her to go on but she didn't; I said, 'You followed him all evening.'

Her fingers crushed the grubby satin of her dress. 'I knew he was going to get drunk. I thought I'd wait until he was so drunk he'd not remember anything, then we'd go back to the inn and I'd get in bed with him. When he woke up, I'd tell him he'd had me. And then I'd say I'd tell everyone I was a respectable girl but I'd keep quiet about him seducing me if he made me his apprentice.' She cast me a sideways glance. '*You* made me think of it – you said he wouldn't remember nothing in the morning.'

So I had. 'That would have been blackmail,' I said, quelling an absurd inclination to applaud. Nightingale might have agreed to her terms; he couldn't have afforded a scandal.

'I saw him when he came out of that place in the Fleshmarket,' she said, 'and I followed him round half a dozen taverns. He can drink,' she said admiringly. 'He picked up a whore too, and they went into an alley and I had to wait till they came out.'

'And then?'

'Lots more taverns,' she said with a sigh. 'Till he could hardly walk. *And* he had his pocket picked on the way. He went down to the Key and then back up to the Turk's Head in the Bigg Market, then off to the Castle Garth.'

'Did he see you?'

'Coupla times.' She rubbed her arms against the cold. 'Told me to get lost, so I made sure I kept out of his sight. He was reeling about and singing. Proper singing, not that stuff he usually does. He found himself another whore in the Garth,' she said scornfully, 'but he couldn't do it – that was the drink talking. She wanted her money anyway and he wouldn't give it her, because he said she'd done nothing for it. So she gave him a push and he sat down in horse shit and yelled at her.'

Nightingale had had an eventful evening, I reflected. The stone doorstep was becoming uncomfortable; I shifted, leant back against the door behind me. 'And after that?'

'A watchman told him to go home, and he said he didn't know how to so the watchman pointed him out the Stair down to the Sandhill. Only the watchman stood there to make sure he went and I didn't want to follow in case he thought I was up to something.' She added darkly, 'Watchmen don't like me. They always think I'm up to no good.'

They were probably right. 'Go on.'

'I didn't think it mattered – I knew he was going back to the Fleece so I sat down on a wall. I thought I'd wait a bit for him to get settled in bed. I know where his room is – he took me there once, the day he ordered the dress for me.'

She stared at the hedge into which the fox had slipped.

'Did you see anyone go down the Stair after him?'

She frowned. 'Two lasses and a lad. They didn't go right down to the bottom though – I heard them laughing in one of the streets off the Stair.'

'Anyone else?'

She thought. 'A man and his wife, old, both of them. And a young man on his own.'

'How tall was the young man?'

She shrugged. ''Bout like you.'

'How old?'

Another shrug. 'Older than an apprentice.'

Maybe early twenties then. 'What was he wearing?'

'Black.'

'You mean mourning?'

'Never asked him.'

Black didn't sound Cuthbert Ridley's style. 'Wearing a wig?'

'Silly little one.' That was more like Ridley.

'Was he fat or thin?'

'Thin,' she said decisively.

'And did he go all the way down the Stair?'

She considered, staring out into the dark empty street. 'The old man and woman went all the way down. She was trailing behind him, like she didn't want to be there. And she had trouble going down the Stair. He just went striding off ahead. Typical man – no help at all! Then the young lad came.' She screwed up her eyes. 'Don't remember what he did.'

'Would you recognize any of them?'

'Nah,' she said. 'Too dark. And I was across the other side of the Garth.'

I hesitated. We were coming to what must inevitably distress her. I'd no doubt she'd seen plenty of unpleasant things in her time but she was still young, no matter how hardened she pretended to be. 'So what happened then?'

She looked down at her hands. 'I got worried. What if he forgot where he was going and went off somewhere else? Picked up another whore, maybe? Took *her* to his bed? So I went after him. And—' Her voice cracked. 'I found him. Lying on his back at the foot of the Stair with blood everywhere.'

'Did you examine him?'

She shook her head violently. 'Couldn't bear to. Didn't need to. Not with all that blood. He's dead, ain't he?'

'Not yet,' I said noncommittally. By her own account, Kate had found Nightingale only minutes after he'd been attacked; if she'd called for help, he would not have lain so long bleeding and, who knows, might have been saved. I didn't intend ever to tell her so.

'So you ran off?'

She stared at the fence where the fox had disappeared. There was something she was hiding, I was sure of it. 'Came here,' she said, indicating the street, meaning *this world*. 'I was scared. Thought they'd say I'd done it.' She added defiantly, 'I didn't!'

I looked at her; she stared back. 'Did you see anyone near the body? Running away, maybe?'

'Nah,' she said. 'Didn't see no one running away.' Another pause. In a low voice, she said, 'You think that gent did it, don't you? The one who's always rude – the one as hit Mr Nightingale at the dinner party.'

'He's top of my list at the moment,' I admitted.

'Why are you so interested?' she demanded. 'Why don't you just go home and forget about it?'

'I can't,' I said. 'I *won't*. And talking of home, I want you to come back with me. You can have something to eat and something clean to wear.'

She hesitated. I got that sense again of something she was concealing; she said begrudgingly, 'You're going to get killed, you are, and then what will I do?'

'Kate,' I said carefully, 'if you're still thinking about that apprenticeship, you saw yesterday how everyone reacted to the idea of you playing in the concert . . .'

'Don't care!' she said defiantly. 'I won't go back to my ma, I won't! I want something better. I deserve it!'

'We can find something else for you to do.'

'You mean, you'll make me a servant. I don't want to be a servant. I want to play the fiddle.'

I sighed and decided there was no point in pressing the matter at the moment. 'I promise you,' I said, 'that I'll think about it. And I won't do anything without your full agreement.'

She stared at me. 'Promise?'

'I promise.'

Begrudgingly, she said, 'All right.'

I stood up. 'Let's go back then. I hope we haven't been missed.'

'*I* won't have been,' she said, with a distinct lack of self-pity. 'No one ever misses me.'

'Can we go back to just after I left?' I asked. I wanted to test the abilities she boasted of, but she looked at me blankly.

'How do *I* know when you left?'

I laughed. 'True. Come on then.'

I got up off the doorstep, feeling stiff, and a trifle chilled. Kate put her small hand in mine; it was very cold. We took a step forward and the blackness washed over us. Then I saw the flicker of stars and a thin curve of moon over rooftops.

We were standing by the same doorstep on Westgate and it looked much the same time of night.

'Do you think he's dead now?' Kate asked.

I stared around. There was not the slightest clue as to what day this was. 'I think we'll go and visit a friend who lives near here,' I said. 'He'll be able to tell us if anything's happened.'

Twenty-Nine

Evil deeds multiply.
[*A Gentleman's Companion*, October 1735]

I knew Hugh would not enjoy being woken – the snores I heard from behind the door of his attic room were too loud and energetic. It took three bouts of banging on the door to wake him, by which time the widow from the floor below was calling up the stairs in protest. When Hugh did come to the door, it was evident he'd had a hard night of it; he'd collapsed on his bed in breeches, shirt and stockinged feet. Kate took one look at his hair sticking up, and cackled loudly.

Sighing, Hugh let us in, rubbing at his injured arm as if it ached. Behind him, one candle gleamed. 'Wake up the widow below, did you?'

'Sorry.'

'You know what she'll think.'

'I'm no whore,' Kate said indignantly, and turned for the door again. 'I'll tell her!'

I grabbed her arm. 'You will not! Hugh, is that piece of pie going spare?'

He looked at the pie on the table and almost turned green. 'Don't talk about food.'

'Too much to drink?' I passed the pie across to Kate who fell on it as if she hadn't eaten for months.

'In your cause,' Hugh said, poking me in the ribs, 'I must have visited every tavern in this town after you ran off last night.'

Well, that relieved one of my anxieties at any rate – we'd not lost too many hours in that other world. 'Did you find anything?'

He grinned. 'Lots! Pour me beer and I'll tell you.'

There was a jug of beer on the table; it was probably past its best by now but I poured two tankards and handed one to Hugh. I stared down Kate's indignant protests, then relented enough to allow her a gulp or two from my tankard. In the glittering candlelight, Hugh sat on the bed to tell his tale, I perched on the edge of the table and Kate wandered about, eating the pie and scattering crumbs across the floor.

'You could have told me what you were going to do, Charles,' Hugh grumbled. 'One minute you're there, the next you're off like a frightened hare and there's no chance of catching you. Still, I shall abstain from complaining. I shan't point out how difficult it is for me to get out of my shirt one-handed without the help of a friend—'

'Hugh—'

'But I understand you've other interests now.' He gave Kate a glowering look. 'Now you're married.'

'Hey!' Kate said. 'Told you. I ain't a whore.'

Hugh looked at me over the top of his tankard. 'Not what people would say. Out all night, turns up at dawn with a girl no better than she should be—'

'I will be,' Kate scowled. 'If folks'll let me.'

'Can we get to the point?' I said. 'What did you find? Where did Nightingale go after the Old Man Inn?'

'I can tell you exactly which taverns he went to,' Hugh said. 'Eight of them. *Eight*, Charles! And he wasn't above trying to wheedle free ale out of the company. Once he even gave a recital in the hope of getting a few pennies, but I don't think he could have been at his best because all he got was three farthings.'

'I hope Jenison doesn't hear of that,' I said. 'His concert soloist demeaning himself by singing in taverns!'

'Had his pocket picked,' Kate said with immoderate glee.

'Was it only drinking,' I asked, 'or did something else happen?'

Hugh gulped down beer, put a hand on his head and winced. 'Someone was following him.'

'Kate was following him.'

'Yes I know,' Hugh said, sighing. 'No one missed her, not in those yellow petticoats.'

'I like yellow,' Kate said defiantly.

'There was a man following him too. It all ended in a fracas in the Turk's Head in the Bigg Market. Some time around ten.'

I looked at Kate; she said, 'Told you he went in there. Didn't see what happened though.'

'Nightingale was on edge when he came in,' Hugh said, yawning. 'Glancing over his shoulder every five minutes. He was pretty drunk by this time. About ten minutes after he'd come in, another fellow arrived and they started yelling at each other. Nightingale made some pretty wild accusations, evidently, something about London but the other fellow just grinned.'

'Is there a description of this other man?'

'Young, fashionable, very full of himself. New to the town, no one there acquainted with him.'

'Cuthbert Ridley.'

Hugh nodded. 'They nearly came to blows, apparently. But the landlord came down hard on them. In the end, Nightingale stumbled out in high dudgeon.'

'Did Ridley follow?'

'Not for a while.'

'How long's that?'

'Half an hour maybe.'

The girl at the Old Man had said that Nightingale and Ridley were both in that night but not at the same time. Had Ridley followed Nightingale up to the Turk's Head? And had he followed him further?

'I could see if I can find out anything more,' Hugh said, rubbing his eyes. 'But, unlike some, I have work to do. I have to put an advertisement in the paper to say I'm back in town, *and* I want to speak to the Steward of the Assembly Rooms about a date for my ball. And a little sleep wouldn't come amiss. If my so-called friends wouldn't mind not interrupting me!'

Kate yawned, a huge, jaw-cracking gape. She was leaning back against the wall and I fancied her eyelids were drooping.

'We'll talk about this again tomorrow, Hugh. I mean, later today.' I took hold of Kate's arm. 'Come on, let's get back home.'

'Charles,' Hugh said, stifling a yawn, 'mind what I say – take care. Don't want Mrs P getting the wrong idea.'

'Thank you for your advice, Hugh. I think Esther isn't prone to wrong ideas. Go back to sleep.'

'Could help a fellow change his shirt,' he said, easing back against his pillows.

'I'll come back later.' I suspected he was asleep before I closed the door.

Kate staggered as we stepped out of the stairwell into the chill night air, yawned again, belched. 'That pie was good.'

'I'm surprised you didn't make yourself sick, eating so quickly.' We crossed the street; she stumbled on the cobbles but righted herself with another tremendous yawn. As we came to the street that led to Caroline Square, I said, 'Can I trust you to get yourself to bed if I let you in the house?'

'Why? Where're you going?'

'I want to see if Nightingale's still alive.'

'Ask a spirit.'

'I'd rather do it myself.' Truth to tell, I wanted another look at that alley and, unlike Kate, I was still wide awake. In my own experience, it was still only late afternoon.

'It's late,' Kate said, yawning again. 'There'll be thieves about.'

'I don't intend to go into any dark alleys.'

'They'll get you,' she said. 'I'll come with you.'

'You're going to bed.'

She yawned again and her jaw cracked.

The spirit in the central gardens was singing quietly to himself as we walked across Caroline Square; as far as I can tell, spirits don't sleep. I fished my key out of my pocket.

The front door was of course bolted on the inside.

I saw little option but to call for George and get him to wake Tom – but that, of course, would cause all sorts of dissension amongst the servants and draw undesirable attention to Kate. As I was hesitating, Kate said, 'Don't fuss yourself. I'll shift to the other world then come back inside the house.'

I sighed. That pang of envy again. 'I wish I knew how you stepped through so accurately.'

She wrinkled up her nose and grinned. 'I'll tell you how – when you make me your apprentice!'

And with a mock curtsey of her soiled yellow skirts – and another great yawn – she winked out of existence. A shiver of intense cold passed over me, so strong I slapped at my arms to warm them. Then both Kate and the cold were gone.

I began to perceive Kate was a problem without an easy solution.

Alone again, I walked down the steep slope of the Side where the torches had reduced themselves to mere glowing embers. The town was nearly deserted; I saw only a handful of miners stumbling sleepily back home from work. The clock of St Nicholas's church struck two.

The Golden Fleece was not entirely quiet; horses shifted in their stables, hooves clinking on hard floors, breath snorting. Two of the torches in the yard had gone out, the others were guttering. The door to the kitchen passageway was wide open; candles burned on a table, showing me the lad, Joseph, comfortably asleep on a chair.

'Keeping watch, Joseph?' I asked loudly.

He jerked awake, grabbed the chair as he almost fell off it. His anxious expression suggested he thought I was the landlord; when he realized I wasn't, he grinned. 'Doing my best, sir, but one beer too many.' The tankard was at his feet. 'Besides, no late travellers tonight. And if one did come, the horses' hooves on the cobbles would wake me. Want to see the old gent? He's hanging on still.'

I mounted the three steps to Nightingale's room, reflecting he would have hated to be called *old*. The door of his room was ajar; I pushed it open and he lay there almost as I'd seen him last time, his breathing stentorian, his face streaked with sweat. There was the acrid smell of urine.

He was alone.

I went back down into the passageway. 'Joseph, do you know why no one's sitting with him?'

He looked surprised. 'Mally was with him. Maybe she's gone to the kitchen for something.'

I resisted the temptation to point out that if he'd been awake he would have seen or heard Mally as she walked down the passageway behind him and know exactly where she was.

In the darkness at the other end of the passage, a pool of light spilled through an open door. I walked down there to find Mally in the kitchen, enjoying the company of two of her fellow servants. Two male servants. They were playing cards and flirting ferociously. To judge by the pile of coins in front of Mally, she was winning.

I coughed.

She grinned cheekily at me. 'Good day, Mr P. Did you want to play?'

'I want someone sitting with Mr Nightingale.'

She shook her head. 'No point, Mr P. Never changes. Not for the better, not for the worse.'

'How do you know if you're not there?'

'I sat there two hours,' she said indignantly. 'Nothing happened. So I thought I might as well be comfortable.' She gathered up her winnings. 'And nothing *will* happen until he passes on, poor gent.'

There was a yell from Joseph in the passageway.

Thirty

Material possessions show the character of those that own them; choose wisely therefore.
          [*A Gentleman's Companion*, October 1731]

I dashed out into the passageway, Mally close behind me. It was pitch black out there; I smelt acrid smoke from extinguished candles. The only light was from the kitchen, and that stretched hardly a foot or two. Flickers of spirits danced in the darkness high up under the ceiling, casting no helpful light at all. One flitted across the wall next to me and I jerked back. 'Get the devil!' it shrieked. 'Get him!'

Even with Joseph's candles extinguished, there should have been light from the torches in the yard. The door at the far end of the passageway must have been shut.

There was a scuffling noise.

'He's in here with us!' Mally said hysterically. 'He's going to kill us all!'

I pushed her back into the kitchen. The two male servants were standing like idiots by the big table. I had to see what was happening out there! 'Candles,' I whispered, waving my hand towards them. One of the servants reached for them – and snuffed them out.

The kitchen was plunged into darkness; Mally stifled a shriek and swore. I gripped her arm. 'Stay here. All of you.'

'Think I'm a fool?' she muttered.

I no doubt was. I edged back out into the passageway. There was no point in hunting round the dark kitchen for the fire tongs or a skillet – by the time I'd done that, any intruder would be long gone. So I went unarmed, heart in mouth.

There was no sound now. Perhaps the intruder was hesitating, as I was, trying to gauge my position as I was trying to gauge his. I crept on, hand trailing along the wall to orientate myself. I could see a vague dark shape near the door to the yard, staggering about as if drunk . . .

My exploring hand met emptiness. I stumbled, grabbed at nothing. Of course! The gap where the steps climbed up to Nightingale's room. I glanced up but there was only darkness. The candles up there must have been blown out too. This must be another attack on Nightingale.

Joseph had to be my first concern. Nightingale was a dead man even if he'd not stopped breathing. I waved my hands about until I found the wall again and edged on.

Brilliant light flooded the passageway. One of the male servants said, 'I lit the candles again.' I stood, dazzled and cursing, a wonderful target for any attacker – I'd never felt so vulnerable. Then my eyes adjusted and I saw Joseph staggering towards me, blood streaming down the left side of his face.

He tumbled into my arms, trying to get words out. 'Hit – hit!' He gestured at his head. 'Yard—'

'Someone came at you from the yard?' He must have been

looking down the passageway towards the kitchen, distracted perhaps by trying to hear what we were saying. Or perhaps he'd dozed off again. Someone had come up behind him, hit him—

'Someone's after the beer!' Mally exclaimed. 'Not again!' She hurried to the door opposite the stairs to Nightingale's room, tried to open it. 'It's still locked. Maybe Joseph frightened them off.'

'Did you see who it was? Where they went?'

He shook his head, groaned, managed to say, 'Fell. Don't remember— Woke up, yelled—'

He must have lost consciousness, perhaps only for a few seconds – ample time for the intruder to do what they wanted before he came round and yelled for help. The beer cellar door was locked, confirming there was only one place the intruder could have gone. Nightingale's room. He could be up there even now . . .

I jerked my head at the male servants. 'One of you go for Gale the surgeon. The other one, help me get Joseph into the kitchen.' The spirits were skittering around in joyous excitement; one yelled from near the door, 'There's a cobble here. Blood all over it!'

The servants looked unhappy. One disappeared into the kitchen; the other said, 'Is he still around?'

'Who?'

'The assassin. The fellow what tried to kill him.'

'Don't fancy dealing with an intruder?' I asked. 'Too much for you?'

He straightened, pulled his coat down. 'Didn't say that.'

Behind him, the other servant came rushing out, dashed past, brandishing fire tongs. He tore open the passageway door and bolted across the yard.

'I'll help,' Mally said, exasperated, and hoisted Joseph's arm over her shoulder. 'If you want a job doing, do it yourself!'

I let them carry Joseph off, took up the kitchen candles and a poker from the fire. Draughts tugged at the flames as I went up the three steps to Nightingale's room, accompanied by a brace of eager spirits, who dashed about, shrieking, dashed out again. I was already tolerably certain I'd find no one there – the spirits would already have investigated.

The candles guttered wildly as I went into the room, my

gaze drawn straight away to the still figure in the bed. It was not the bloodstained scene of slaughter I'd anticipated. Nightingale was still alive, lying on his back as ever; I drew back the sheet and saw the bandages were undisturbed. His breathing was more laboured than ever, his face white as ice, his hands as cold as the grave.

The candles flared again. I looked about the room. The chair Mally should have occupied had been pushed back. Nightingale's trinkets still lay on the bedside table beside a jug of water and a glass. His pink clothes were folded on one end of the travelling trunk that stood under the window.

The window was open. Wide open. That was what was causing the candles to flare. And the pink coat had slipped from its neat folds; part of it was hanging over the edge of the trunk.

I left the candles and the poker on the washstand near the door, went to the window. As I touched it, it swung open wider, unsecured. I looked at it, and at Nightingale's trunk that stood beneath it. Cautiously, I stretched to peer out of the window, looked out on the alley where Nightingale had been attacked. There was little to be seen in the darkness but I remembered it was barely two or three feet down to the ground. This was the way the intruder had escaped; it would have been all too easy to clamber up on top of Nightingale's trunk, the window was wide enough even for a bulky man and then there was only that low drop to the alley below. The intruder could have been away before Joseph shouted out.

But *why* had the intruder been here? I'd assumed he'd come back to finish Nightingale off but Nightingale was unharmed. Had the attacker fled in panic after hearing Joseph call out? Or—

There was something wrong about the room, something missing. Something not as I'd seen it the previous day, at any rate. I pushed the window shut as the candles flared again, and turned to scan the room. Water in a jug on the table, a slip of paper containing powders left by Gale. A newspaper tucked under the foot of the bed next to the chamber pot.

My gaze came back to the table. A few pennies, a bill from the dressmaker's, presumably for Kate's dress. What else had been on the table before, that was missing now? I'd barely glanced at it on my last visit but—

There'd been a watch. Nightingale's watch had gone.

Thirty-One

Do not believe everything you hear; the lower orders do
not know the difference between truth and falsehood.
[*A Gentleman's Companion*, January 1730]

I fingered the empty space as I heard someone come cautiously
up the steps from the passageway. Mally peered round the corner
of the doorjamb, looked relieved when she saw Nightingale
unaltered. 'Spirits just sent a message from the surgeon,' she
said. 'He's on his way.'

I shifted so the table was behind me and she couldn't
see it.

'I was wondering if we shouldn't put Mr Nightingale's watch
somewhere for safe keeping.'

She glared, no doubt thinking I was casting doubt on her
honesty. 'Suit yourself,' she said. 'It's on the table. I wouldn't
bother – it's cheap and nasty.' And she flounced out.

I didn't remember the watch very well but I was inclined
to think Mally was right. But who'd go to such lengths to
steal a cheap watch? Was it worth attacking a lad and leaving
him injured? And if so, why?

I closed the window and drew the curtains – they didn't
quite meet in the middle – and went back down the stairs. In
the passageway, Mally was flirting with the excited spirits; the
remaining male servant, clearly disgruntled, was straightening
Joseph's chair and generally removing any evidence that might
have been there.

I interrupted Mally. 'You didn't see anyone loitering outside
the inn before any of this happened?'

'Not been out for hours,' Mally said.

'Catch him, catch him!' shrieked one of the spirits. 'Call the
constable!'

The other spirit sounded smug. 'Never saw a thing. I was
upstairs, in the attics.'

'And we all know why,' Mally said, giving me a look.

'I was *conversing* with the maids.'

'Giving them the once over, you mean.'

'A little friendly admiration,' the spirit conceded.

'Don't know why. It's not like you can do anything about it.'

'Oooh!' shrieked the first spirit in outrage.

'All talk and no action,' Mally said. 'What good's that to a girl?'

This had the sound of an old argument and I got out of it quickly. I went outside, a candle in hand. The yard was darkening still further; one of the remaining torches had burnt out. Gale the surgeon was walking through the arch, looking tired and irritable.

'Joseph's in the kitchen,' I said, indicating the passageway. Gale grunted and went in.

Just outside the door, in the yard, was an area of damaged paving. Cobbles had been prised from their settings and a hole dug into the earth beneath; dirty water glinted at the bottom. The servant had tossed the cobblestone used to hit Joseph back on to the pile — it was obvious from the dark splash of sticky blood on it. A half-cobble with a very sharp edge; Joseph had been lucky — it must only have been a glancing blow.

I tried to reconstruct what had happened. The attacker must have walked into the yard not long after I had. The passageway door had been open; the intruder would have seen Joseph lit by his branch of candles, dozing, or distracted by what was going on in the kitchens. The sound of his own footsteps on the cobbles need not have been loud if he'd gone carefully, and would not have alerted Joseph. He'd picked up the cobble, hit Joseph with it, slipped up the stairs to Nightingale's room and taken the watch, then made his getaway through the window.

I walked out into the street, taking the candle with me. A breeze had risen, and tugged at the candle flame; I sheltered it with my hand. In the dark alley, light from the window of Nightingale's room pooled across the cobbles. I stooped to peer in. Through the gap where the curtains did not quite meet, I could see the man in the bed, the candle on the table, the space where the watch had been. And the girl's chair, pushed back and unoccupied.

The most obvious conclusion was that it was Nightingale's original attacker, come back to finish off the job. But Nightingale had not been attacked again; instead his watch had disappeared.

Was it then simply an opportunistic theft? A drunken man wandering down the alley, peering in and seeing the watch? If the window had originally been closed, then he'd have had to go in through the yard. A weapon lay ready to hand in the pile of cobbles. That alone suggested an impulsive act; if this had been planned surely the attacker would have brought a weapon with him.

At least one thing was tolerably clear – the intruder was not Kate. If her abilities were as good as I thought, she'd no need to sneak into Nightingale's room; she could simply have stepped through from the other world.

But the intruder, whoever he was, would have had to be acquainted with the Golden Fleece to know how to reach Nightingale's room. Would an opportunistic thief not simply have broken the window and climbed in? Though how would he have known Nightingale wouldn't wake and apprehend him? At a casual glance, Nightingale looked as if he was merely sleeping.

Ridley would have known Nightingale would not stir, but would he have known where the room was?

I went back into the street. Lights were dancing in the darkness beyond the Guildhall; I heard raucous laughter. I blew my candle out and left it on a windowsill in the Fleece's yard, walked across the deserted Sandhill to the Guildhall. Behind the building, three or four young fellows were stretched out on steps overlooking the Key; a fishing boat bobbed at its mooring. It wouldn't be long before the tide turned; they must be preparing to sail.

They looked up when they heard my footsteps. They'd stuck two or three candle stubs to a step and were playing dice in the flickering light. I nodded in greeting. 'Seen anyone pass in the last half-hour?'

One of them wiped his nose with his sleeve, and grinned. 'Who's asking?'

They didn't look particularly respectable characters – rough men in their twenties, dressed in shabby clothes, with the smell of gin about them. I suspected they'd probably wish a thief good luck. I produced a shilling from my pocket, feeling as if money was slipping through my hands like water. Much more of this and I'd be as blasé about it as Ridley.

'Just a couple of old wives passed a while back,' said one of the men, eying the shilling. 'On the way to a laying-out.'

'There was that old fellow,' another said, stretching out lazily and kicking at the cobbles of the Key. 'The one as lives on the doorstep of the Printing Office.'

I contemplated them thoughtfully. They grinned. I put the shilling back in my pocket.

'Oi!' said one of the lads.

I let the silence grow. One of the candles expired in a hot pool of wax. They looked at each other, shrugged. The lazy one lit another stub and said, 'One of your stupid foppish fellows, all smiles and friendliness.'

'Sneering,' said another.

'Trying to pretend he's one of us,' said a third. 'As if!'

I produced the shilling again. 'When did you see him?'

Frowns and shrugs. 'Didn't see him come,' one said at last, 'we was loading her up,' nodding at the boat. 'But when we finished, he was hanging about the Fleece.'

'When was this?'

He shrugged. 'Maybe half an hour back.'

'Nah,' said the lazy one. 'Less than that. Only went off five minutes ago.'

'What did he say?'

'Wanted to know where we were going.'

'Where we lived.'

'What our names are.'

'Nosy,' said the lazy one, yawning. 'Don't trust no nosy fellows.'

'Did he go into the Fleece?'

A shrug. 'Didn't see. Too busy.'

'And he left five minutes ago? Which way did he go?'

They waved along the Key. 'Went dashing off all of a sudden.' The lazy one cackled. 'Reckon he saw a nice piece of flesh.'

'Gave us a wave. Said he hoped we enjoyed the trip.'

'Like he ever did a day's work.'

'If he's who I think, he never did,' I agreed and gave them the shilling. I wasn't out of earshot before they started squabbling over it.

Wearily, I climbed the Side in the chill night air and headed homewards. Ridley would have had the audacity to do the deed; he'd not particularly have cared about Joseph's welfare, and the impulsive nature of the affair was the sort of thing that would appeal to him. But I wasn't satisfied. Why should Ridley have wanted Nightingale's watch? It was hardly the sort of expense his mama would have objected to – he could have bought his own.

But, more importantly, why had Ridley so deliberately drawn attention to his presence? As if he'd known I'd ask about it—

Of course he'd known. He'd known I was there; he'd seen or heard me, talking to the servants. Was this more of his *fun*? Had Ridley seen me go into the Fleece, heard me talking, attacked Joseph, stolen the watch from Nightingale's room? Had he done it all for devilment? And then deliberately drawn attention to his presence by making sure the sailors would remember him?

Or was it something more personal? Mrs Annabella had mentioned my penchant for mysteries in Ridley's presence that day we were first introduced; had he taken it into his head to take me by the nose and lead me astray? He might have guessed I'd question any witnesses about. And if I didn't, then nothing had been lost, and he might find some other way to draw himself to my attention.

Was that all it was? A performance put on especially for my benefit?

Thirty-Two

A gentleman always acknowledges when he is in error, but he should not be in error frequently.
                              [*A Gentleman's Companion*, July 1733]

I snatched a few hours' sleep and woke to find a note from Esther on my pillow. *Have gone shopping with Kate. Tell me later how you found her.* I stared at the note in resignation. In one way or another, Kate was becoming a part of our household. The note also said that last night Hugh had sent Esther a message. *He told me where you have gone* was underlined, meaning, of course, that he'd told her I'd dashed off in search of Kate and probably gone into that other world.

The note brought me up short. When I'd been unmarried, I'd never had to worry about telling anyone where I was going; now it occurred to me that Esther might have been lying awake worrying about me. The gentle rebuke stung. And I'd a shrewd idea she was also hinting she might have liked to come with me.

I was going downstairs to the breakfast room when George slid down the banister. I snatched my hand away as the cold spirit skimmed past.

'She didn't come in till dawn, master!'

I sighed. 'George—'

'She's a nasty girl! She's rude to me!'

I warmed to Kate. 'Well, of course, she *shouldn't*—'

'Ask her what she was doing, master!' George's tone said he thought he knew exactly what Kate had been doing. 'She came in even later than you did! And that was really late!' he added snidely. 'Were you having fun, master? I thought you weren't supposed to do that after you were married.'

I was rigid with fury. Commenting on Kate's movements was bad enough; criticizing mine was intolerable. 'George—'

The spirit started to speak again but at that moment Tom appeared from the back of the house, looking determined. He interrupted the spirit ruthlessly, raising his voice to do so. 'Will you be requiring breakfast, sir?'

'No,' I said. 'I'll eat out.' And I walked out of the house, ignoring the calls of the spirit behind me.

Claudius Heron waved to me from the far side of the busy coffee house. He signalled for more wine as I dropped into the chair opposite him, feeling a little dishevelled from the brisk breeze that had sprung up. The bruise Ridley had inflicted was livid in black and yellow on Heron's cheek; he looked piratical. 'I hear there was a robbery at the Fleece last night,' he said.

I nodded. 'Nightingale's watch is missing.'

'And Ridley was seen outside.'

How the devil did he know that? Charlotte brought the wine, winked at me and took herself off to deal with an elderly gentleman. 'He made sure he was seen. He approached a group of sailors and drew himself to their attention. Is the tale the talk of the town?'

'The spirits know it, certainly.'

I contemplated this; was that Ridley's doing too?

Heron poured me wine. 'He is a young man who likes to provoke others.'

'He's very talented at it.'

'But why should he take Nightingale's watch? Why not make another attempt on his life?'

'Perhaps he merely wanted a souvenir,' I said flippantly.

Heron acknowledged this pleasantry with the slightest of smiles, and nodded to a passing acquaintance. 'I have just had a message from Jenison. I think he was hoping to see you.'

By which I suspected he meant Jenison had demanded my presence. I sighed. 'I was hoping to visit a few more possible subscribers to the concerts.'

'Naturally,' Heron said lazily. 'It is, after all, one of your favourite occupations.'

I made a face.

After I'd eaten, we walked up together to the Jenisons' house on Northumberland Street. The breeze was hustling fleecy clouds across the blue sky. Heron was anxious that I start his son's harpsichord lessons again after the summer break; I dutifully agreed, though the son is not as eager, or as musical, as the father. He'd also heard of a *young female*, as he put it, who sang *tolerably well* at Bath earlier in the year and passed her name on to me as a potential replacement for Nightingale. His quiet conversation soothed me, particularly in contrast to George; by the time we reached the Jenisons' I was feeling reasonably human again. Until he asked if *we* – he used the plural, meaning both myself and Esther – had sorted out the estate business with Armstrong. I said, curbing my annoyance, that the matter was in progress.

The Jenisons were all in the drawing room. Jenison looked out of place in so feminine a room and was rustling a newspaper loudly to assert himself. Mrs Jenison, still looking tired, held a book of sermons, which is the usual resort of women when they want to indulge their own thoughts without interruption; Mrs Annabella, who was rather more lively, had a piece of embroidery spread across her lap and was trying to match silks. As we were announced, I heard her say, '. . . do you think this rose is too dark?'

They looked up, and Jenison pushed himself to his feet. Mrs Annabella said, 'Oh!' and put her hand to her breast, looking suddenly stricken. Esther was right – she did like an audience. Mrs Jenison turned a dulled weary look on us.

We sat down and I explained what had happened while Mrs Jenison asked the footman to bring refreshments.

'His watch?' Jenison echoed. 'Then it was a common thief.'

'Apparently,' Heron said.

'How dreadful,' Mrs Jenison said automatically. She was holding the book tightly, as if the pain was welcome.

'The curtains of the room were not drawn properly,' I said. 'He probably looked in from the alley and saw the watch on the table.'

'But how did he know which room to go to?'

'Oh, indeed,' Mrs Annabella said, 'the place is a warren. Do you remember last year, Robert, when we came back from London and we were going to breakfast there and took quite a wrong turn?'

She put her hand down again and hunted amongst the silks, pulling out a bright purple. A pair of small embroidery scissors clattered to the floor; she stooped to pick them up. 'I really can't find the right colour for your embroidery, my dear. Not if you wish to match the roses you did before.' She glanced at Mrs Jenison, who was absorbed in her own thoughts again and didn't appear to hear her. Mrs Annabella lifted the top of the workbox on the table between the two women and waved the scissors. 'Where do these go? They're rather dirty, you know.'

'This is intolerable,' Jenison said. 'I cannot conceive what the world is coming to. That such a fine man should be attacked at all is astonishing enough, but to then rob him while he lies helpless . . .'

'Shocking,' Mrs Annabella said. She gave Heron a speaking look. I rather thought it wouldn't be long before she exhausted her grief and turned her attentions to another target. 'A wicked world,' she said. Heron looked away from her but she didn't seem abashed.

The door opened. A servant came in with a tray of that sweet wine women seem to like. Mrs Jenison came out of her daze and directed where she wanted the wine set down. A footman in the doorway announced sonorously, 'Mr Cuthbert Ridley.'

We all jumped, except for Heron, who said dryly, 'Talk of the devil.' It was plain who *he* thought had attacked Nightingale. We all turned our heads to stare at Ridley who was hesitating in the doorway.

'Oh— I rather— I would not—'

Jenison stood up convulsively, knocking over a footstool. 'How dare you come here again, sir! Your behaviour last time was totally unacceptable!'

'Oh— I— er— I really—' Ridley's gaze slid round the room until it lighted on me, then skittered away again. '—apologize—'

Jenison looked apoplectic but ground out, 'Apologize?!'

'I thought— I wanted to . . .' He was twisting his hands together nervously, even blushing. 'To appear before the ladies in such an inebriated state—'

'Drunk,' Heron said uncompromisingly.

'. . . not the thing—'

'Disgraceful,' Heron said.

Ridley bobbed as if accepting the rebuke. He cast another glance at me from under his eyelashes, a challenging amused look. 'The lady—' Both ladies looked puzzled. 'About Mr Nighting . . .'

Mrs Annabella shrieked. 'He's dead!'

'Alas,' he hesitated. 'No. I haven't— have you—?' He turned to me.

Heron said, 'Perhaps you would care to explain yourself more coherently.'

Ridley flashed him a venomous look. Jenison had subsided. After what had happened previously, no one would have argued if he'd thrown Ridley straight out into the gutter. But Ridley's mumbling, helpless, peaceable demeanour had evidently reassured him that nothing dreadful would happen, at least not immediately.

'I wanted,' Ridley said, enunciating with painful carefulness, 'to com-mis-er-ate with the lady.' He bowed to Mrs Annabella. 'I know she— her interest in the gentleman—'

Mrs Annabella flushed vividly, clutched at the embroidery on her lap.

'His interest in her—'

Heron unfolded himself lazily and rose. 'I think we will go, Ridley.'

'If he had indeed survived . . .'

Mrs Annabella was going as white as she'd been red.

'I'm sure we would have had an interesting announcement—'

He'd not come to apologize at all. He'd come to have some fun at Mrs Annabella's expense. This was cruel. We all knew Nightingale's interest in Mrs Annabella had been minimal; I had myself seen him abandon her at the concert in favour of younger prey. If she had indulged a few fantasies in that direction, it was hardly surprising; she was in an invidious position, dependent on her family financially, always having to please them with little favours, like sorting her sister-in-law's embroidery. For Ridley to taunt her like this was unforgivable. She was a woman who had no hope of a change in her circumstances; to point it out so blatantly was adding insult to injury.

And I suddenly perceived what his motive for stealing the watch must have been. *Adding insult to injury.* He'd not intended to attack Nightingale again; he didn't need to – the man was plainly dying. But to steal the watch; even though Nightingale himself would never know – that was the ultimate gesture of contempt.

Heron bowed to the ladies, took Ridley's arm. 'I regret we must leave.'

'No, no,' Ridley said. 'Must speak to the ladies— cannot be silenced—'

'You underestimate me,' Heron murmured, and steered him towards the door.

We were left in an awkward silence. Mrs Annabella was fingering her sister-in-law's embroidery silks. She hunted for her lace handkerchief. 'Oh – it has brought it all back—' She started to sob; Mrs Jenison looked at her with the stony gaze of a woman tried beyond endurance.

Jenison said, 'You will of course let me know at once if Nightingale's condition worsens?'

He was unmistakeably dismissing me. I got up, bowed to the ladies, and went out into the street. On the sunlit cobbles, Heron and Ridley were facing each other off and Heron's hand was on his sword. I saw why. Ridley was smiling at every sharp word, making little *moues* of amusement, patently not in the least unnerved. I wouldn't have been so sanguine; I've seen the consequences of Heron's anger.

Heron stopped in the middle of a sentence, stared at Ridley's unperturbed amusement. 'You will not live a long life,' he said.

Ridley grinned and threw Heron's own words back at him. 'You underestimate me.'

And he strolled off as if nothing had happened.

Thirty-Three

A gentleman should aim to marry a rational woman, whose chief concern will be his comfort.
[*A Gentleman's Companion*, August 1736]

Kate and Esther were in the library when I got home. From the hall, I heard the ping of isolated notes on the harpsichord and a kind of ritual chanting: A, B, C. Pausing at the library door, I realized Esther was teaching Kate how to read music. Or trying to, at any rate.

They sat side by side on the harpsichord stool, Esther very fair, Kate's dark curls a vivid contrast. Esther had bought Kate a simple white dress, very suitable for a young girl, and she looked demure. A pity it was only an illusion.

She prodded a note viciously and said, harping on an old theme, 'Why is this one called B? If I wanted to call it something else, why shouldn't I?'

'Because you'd be wrong,' Esther said. 'Charles, you look tired. Let me ring for wine.'

I strolled across while she spoke to the servant; peered over Kate's shoulder at one of Mr Handel's easier pieces. Kate said, 'Playing the harpsichord is boring. Why can't I play the fiddle?'

'I've told you, it's not a suitable instrument for a lady.'

'I don't care,' she said obstinately.

'How is Mr Nightingale?' Esther asked.

'The same.'

I sat in the window embrasure and over my glass of wine explained the events of the day, ending with my visit to the Jenisons. Esther listened attentively, while Kate pinged indifferently away at the keyboard. I thought she was listening more than she cared to let on.

'And to cap it all, Ridley turned up and set everyone in an uproar. I thought Mrs Annabella had reconciled herself to the state of affairs, but he set her off again. And deliberately too. The man is—' I glanced at Kate and amended what I'd been going to say. 'Vicious.'

'I suppose I had better pay the Jenisons another visit,' Esther said reluctantly.

'Mrs Annabella should be left to her own devices. She's playing to the audience.'

'It's not Mrs Annabella I worry over,' Esther said. 'Does Mrs Jenison look well to you? I think she finds her sister-in-law very trying. If I can take the burden from her for a few minutes now and again it may help.'

'Who's Mrs Annabella?' Kate asked. 'Is she the old witch who was all over Mr N at the concert? Dressed in lots of frills?'

'She's not a witch,' I said curtly. 'And you have something to explain. Where did you go after I left you at the door of this house last night?'

'I came in,' Kate said with an unconvincing air of innocence. 'Went to bed.'

'No, you did not. George says you came in after I did, which must have been an hour or more later.'

She flared up at once. 'George, George, George! Hate him, hate him, hate him!'

'Where did you go?' I repeated.

'None of your business!'

'It is if you want to stay in this house.'

She leapt up, glared at me. 'You ain't going to let me anyway. You're stupid, you. Know that?'

'Kate,' Esther said sharply.

'You're gonna get yourself killed.' She was standing, fists clenched, face going red. 'You dash off on your own, down to the Key—'

'You followed me!'

'Could have been anyone there – thieves'd strip those clothes off, soon as look at you.'

'Kate, calm down—'

'Well, get yourself killed then!' she yelled. '*I* don't care!' And she stormed out of the room, slamming the door.

There was silence.

Esther sat down in the window next to me and put her hand on mine. She was warm; her scent – faint lavender – teased me.

'She's feeling very insecure, Charles. She thought her whole future depended on Nightingale and now he's gone. Treat her gently.'

'She knows something she's not telling.'

'Perhaps.'

'All that nonsense about the town being dangerous at night. Certain areas of it, certainly, but plenty of honest folk walk out after dark!'

'Be patient with her.'

'She cannot play the violin,' I said. 'And she cannot be my apprentice.'

Esther hesitated, her gaze intent on me. 'Why not?'

'You know why not.'

'You once said you could not marry me.'

'That's different.'

'Really?' she said, amused, and let me stew on that for a moment.

Tom had brought two glasses; Esther poured herself wine and refilled my glass. Outside in the garden, the breeze ruffled the bushes, bowled a dead leaf or two across the neatly scythed grass. 'We'll see,' Esther said, after a moment. 'I have talked to Kate about her ability to step through into the other world, by the way. She is rebellious, of course, but I believe she will come round to my way of thinking in the end.'

I believed she would too. People generally do. Including me. I sighed and took her hand again, rubbing my thumb across the smooth skin. 'Which is?'

'That it is an ability to be used sparingly and only in times of real need.'

I thought Esther didn't quite appreciate how *stepping through* could take hold without warning. But I was enjoying the feeling of having her next to me, didn't want to argue. I put my arm around her; she shifted closer.

'Now,' she said, 'what proof do you have that Ridley first attacked Mr Nightingale and then later stole his watch?'

'None whatsoever,' I admitted. 'Except we know he argued with Nightingale. Twice, once at the Jenisons' and then at the Turk's Head on the evening Nightingale was attacked.'

'Half a dozen others may have argued with him too.'

'He made sure the sailors saw him and could tell me about him.'

She frowned – I loved the way the skin around her eyes crinkled. 'Why should he want you to know he was there? Surely if he had stolen the watch, the opposite would be true?'

'He's taunting me.'

'I can see he would consider that entertaining.' She sipped her wine. Her closeness was distracting me; I drew her closer. She smiled mischievously up at me but said, 'Ridley's presence outside the Fleece is no proof he stole the watch.'

'He has the audacity to do something of the sort.'

'Still no proof,' she said. 'Why do something clandestinely – to the extent of hitting a poor defenceless boy – presumably so he would not be caught, then deliberately make it clear to you he was the culprit?'

'If he didn't steal the watch, why was he there?'

She gave this serious thought, while I looked at her: her pale hair wispy against her neck, the graceful line of neck and shoulders, the bare smoothness of her forearm beneath the fall of lace. I knew that body now as well as I knew my own, and loved it a great deal better. 'I'm sorry I left you wondering where I was last night,' I said.

She smiled wryly. 'You could hardly have sent me a note.'

'Still—'

She shook her head. 'I knew what I was getting myself into when I married you, Charles. I knew what kind of a man I was taking on.'

'An irresponsible, inconsiderate tradesman with no manners.'

'No, no,' she protested. 'Your manners are excellent.'

Reluctantly, I laughed.

'Back to Ridley,' she said sternly, not quite contriving to hide her satisfaction at this little triumph. 'He might have seen the real culprit and decided to play with you, tempt you to think he did it. He wanted you to go awry.'

'But then his presence there was mere chance. He *happened* to see the culprit run off, *happened* to see me there – I don't believe in coincidence.'

She shook her head. 'As far as I can judge, Ridley spends most of his life amongst the taverns and brothels on the Key and round about. Is it surprising he should venture on to the Sandhill and look at the Fleece, perhaps even ponder going in to see Mr Nightingale – and then by chance see the thief run off?'

I sighed. 'I can't believe it.'

'Then—' She hesitated. 'Perhaps he was following you.'

'Dear God, I hope not! Kate had just led me a merry dance through that other world.' I thought back, as best I could, to the events of the previous night. 'I don't recall anyone following us. I don't see how it would be possible. Even if Ridley knows about our ability to step through, he couldn't have known when and where we would *re*appear in this world.' I sat upright suddenly. How had I been so stupid as to not see the truth? 'Of course! He wasn't following *us*! He was following the thief!'

Esther paused, glass at her lips. 'But that would mean he knew a crime was going to be committed *before* it was done!'

'He was following Nightingale's *attacker*,' I said. 'He saw the fellow, suspected he might intend to have another go at Nightingale and followed him to see what happened.'

'But I thought you believe *Ridley* the attacker,' she said, bewildered. 'Did he not give you an accurate account of what happened?'

'Let's suppose for the moment he's not.' I leapt up, walked about the room. Esther caught at a bowl of dried rose petals as I knocked against a small table. 'We know he encountered Nightingale during the evening, and they argued. Suppose he then followed Nightingale with a view to taunting him further and *saw the attack take place*. That would explain how he knew the details. Then what would have been his reaction?'

Esther frowned. 'Any sane person would have told the constable.'

'I'm not sure Ridley's sane,' I said. 'But in any case he's very short of money – so short he steals from his mother and tries to persuade me to give him a loan.'

'You never told me that,' she said, bemused. 'You refused of course?'

'He wanted fifty pounds. I don't have fifty pounds.'

She sighed. I hurried on. 'So what *did* he do? He blackmailed the attacker.'

She stared.

'Ridley would enjoy having someone at his mercy. And of course he suspected the attacker would want to finish the job.

Therefore he took to following him, saw him go in to the Fleece, saw me go in too—'

'Would he not have tried to stop the attacker making another attempt on Nightingale?'

'Not at all – he doesn't care what happens to Nightingale. And the worse the attacker's deeds, the more scope there is for Ridley to blackmail him.'

'No, no!' Esther sat up straighter. 'Consider, Charles! The intruder who stole the watch cannot be the original attacker. He had the chance to finish Nightingale off but did not do so. Why should he have changed his mind? It must have been a thief, nothing more.'

'Are you suggesting there are *two* people involved?'

'The original attacker and an opportunistic thief. Why not?'

'Because Ridley's presence cannot be explained unless he was following the attacker.' I slumped against the mantelshelf above the unlit fire. 'Dear God, we're arguing in circles.'

Esther absently rearranged her petticoats. 'Perhaps Ridley had other fish to fry? If he is himself the attacker, he may have been waiting outside the Fleece for the opportunity to attack Nightingale again. Then his spotting of the thief, and of you, would not be a coincidence – which would answer your objection.'

I drained my wine, put the glass down on the mantelshelf. 'There's one certain way to clear this matter up.' I strode for the door.

'Charles! Where are you going?'

'To find Ridley and ask him.'

'Is that wise?' she asked, alarmed. 'Charles, he could be dangerous!'

I turned at the door. She was rising from the sofa. 'What else can I do?' I asked. 'Is there any other hint as to the identity of the attacker? And I've not forgotten the death of that baby, Esther, even though everyone else seems to have. Ridley was the villain of *that* little episode. He's at the heart of this, Esther – attacker or not, thief or not, he knows what's going on. And I mean to get it out of him!'

Thirty-Four

Family relations should be strong; respect should be culti-
vated for the elders, and discipline inculcated in the young.
[*A Gentleman's Companion*, June 1735]

And of course I couldn't find Ridley anywhere. I spent several
hours looking for him without success – the only sniff I had
of him was when the landlord of the Fleece told me he'd been
there earlier, asking after Nightingale's health.

'Something odd about him,' the landlord said. 'A kind of
knowing look, if you see what I mean. Like he was about
to wink and nudge me.' He looked measuringly at his ostler
who was leading a horse to a coach. 'A pity – his mother's
a good woman.'

While I was there, I went in to check on Nightingale. The
room looked funereal. The curtains were still drawn; a single
candle flickered on the bedside table. Gale was standing over
the bed; the sick man's breathing was so shallow I looked twice
to be certain he was still alive.

'I don't know how he's still here,' Gale said.

'Nothing you can do?'

He shook his head. 'The curate of All Hallows came in and
said a few prayers over him, and for all I know that did better
than I can.'

'But he won't survive?'

'An hour or two at most. But I said that last night and I was
wrong.' He nodded at the trunk that stood under the window.
'I was thinking we should look in there. He must have some
family who'd care to know what became of him.'

I hesitated. I'd never heard Nightingale speak of any family
and I didn't want to get myself involved in awkward correspondence of that kind, but the only other person who might feel
obliged to do it was Jenison and he was not a man to write a
letter of sympathy. A business letter, yes, he'd be good at that,
but a letter of condolence would be beyond him.

'I'll do it,' I said. 'If he dies.'

A ghost of a smile touched Gale's lips. 'When,' he corrected me.

I'd promised Jenison I would keep him up to date and I went up a windy Westgate to his house, feeling that the trip was becoming very familiar. But as I raised my hand to knock at the door, Claudius Heron came up behind me.

The breeze was flicking his hair across his forehead; he said without preamble, 'I have been looking for you – Gale told me where you were headed. Ridley is nowhere to be found. No one has any news of him, neither living man or spirit.'

I had no time to say anything; the door swung open and a footman stood back to let us in. We were left in the elegant hall while he went to see if his mistress was at home. There was a new picture at the foot of the stairs, a fine portrait of Jenison himself.

'I have been presented with a dozen bills today,' Heron said, lowering his voice. His hand was tapping regularly against his thigh in barely repressed anger. 'He has told all the tradesmen I would pay. Tailor's bills, wine merchants, shoe-makers – even a butcher's bill. He is racking up impressive debts already. This cannot continue.'

'He could still be at the Old Man,' I said. 'I don't trust the people down there one little bit. And the spirits on the Key can be uncooperative.'

Heron nodded. 'I have sent my manservant down to enquire. He may hear something different.'

A noise behind us; we both turned. The door to a side room had opened. Mrs Annabella stood in the doorway, looking disconcerted. She was wearing one of her girlish, befrilled gowns. 'Oh, I had no idea.' Her gaze settled on me, a watery gaze ready to shed tears at any moment. 'He's not—'

'No,' I said, firmly. I hoped fervently I'd not be the one to tell Mrs Annabella that the object of her affections had indeed passed away. Though I thought she looked a little disappointed – failing a true love culminating in the triumph of marriage, a love lost for ever would probably suit her inclinations very well. I immediately felt ashamed of my cynicism; I was as bad as Ridley, ridiculing her in such a fashion. But in an odd way, Nightingale's death would be a blessing for her; if he'd lived, she would have been doomed to disappointment and distress; now she could hold on to a dream of what might have been.

The footman came back and ushered us into the drawing room where we had one of the most tedious conversations of my life. Jenison was apparently out on business and once I'd delivered my message we none of us had anything to say. Mrs Annabella wavered between eagerness for the latest details and the faltering air of a woman doing her best to forget her woes. Heron was almost silent, patently impatient. Mrs Jenison looked more haggard than ever and more withdrawn, although she did her duty by us as guests conscientiously; I wondered if I should suggest to Esther that she should pay another visit. Even my compliments on the new portrait of Jenison aroused no enthusiasm; Mrs Annabella managed to say that it was 'very like' but her tone was doubtful.

We escaped at last. Heron muttered in exasperation as we stood on the street again. 'I have had sufficient irritation for the day,' he said brusquely. 'Come to dinner. Bring your wife and let us have some music. Ridley and Nightingale may go to the devil for a few hours.'

Perhaps I should have spoken to Esther before agreeing; when I told her later, in the drawing room, she shrieked. 'Charles, why didn't you tell me earlier! I cannot possibly get ready in time!'

Kate was painstakingly copying out notes on to manuscript paper; it was difficult to tell the notes from the blobs of ink she'd spilt. 'Am I going to wear my yellow dress again?' she said, frowning. 'It's dirty.'

'You're not coming,' I said.

She fired up at once. 'Why not?'

'It's a private dinner.'

She looked stubborn. 'I want to come.'

'No.'

'I will!' she shouted.

'No,' Esther said.

Kate stood breathing heavily, biting her lip. As I thought, Esther was already licking her into shape.

'Mr Heron is not holding a dinner party,' Esther said. 'It is merely for his intimates.'

'Heron?' Kate said sharply. 'Is that the gent with the sword?' She surprised me by adding, 'I like him. He's dangerous.' She sounded as if she relished the idea. 'If I stay, can I have some pie for supper?'

'I'll get cook to send your dinner to your room,' Esther agreed.

'All right, I'll stay,' Kate said as if it was a great favour, and danced out.

Esther looked after her with some amusement. 'Do you think Heron would like to be thought of as dangerous? It is not a very gentlemanly attribute.'

'Perhaps not, but I agree with Kate. And I think Ridley is likely to find it out soon enough.'

Kate was waiting in the hall to see us off when I came down an hour or so later. Tom was busy lighting candles; I lowered my voice, said to Kate, 'I know you're hiding something from me.'

She reddened but glared. 'I'm not!'

I bore in mind Esther's injunction about treating her gently. 'You'd do better to tell me now.'

'There's nothing,' she said sullenly.

'Very well. But remember you can tell me at any time, whenever you wish.'

She looked obstinate.

Esther came down the stairs in a gown of white silk spotted with tiny pink roses with even tinier green leaves. 'Here,' Kate said, eyes narrowing. 'You ain't walking to the dinner, are you?'

'Not in this dress,' Esther said, with amusement. 'Heron has sent his carriage. We must go, Charles. We must not keep the horses waiting!'

'A carriage!' Kate said eagerly, and dashed outside to stare in admiration at the magnificence in the street. 'I'm going to have a carriage,' she said, marvelling. 'Not this colour though.' Heron's carriage was a dark plum colour. 'I'm going to have a pale-blue one,' she said. Out of the corner of my eye, I saw Esther shudder.

I was surprised, but pleased, to find Hugh in Heron's stylish drawing room, drinking his host's best wine appreciatively and swapping tales about fencing. Dancing masters frequently teach fencing too, and the only reason Hugh does not, as far as I can tell, is that he doesn't need to – there are more than enough young ladies desperate to make eyes at him, to keep him dancing from morn to night. Before I knew it, both Heron and Hugh were pressing me to buy a sword and offering to teach me how to use it. Esther, unfortunately, thought it a good idea. 'All gentlemen carry swords, Charles,' she pointed out.

'But not if they can't use 'em,' Hugh said severely.

Heron nodded. 'Carry one and you *will* one day have to use it.'

'Only trouble is,' said Hugh grinning, 'Charles is an abominable dancer. No sense of rhythm. And if you can't use your feet properly, it's a bit of a handicap for a sword fighter.'

'I don't want to fight,' I said. 'I'm quite happy without a sword.' Truth to tell, I was feeling uneasy. Heron was smartly, and expensively, dressed as befitted a gentleman; Hugh was magnificent in lilac and plum, and Esther's gown was new and gorgeous. My 'best' coat was dull and patently cheap; as I had at the Jenisons', I felt distinctly shabby, particularly amongst the elegant sophistication of Heron's Chinese wallpaper and Roman statuettes. I wondered whether I could encourage Mr Watson the tailor to produce my new coat more quickly by the payment of a little extra something, then reflected I was thinking exactly as Jenison would. Or Heron. No, Heron would just look at Watson in a certain way and have the man volunteering to deliver the coat in minutes.

Heron said repressively, 'All skills can be learnt if the inclination is there.'

I hardly dared look at Esther. Swordplay, estate management – Heron had hit on the nub of the matter. I had no inclination to learn either.

I managed to change the subject and we went in to dinner in a panelled, very masculine dining room, with a polished mahogany table and heavy silver cutlery that shrieked expense. Heron's taste in food runs to the elegant too – he has a French cook apparently – a fact which sparked off talk of Paris. Esther had lived there as a child and longed to see it again. Hugh and Heron both know it well and advised me extensively on where to stay and what to visit; they seemed to assume we'd take a somewhat belated bridal trip there. I was gripped by a sense of unreality. Paris, Rome? Devil take it, I was a provincial musician with an income of under a hundred a year and the likes of me don't go to Paris.

We didn't banish Esther alone to the drawing room after dinner; instead we all repaired to Heron's library. He got out his violin and I opened up the harpsichord. Esther and Hugh murmured disconcertingly in a corner. I thought I heard Hugh mention my name; I glanced up at them – and saw, through a window behind them, a pale face.

The window looked out on to a terrace and night-shrouded gardens. I went across to draw the curtains. It was difficult to see anything outside; all I could see in the window glass was the reflection of the candles and Esther's pale dress. Had I imagined it? I was certain I'd seen something, *someone*. Someone small. Childlike. Was Kate following me again? How had she got it into her head I was in danger? What was she not telling me?

In the reflections, I saw the drawing-room doors open, and a footman look round for Heron. I drew the curtains and turned back. Heron was just dismissing the servant.

'I regret,' he said, 'we must postpone our music. Someone has tried to kill Ridley.'

Thirty-Five

Gentlemen never frequent low taverns.
[*A Gentleman's Companion*, February 1731]

I felt, as always, uneasy in the Old Man Inn, very much a fish out of water. Heron kept his hand on his sword throughout and, oddly, looked much more at home despite his fine clothes. I began to think Kate was right – he did look dangerous. And the livid bruise that branded his left cheek gave him a certain credibility with the regulars here – I saw them admiring it.

It had plainly been out of the question for Esther to accompany us. In her costly dress, she'd be an easy target for the insults of the ruffians at the Old Man, and while that wouldn't probably concern her in the least, it would distract me. She'd not even raised the suggestion but immediately accepted Heron's offer of his carriage home. Hugh had been harder to persuade but, eventually, reluctantly agreed that a one-armed man would be severely handicapped if it came to a fight. I fancied he was feeling more tired than he liked to admit.

Ridley had been carried to an upstairs room, so small it barely accommodated the bed and a cane-bottomed chair riddled with mildew. A window looked out on to the filthy chare to the side of the inn and was speckled with dead flies hanging in ancient spiders' webs. The room plainly didn't please Gale the surgeon, who was fastidiously avoiding touching anything he didn't have to.

Ridley himself lay on the bed, grinning at Gale's mutterings over the wound in his shoulder and occasionally pinching the serving girl who was primly standing holding a bowl of blood-stained water. Heron and I waited in the doorway while Gale worked; Heron set his back against the doorjamb so he could glance easily down the passageway to the stairs, plainly ready for possible trouble. I saw Ridley's gaze stray to Heron's sword and then to his profile, and I glimpsed – fear? surprise? But then the insolent grin slipped back into place.

Gale put a wad of cloth over the wound and held it in place with one hand while he wound bandages round Ridley's chest. 'It's only a scratch.' He glanced at me. 'Done with something none too sharp again.'

'Blunt be damned!' Ridley protested, laughing. 'It nearly killed me!'

'Nonsense,' Gale said curtly, gesturing at a bruise on Ridley's forehead. 'You fell and knocked yourself out – the villain must have thought he'd done enough damage and run off.'

The girl, dismissed, sauntered past us with her bowl of water, allowing it to slop over the sides as she went. Both Heron and I were on the lookout for mischief, however, and stepped back in time to prevent ourselves getting splashed.

'I'll put in my bill first thing tomorrow,' Gale said.

'As you wish,' Ridley said, grinning still.

Gale hesitated. 'And I'll tell the boy who brings it not to leave until he has his money.'

'He'll have to wait a long time,' Ridley said. 'I don't have a penny.' He looked up at Gale's scandalized face. 'So what now? Are you going to unwrap me and take the soiled bandages away with you?'

'I'll pay,' Heron said, wearily. 'On his mother's behalf.'

Gale muttered his thanks, gathered up his instruments and left with affronted dignity.

'I don't intend to be grateful, you know,' Ridley said.

I strode across to him, lifted up his right hand. He was too surprised to resist. The hand was scratched: one substantial graze across the palm, two or three smaller scratches across some of the fingertips. I checked his left hand; that too was scratched, though not so badly.

'The wound is in your left shoulder,' I said. 'You were attacked from the front by a right-handed person. You put up your hands to defend yourself and caught hold of the knife, at least once, perhaps more.'

'That's very clever,' Ridley said with mock admiration. 'Or were you hiding behind a heap of baskets, watching?'

'You were attacked on the Key?'

'Alas,' he said. 'I was drunk!'

'And still are,' Heron muttered.

'And your attacker?'

'Caught me by surprise!' Ridley said, beaming. 'Never saw a thing.'

'So you can't identify him?'

'Haven't the slightest idea.'

'But, as we've just agreed,' I said, 'you were facing your attacker. Moreover, you grabbed hold of the knife, which means you can't have been further than arm's length from him. So what did he look like?'

He was amused. 'The fellow was too short.'

'What?'

'A midget. No more than two feet tall. His face was on a level with my knees – never saw it.'

'Then how did he manage to stab you in the shoulder?'

'Perhaps he was aiming for something closer,' Heron mused. 'Somewhere more permanently damaging. A pity he missed.'

Ridley was furious at that. He snarled, started to swear.

'So why didn't you see his face?' I asked again.

'Too tall,' he said savagely. 'A giant. Eight feet tall at least.'

Silence. We heard the sound of laughter from the taproom below.

'So you knew him,' I said.

'Go to the devil!'

'It's Nightingale's attacker.'

He struggled up further in the bed. 'Get out! Get out of here!'

'You didn't knife Nightingale,' I said scornfully. 'You wouldn't have the nerve – you're all bluster. But you know who did and how – you saw it happen. And you saw the chance to make a little money so you sent him a note suggesting he might like to buy your silence. Only he didn't want to be blackmailed. He'd already disposed of one man; he thought he'd do the same to you.'

'I said, get out!' Ridley was reaching across the bed, evidently intent on seizing hold of the heavy candlestick on the bedside table, presumably to hit me with. He grunted in pain. Sweat broke out on his forehead. 'You want to watch yourself. One day someone'll have a go at you – and it'll damn well be me!'

Lazily, Heron flicked out his sword. A thin line of red sprang out along the back of Ridley's hand. He yelped, snatched his hand back from the candlestick, cursed, sucked at the cut.

'Of course, I could be wrong,' I said conversationally. 'Your wound could have been inflicted by one of the ruffians down-stairs – maybe you made advances to his girl. In which case, just tell me and we'll go.'

He said nothing, still licking the blood from the scratch.

'You're playing with fire,' I said. 'This is a dangerous man. He's made one attempt to kill you – it won't be the last.'

He snarled. 'I'll get my blow in first!' He pressed a corner of the grubby sheet to the back of his hand; a red line grew along the cloth. 'I'll do what I like,' he said. 'I'm not beholden to anyone and I'll not have anyone saying what I can and can't do. I'll break the attacker who killed the tweeterer and I'll get every penny I can. And then I'll be out of this damned town faster than you can see me.'

He raised his voice, yelled raucously for the girl. 'Bring me paper and ink – I want to write a note!' He sneered. 'I've a way out of here no one knows of. Not you, not him—' a jerk of his head at Heron '—and certainly not the law. I'll be off and no one'll be able to follow me.'

He leant back against the pillows, that obnoxious grin widening still further. 'You might say, I'll be out of this world!'

Thirty-Six

A wife always defers to her husband.
[*A Gentleman's Companion*, July 1734]

Heron's gaze met mine; the next moment, the girl came back with a platter piled high with food – half a chicken, a huge wedge of bread, pickles, an apple. She gave us a saucy eye. 'You two staying? I'm told you get three times the fun with three gentlemen.'

Convulsively, I spun on my heels, out of the room, down the stairs, through the taproom, into the blessed fresh air of the Key. Through the passers-by to the edge of the river. I stood on the wharf looking across the water to the lights of Gateshead on the opposite bank. It was almost midnight and the Key was not as crowded as during the day, but there were still sailors about, most of them drinking hard, some standing in serious conversation over smoking pipes. Whores touted for custom.

I was standing almost on the spot where Kate's mother and her child had been sent flying into the river, where the child died. Damn it, I would not let Ridley get away with murder!

Heron came up behind me, hand still on his sword, glanced around to make sure no one could hear us. 'He can step through to that other world?'

I turned my back to the river, stared at the Old Man, brilliant with candles and torches, and bubbling with noise.

'The evening Nightingale was attacked, Kate followed him,' I said. 'She saw him go down the Castle steps but didn't immediately go after him. She watched everyone who went down and saw no one suspicious – a middle-aged man and woman, a drunk. She didn't see Ridley – of course she didn't! He stepped out of that world into ours at some point on the steps!'

'Is that possible?' Heron asked. 'I had the impression it was a random business.'

'Not always.' I cursed, remembering something else. 'When I saw Ridley yesterday morning, he looked confused, disorientated – he even asked me the time! He must have just got back from the other world!'

Heron considered in silence for a moment then shook his head. 'This changes little. It explains how Ridley came to see the attack and to know the identity of the person concerned—'

'It makes him more dangerous,' I said. Ridley! Able to escape when he chose!

Heron nodded. 'And the task of dealing with him is therefore more difficult. But nevertheless, what has happened tonight merely confirms what you surmized. Ridley knows the identity of the attacker. And the attacker objects to being blackmailed and is seeking to dispose of Ridley.' He grunted. 'I always knew him for a fool. What now?'

I looked up at the second storey of the inn. Ridley's room was round the side, looking out on to the narrow chare. 'Now he'll eat that ridiculously large meal and drink himself stupid and probably give himself a fever. Then he'll no doubt enjoy himself with the girl.'

'And then?' Heron said patiently.

'And then, in a couple of hours' time, when he's feeling more himself, he'll get up from his bed and stagger out into the street.'

'You think he will seek out the attacker?'

'I think he'll put up the price of his silence.'

'So we follow him?' Heron looked down at his own magnificence. 'I shall be somewhat obvious, as indeed will you be in so light a coat. Do we have time to go home and change?'

I nodded. 'I know a spirit here who'll keep us informed if anything happens in the meantime.'

By the time I got home, I'd talked myself into a much better state of mind. The prospect of laying my hands on Nightingale's attacker revived me. And after that was done, I could return to the matter of the dead child, and Ridley. I flung open the bedroom door – and there was Esther, standing in front of the mirror in the candlelight, hair hanging loose in a shimmer of gold about her shoulders. She was dressed in shirt and breeches and concentrating on adjusting her cravat.

'No,' I said.

'Do not be ridiculous, Charles,' she said, patting the cravat. She reached up to coil her hair into the nape of her neck. 'I am coming with you. You know you cannot shoot straight.' She gestured towards the dressing table. Amongst the bottles of scent, the hairbrushes and pins, sat the brutal metal shape of one of her duelling pistols.

'How do you know I'm going anywhere?'

She sighed. 'You insult my intelligence, Charles! It is not difficult to see what has happened. Your blackmail theory must be correct, and Ridley's victim has turned on him. Now you have dragged information out of Ridley, and are off in pursuit. It is plain that neither you nor Heron would dash off in your best clothes, so I knew you would come back to change and have organized myself accordingly. Really, Charles, anyone with even a little knowledge of you would find it *so* easy to predict what would happen!'

She was right of course. And she and I had been out hunting a villain before; I knew she could take care of herself. She loved to cast off convention from time to time, along with the skirts she sometimes found confining; that freedom of mind was one of the reasons I'd fallen in love with her. I sighed, turned my back on the all-too attractive sight of Esther in her breeches, pulled off my coat.

'You don't have the story quite right.' I explained what had happened while she arranged her hair to her satisfaction.

When I'd finished, she nodded. 'Ridley is plainly one of those men who are always in trouble.'

'He leaves havoc in his wake,' I said. 'First the child, now this. And I've no doubt he'd claim none of it was his fault.' I hesitated. 'There's worse.'

She raised an eyebrow in query.

'He can step through to the other world.'

'He and Kate both?' she said blankly, pausing as she reached for her coat. 'Charles, until this week I knew of only two people who could move between this world and the other: my late cousin and yourself. And now there are two more? This is by far the most worrying thing you have told me.'

'I agree.' I was hunting for my oldest coat; I couldn't find where Tom had put it – devil take it, he couldn't have thrown it away!

'Kate is young and silly,' Esther said, 'but she is not

malicious. We can teach her not to do something foolish with her ability—'

'You seem to have taken the girl under your wing!' I protested. 'Can't you see how impossible it is?'

She came across to me, took my hands. 'We cannot afford not to! You must teach her to use her ability wisely.'

'I'm hardly a good teacher. She's far more accomplished in this than I am.'

'But Ridley!' she said, clearly hardly hearing me. 'Dear God, how can we possibly stop him doing whatever he chooses?'

I found the old coat and dragged it on. It wasn't much darker than the other but if it was damaged I'd regret it less. My greatcoat would help cover it up. 'We can only deal with one thing at a time,' I said, fully aware I was putting unpleasant matters aside again. I seemed to be making a habit of that. This time at least there was patently nothing else to be done. 'Ridley's not one to cower at home. He'll go out and press the attack.'

'So we follow him and find out who this other person is?'

'*I* follow him.' I reached for the duelling pistol.

'As I said, Charles.' Esther shrugged on her own coat and took the pistol from my hand. 'I am a *much* better shot.'

We were halfway down the stairs when the gleam of the spirit shot over our heads, hanging on the top of a mirror. 'It's her again, master!' George shrieked. 'She sneaks in and out whenever she likes!'

'George,' I said, losing patience. 'I don't want to hear any more from you about Kate.'

'But she's been getting notes! Writing to people!'

'And don't shout!' I snapped. 'You'll wake the household!'

'Honest, master—'

'Notes,' I said, impatiently.

'Yes, master.'

'That's very interesting,' I said. 'Considering Kate can neither read or write. Goodnight, George.'

And I shut the door firmly as we went out on to the street.

As we came along the darkened Key, I couldn't see Heron; I scrutinized the knots of sailors and whores while Esther hunched inside her greatcoat and pulled her hat down to shadow her face. Then I spotted him, leaning against the huge timbers of a pulley set up by one of the moored boats. He too had donned a hat, for fear presumably that his fair hair would glint in the torchlight, and he wore a voluminous greatcoat which swung open to allow him access to his sword.

He frowned when he saw Esther, seemed about to say something but she forestalled him with a murmur, patting the pocket where she had stowed the pistol. 'You know Charles can't shoot straight.'

A smile tugged at the corner of his mouth.

'Is he still in there?' I asked.

'Your friendly spirit says so.'

Esther glanced about anxiously. 'Will he not spot us?'

'His room looks out on to the chare at the side,' I said. 'He won't be able to see us before he gets to the inn door.'

She turned her back on the inn. 'We have one advantage – he will surely be looking for a single pursuer, not a group.'

I said, 'Don't move suddenly. He's just come out.'

Ridley hesitated at the door of the inn, his glance sweeping the Key. Esther gestured towards Gateshead Bank as if she was pointing something out; Heron turned as if to look, but I saw his gaze drift quickly back to the Old Man. I drew my coat about me as if cold and kept an eye on Ridley.

He looked pale, as far as I could tell in the flickering light of the torches that lit up the Old Man; there were no bandages visible but he held his left arm stiffly. After a moment, he turned and strode off along the Key.

We turned to follow. Heron drew off to the left, strolling away from Esther and myself, and gaining rapidly on Ridley.

'He cannot be going to accost him surely,' Esther whispered, hand on the pistol in her pocket.

Heron overtook Ridley, using a group of apprentices to shield him as he passed. Ridley's attention fortunately was on his back; he glanced round constantly, clearly to see if he was being followed. Esther and I strolled out to the edge of the Key and paused to debate over a pile of Baltic timber that lay alongside a seagoing ship.

Ridley put on a turn of speed.

I seized Esther's arm. 'He's going on to the Sandhill. I suspect he'll walk up the hill towards St Nicholas. You stay behind him – I'll cut through the back alleys and try to pick him up by the church. If you see me do that, take another turning and catch up with us again later. He mustn't see the same person behind him for too long!'

She nodded, strode off behind Ridley's receding figure. I hurried into an alley; zig-zagging to avoid the worst of the villainous chares just off the Key, I climbed up to Butcher Bank and thence, eventually, to the top of the Side. There I hovered in the mouth of an alley, peering cautiously out. For a moment, I feared Ridley had gone another way, then I heard footsteps and drew back; moments later, he passed the end of the alley. I gave him time to get ahead of me then strode out into the street.

I almost collided with Esther. 'He's off to the Bigg Market,' she predicted scornfully. 'Just out for a drink!' And crossed the road at once to a side street beside the Post Office.

For a moment or two, I feared she was right. Ridley cut round Amen Corner behind St Nicholas's church and came up towards the Clothmarket. As I crossed the street to follow him, I saw Heron, striding out in a businesslike fashion. He didn't so much as look at me, although we came within three feet of each other.

Ahead, Ridley paused outside a tavern as if he was tempted to go in. One hand strayed to his hip and began to scratch. With any luck, he'd picked up fleas from the beds at the Old Man.

I realized my danger almost too late. If I stopped too, Ridley might realize I was following him. There was nothing I could do but walk steadily past him and hope he didn't look too closely at my face. I pulled my hat low on my forehead and was lucky; he didn't look round. He was frowning at his waistcoat pocket, dipping his fingers in as if in a vain search for a coin or two. It looked as if he'd have to sing for a drink, as Nightingale had. I walked on then, at the point where the Clothmarket meets the Bigg Market, stopped and sneaked a look back down the street.

Ridley had disappeared.

Thirty-Seven

A gentleman's reputation precedes him . . .
[*A Gentleman's Companion*, September 1730]

Heron was striding across the Clothmarket; when he saw me start back, he waved his hand, pointing at a building about halfway down the street. I got there before he did and found a small alley between two shops, barely wide enough for a man. Light from a torch burning in the Clothmarket barely penetrated the alley but I thought it turned almost immediately to the right. Once we were round that corner, it would be pitch black.

Heron came to my shoulder. 'It is too dangerous to go in there. I will cut round the other side of the shops and see if there's a better way in. Stay here.'

He was just moving off, leaving me, annoyed, at the entrance to the alley, when we heard a clatter.

I plunged in.

My shadow blocked out most of the torchlight. I trailed my hand along the bricks, straining to see. Ahead was a blank wall with the tiniest of windows high under the eaves. I could have done with the help of a friendly spirit but didn't want to call for one in case Ridley heard me. None came dashing to see what was going on so perhaps the alley was unspirited.

I came to the corner, took a deep breath and swung round it. Heron came up behind me, swearing. I drew back, said, 'There's no danger. Look.'

It was a dead end, closed off at a doorway that had been bricked up decades ago. The staves of a broken barrel were still rocking where they'd been knocked over. There was no way out and no Ridley.

Heron said, 'He has stepped through. We must do the same.' He gripped my arm, his thin fingers bruising me through the material of my greatcoat. 'Without delay.'

He was right. God knows what havoc Ridley might wreak on an unsuspecting world. We had to follow him. And at once, because of that disconcerting habit of the worlds being slightly out of step. I took a pace forward. Heron, still gripping my arm, took that pace too. There was the familiar sense of cold and a flash of darkness, then we were standing in the same alley – only it was daylight and rain was lashing into our faces.

At least we were dressed for it, I thought wryly as we huddled at the place where the alley debouched on to the Clothmarket. Which Ridley was not – he'd be getting very wet. And the heavy rain meant too that there were fewer people about, and they were hurrying past with heads down. No one seemed to notice us.

Heron, beside me, was shivering despite his thick greatcoat. I stared out into the sodden street, remembering, too late, that Esther would be walking about the streets of our own world on her own, in the small hours of the morning, wondering what had happened to us. I took a firm control of my anxiety; she was a sensible woman and she had a duelling pistol. Heaven help anyone who tried to take advantage of her!

We splashed up the cobbles to where the Clothmarket meets the Bigg Market and stood in the shelter of a shop doorway to stare about for Ridley. We could be directly behind him, or hours too late. The heavy rain stung my exposed hands and face. If this was our own world, I'd ask a spirit to trace Ridley's movements but there were no spirits here. And if we accosted a passer-by they might mistake us for our counterparts and ask awkward questions.

Heron said suddenly, 'There!'

Ridley was dressed in sombre brown, which was not easy to spot in the driving rain but he was also the only person not sensibly wrapped up against the weather. He was just disappearing round the corner where the Bigg Market dog-legs to the right, leading up to the dead end where the Turk's Head lies.

'Esther was right,' I said grimly as we hurried from our shelter. 'He's looking for ale.'

We were walking into the rain. A vicious wind tugged at our clothing; I was forced to keep one hand on my hat to prevent it blowing away. My greatcoat flapped open; the rain quickly soaked the knees of my breeches and stained my white stockings a muddy brown. A man hurrying past raised a hand

and shouted something. The wind whipped away his words but I distinctly heard my own name.

'I hope to God we do not come face to face with our own selves,' Heron said.

I'd met my counterpart in this world once before, the briefest of encounters – we'd come face to face on a doorstep – and it had been one of the most frightening experiences of my life. And one of the most humbling. My counterpart in this world is wealthier than I—

And I almost came to a halt as I thought: *Not any more.*

The street was less exposed when we turned the corner – the Bigg Market narrows progressively as it twists towards the Turk's Head, and the worst of the rain splattered against the walls above our heads. The door to the inn stood open but an inner door was firmly shut against the weather; I pushed on it, feeling water dripping from my hat down my back. Noise hit me as the door swung open: laughter and the rumble of conversation, the clatter of tankards, the calls of serving girls.

Ridley had his back to us. If we'd any doubts the sodden figure was his, they would have been dispelled by his behaviour. He was ranting and raving at the landlord, Parker, demanding beer on account, and game pie too, and where the devil was Maggie? Judging by Parker's squint of puzzlement, Maggie had no counterpart in this world. Some do not.

'It's no use you going on, Mr Ridley,' Parker said levelly. Parker has a big black wig which looks as if it was left over from King Charles's days, and a shock of eyebrows to match. 'I told you last time you'd get no more credit from me. Not until you pay what you already owe.'

'I can give you wealth beyond your imaginings,' Ridley said, gesturing drunkenly. 'I can show you the entrance to another world—'

I started forward but Heron put out a hand to hold me back.

'Yes, I know,' Parker said sighing. 'You want to show me the land of the fairies.'

A man with a tiny wig and a huge belly grunted with laughter.

'No!' Ridley caught Parker's sleeve. 'A world like this one but with unimaginable wealth!'

Parker looked at him until he took the hand away. 'There are only two worlds, Mr Ridley, this one and the next, and I can hear all I need to know about the next world in church on Sunday mornings.'

'Oh my God,' I muttered to Heron. 'What day is this? In our own world, I mean.'

He stared at me as if I was mad. 'Saturday. No – it must be Sunday morning now.'

I groaned. 'I've promised to play the organ at All Hallows today.' Would I be back in time, I wondered. Who could tell? I'd never yet fathomed how to guess when I'd get back to my own world. Perhaps I did need Kate to give me a lesson or two.

'I want a beer!' Ridley growled.

'No, sir,' Parker said, very deliberately. 'And if you don't leave this inn now, I'll personally throw you out of it. And you'll know from the last time that it's none too pleasant an experience.'

Heron strolled forward. Startled, I trailed after him. 'Parker,' he said cordially. He took off his hat and shook himself. 'Dreadful weather.'

Parker looked relieved. 'It is indeed, Mr Heron. Good day to you. And to you, Mr Patterson – I didn't see you there.'

Thanking providence my greatcoat hid my shabby clothes, I nodded warily. I don't have Heron's inbred confidence that immediately makes him master of every situation.

Ridley was staring at us and I didn't like the slow grin that spread over his face. 'Here you are, Parker. These are the very gentlemen to confirm what I've been telling you.' He prodded me in the ribs. 'You tell him, Patterson. You tell him we've just come from another world.'

'Yes, yes,' I said soothingly and winked at Parker. 'Another world entirely.'

'With spirits on every corner.'

'What's special about that?' Parker sighed. 'There are enough taverns in this world. I wish there weren't – too much competition.' His large customer grinned.

'Spirits!' Ridley cried. 'Not brandy or— or— not *those* spirits. The spirits of the dead!'

'I was told he has been hearing voices,' Heron said, regarding Ridley dispassionately.

'Sad case,' Parker said, more as a matter of politeness than anything else. The look he bestowed on Ridley was not sympathetic. The large customer looked thoughtful, ε professionally interested. I wondered if he was one of the gentlemen who look after the deranged in such places a Bedlam. Perhaps we ought to enlist his help.

'Real spirits, damn it!' Ridley burst out.

'Drunk as a lord,' Heron said.

I took Ridley's arm. 'Time to go home.'

Ridley staggered. 'I won't go with you! Got to get to the field.'

This puzzled me. 'Which field?'

Ridley clutched at me. A faint pink stain disfigured the shoulder of his coat, I noticed; the wound must still be bleeding. I thought of the field Kate and I had stepped through to – was that what he was referring to? But how could he know about that?

'Shall I call a chair?' Parker asked.

The vision of Ridley being carried to our own world in a sedan chair briefly diverted me. 'No, no. The walk will do him good. The rain will help sober him up.'

Ridley shrugged me off. 'I said I won't come. I want to go to the field.'

'Maybe he doesn't want to see the spirits,' Parker said humorously.

'Does one *see* spirits?' Heron said, frowning. 'I would have thought that by its very nature the human spirit is incorporeal. Surely, like the rest of the spiritual world, it is invisible, beyond our perception?'

We all stared at him. I suddenly realized he was trying to distract Ridley and was succeeding. I snatched at Ridley and got a good grip on his arm. He struggled to get free. 'Let go of me, I said, let go!'

'Jem!' Parker said imperiously.

And the large customer lifted a massive fist and brought it down on Ridley's head.

He slumped into my arms.

Thirty-Eight

Independence of mind and action are the sure sign of a
gentleman.

[*A Gentleman's Companion*, June 1734]

We staggered out into the rain-lashed street with Ridley lolling
between us, a dead weight. The thought of carrying him even
a hundred yards was not appealing.

'Take us back to our own world,' Heron said peremptorily.
'Now!' A rough-looking man pushed past us.

'I can't! Not with so many people about! We need a deserted
alley.'

That should have been easy, particularly in this rain. But it
seemed that half the town was heading for the Turk's Head to
shelter from the weather; every time we turned down a side
street or alley, someone was coming the other way. Heron
cursed and Ridley began to show signs of coming round.

In the Bigg Market again, we came face to face with a
group of five or six apprentices causing havoc, yelling and
shouting at passers-by and trying to splash them as they
trudged through the puddles. Heron almost exploded with
rage and frustration. 'What the devil are they doing out at
this time of day!'

I tugged at Ridley. I'd pulled his arm round my shoulder
but his weight was dragging me down. 'Let's cross to the other
side.'

Avoiding confrontation is not in Heron's nature. 'Devil take
it! Get back to work!'

The boys sneered; one struck a defiant pose. With water
dripping off his hat and running down his face, Heron was not
an impressive authority figure.

'We'll call out the Watch,' I threatened, trying to tug at
Ridley and, through him, at Heron.

The effect of my words was startling. One of the lads started
stammering. 'Mr Patterson. Sorry, sir, I didn't recognize you.'
Rain was running down his cheeks but I rather thought there

were beads of sweat there too. 'I was just off to get that ruled paper for you, master. I just happened to meet—'

His voice trailed off. I thought it best to say nothing; I looked at him. 'Yes, sir,' he said quickly and dashed off into the downpour. The other boys, maintaining their dignity, sauntered after him and didn't laugh or smirk until they were at a safe distance.

'You patently do not keep a sufficiently hard hand on your apprentice,' Heron snapped, staring after the boys.

'My *counterpart* doesn't,' I said annoyed. Thinking of George. And Kate.

At which moment Ridley kicked me on the ankle bone.

I yelped, involuntarily let go of him, and he set off running. Heron still had his other arm and held on grimly. Ridley swung in a circle, slipping on the wet cobbles and almost tumbling over. He swung a wild punch. Heron swayed back out of reach.

My ankle throbbed furiously. I made an ineffectual grab for Ridley. His arm took me full in the face, sent my hat spinning and knocked me to the ground. I landed in a pool of rain; water soaked straight through my clothes to the skin. I heard Heron swear, then the rip of cloth, and Ridley dashed past me.

Heron bent to help me up. I waved him away. 'After him!'

He raced off. The Bigg Market runs downhill and Ridley was fast, skidding on the slick stones, dodging and weaving between startled passers-by. He had the advantage in years on Heron but I didn't believe for a moment he had more tenacity. He'd be hard put to escape.

I crawled to my knees. My jaw had taken the full force of Ridley's blow and was aching. My hair was streaming with rain; the damned stuff had soaked through my coat and was sticking my shirt to my shoulders. My hat lay sodden and misshapen a yard or so away; I dipped for it, grunted as the world threatened to spin around me.

A voice was calling, 'Master! Master!' The boy came running up, looking anxious. 'Are you all right, master?'

'I am,' I said. 'But Cuthbert Ridley won't be when I get hold of him.'

He looked awed. 'Was that Mr Ridley? But he says he never drinks.'

That was not what Parker in the Turk's Head believed. 'Ruled paper,' I said thoughtfully.

'Yes, master.' And he dashed off again.

Ridley and Heron had disappeared, running down into the Clothmarket and out of my sight in the driving slant of rain. I followed more sedately, cramming my sodden hat back on my head, trying to avoid the worst of the puddles and wondering what best to do. The crucial thing was to find Heron again; he couldn't return to our own world without me. In that sense, Ridley was not so important as he could find his own way back.

But then, I thought, why hadn't he already done so? He was foolish to begin with, and wild, and now he was drunk besides; no scruples would prevent him stepping between worlds, even if there were people about. It was clearly the easiest way to escape myself and Heron. He must want to stay in this world very badly. Why had he come here?

To go to a field, apparently. A field, I thought, would be a good place to hide something, in a hedge, under a few stones or even in a hole dug for the purpose. Like a weapon you'd just stabbed a man with, for instance. Or that someone else had stabbed a man with. The attacker had tried to get rid of Ridley tonight and Ridley's first impulse had been to recover the weapon used on Nightingale to bring even more pressure to bear.

I splashed on down into the Clothmarket. Past a draper's shop. Quickening my pace, I came out opposite St Nicholas's church. The veil of rain obscured the gilded points of the crown on top of the church. Which way would Ridley have taken from here? I looked about in some despair, then saw someone I recognized – Philips, the new constable of All Hallows' parish, wrapped in a voluminous greatcoat and looking miserable as he tramped through the torrents. I hesitated to speak to yet another person who knew me but surely a mere civil enquiry could not hurt. 'Mr Philips!'

He stopped and bowed, even reached for his hat but clearly thought twice of taking it off and getting his wig wet.

'I'm looking for Mr Cuthbert Ridley. I was told he came this way.'

'He went down the Side to the Key, sir,' Philips said. 'Saw him not a moment ago. Looked like he was in a hurry.'

'Thank you,' I said and he walked off. I went on my own way, reflecting on the encounter. Philips had just spoken to a man from another world and would never know it.

The stones of the steep Side were treacherously slick; I tottered down, concentrating on my footing, only belatedly realising there was a man standing at the foot of the street, staring into the window of the breeches maker as if the rain was not sluicing down. He turned his head. Ridley. But I knew at once it was not *our* Ridley, for he was wearing a greatcoat and hat against the weather; the clothes were sober to the point of dullness and his wig unfashionable, even staid.

He had a sour look which deepened into disapproval as he saw me. I nodded and made to pass. The rain slashed against my back and threatened to make off with my hat. I put up a hand to secure it. My face ran with raindrops. Ridley stepped in front of me. 'Mr Patterson,' he said in a peremptory fashion, 'I want a word with you. You have been traducing me, sir!'

I sighed. 'No, I haven't.'

'You have been telling the world I am a drunkard and a lecher. You have been prejudicing the ladies against me! Particularly Mrs Jenison. I have a stake there, sir, one of those daughters is mine!'

Revulsion rose up in me. 'Money, I daresay,' I said.

'Damn it, I will have the girl!'

His face was purple; I said carefully, 'I assure you that I never speak of you at all.'

I tipped my sodden hat, and walked away. He even shouted after me, but I let the wind and the rain take his words and hurried on down to the Key.

Heron was standing by the slope that led up on to the Tyne Bridge, apparently oblivious to the rain lashing down. He was scanning the few scurrying passers-by without a great deal of hope. 'Damn him to hell, he's disappeared!'

I was wet and wretched, and didn't want to encounter anyone else I knew, or ought to know. 'Let's go back. Ridley will follow in his own time.'

Heron had his hand on his sword hilt. 'And if he doesn't?'

I sighed. 'We'll be well rid of him.'

He stared at me. 'We cannot leave him here! God knows what damage he could do.'

'We can't comb the entire town for him!' I pointed out.
'We could miss him half a dozen times. Much better to get
back home. Besides, he can't stay here for ever, not if he hopes
to get money out of his attacker.'

'Then why the devil did he come here in the first place?'

'To get the evidence he needed to damn the real villain of
this crime.' I glanced round as a merchant, hurrying past,
greeted us both. He was plainly in no mood to linger, but the
encounter decided Heron. He nodded. 'I know where we can
go back without being seen.'

I followed him into the Guildhall. At the front of the
building, wide stone steps wind up from the Sandhill to a
covered balcony from which one can survey the wide expanse
below. But Heron led me past the first flight of stairs and
behind, to a cramped dark passage with two doors leading
from it. It was deserted.

'This will do,' I agreed. Heron put his hand on my arm and
I started to take that one step forward that would take us back
to our own world—

A heavy weight descended on my shoulders, and bore me
down, down . . .

Thirty-Nine

A truly civilized society is one in which every man and
woman knows their place.
                    [*A Gentleman's Companion*, October 1735]

I hit hard flagstones with a force that took the breath out of
me. Heron was shouting somewhere close by. For a moment
the crushing weight lay heavy on my back; I heard a grunting
breath in my ear, and something else, almost like a sob.

Then the weight lifted; I heard Heron say, 'Move one inch
and I'll put this sword straight through your windpipe. And
don't think I won't do it.'

I managed to roll on to my back, wheezing for breath.
Behind me, in the faint light of dawn, Ridley stood cringing,
the point of Heron's sword at his throat.

I tried to speak but I didn't have breath enough. Heron said, 'We are back. All three of us. Ridley played piggyback to get here.'

I squinted at them, managed to drag myself to my feet with the help of the stairs. 'But that means—'

'Exactly,' Heron said. 'He cannot come and go on his own.'

'But he did!'

'Actually,' said another voice, sounding amused, 'he did not.' And Esther, still in greatcoat and breeches, appeared on the other side of the steps.

With her hand on Kate's shoulder.

Hugh's lodgings were unquestionably the best place to go, being nearest, but he was not best pleased to be woken at dawn yet again.

'What the devil are you doing here!' he demanded, staring at my sodden clothes. 'Been taking a dip with your clothes on, have you?'

'It is Sunday, isn't it?' I asked, supporting myself wearily on the door jamb. 'Sunday morning?'

Hugh was bewildered. 'Yes.'

'That's good.' I heaved myself off the doorjamb wearily. 'I'm supposed to be playing the organ at All Hallows today.'

We trooped in. Hugh stared at Kate and Esther, frowned at Heron's dishevelled and wet state, then opened his eyes wide when he saw Heron's sword at Ridley's back.

'We didn't want to have to drag Ridley through the streets at swordpoint any further than we had to,' I explained.

'I can see that might cause comment.'

'He deserves it!' Kate said mutinously. 'Spit him! Run him through!'

Heron pushed Ridley down on to the one hard chair Hugh possessed. He put down the sword, but didn't sheath it, standing guard. Ridley glanced around the room, quick eyes darting here and there as if he was contemplating an escape plan.

'Besides,' I said, 'this is an unspirited house. No one can overhear us.'

Hugh sighed. 'Except the widow below. You didn't wake her up again, did you?'

Fortunately, Hugh had gone to bed wearing shirt and breeches, still presumably finding it too much of a struggle to get out of his clothes one-armed when he was tired; he was decent enough for female company therefore. Esther and Kate sat on the edge of the bed; Hugh stood by the door and I leant against the wall near Ridley, ready to react if he tried any tricks. My shoulders were stiffening from carrying his weight and I felt bruised all over. I was dripping water on Hugh's floor and my wet clothes were beginning to feel clammy and my skin chill.

It was not a pleasant atmosphere. With six of us in the tiny attic room it was decidedly stuffy and the smell of wet cloth began to be overpowering. Ridley, with a grin, wrung out the skirts of his coat on to the floor. Hugh glared.

'He used Kate,' Esther said. 'Made her take him into the other world.' She turned a sympathetic gaze on the girl.

Kate was still wearing the white dress but it was grubbier than it had been. She looked slightly damp but had patently escaped the worst of the rain in the other world. She kicked at the edge of the bed. 'I ran off, didn't I?' she said sullenly. 'Soon as we got there. Thought he'd be stuck there for ever!' She glared indignantly at me. 'And you had to bring him back!'

'It wasn't entirely voluntary,' I said. 'Start from the beginning and tell me everything. How did he know you could step through into the other world?'

She squirmed, started kicking the bed again. Hugh seized an old cloth and rubbed it along the wet floor with his foot.

'Go on,' Ridley sneered. 'You tell 'em. Tell 'em how I found you standing over the body.'

'I never!'

'Blood all over her,' Ridley said gleefully. 'And the knife in her hand.'

'You— you—' Words failed Kate; she stared at us wildly. 'I didn't do it! Honest, I never touched Mr Nightingale!'

'Kate was wearing the yellow dress,' I said, starting to shiver. 'I saw her later and there was no blood on the dress. And I doubt very much Nightingale was stabbed with a *knife*.'

'It was scissors,' Kate said, sticking her tongue out at Ridley. 'A big pair.'

'Kitchen scissors?' Esther suggested.

'Which would explain the tearing around the wounds,' I said. 'Kitchen scissors would be sharp but not as sharp as a knife. So what did happen?'

Ridley was grinning but he let Kate have her say. 'I went

down the Stair like I said – when I thought Mr Nightingale might have gone off the wrong way. And I found him with the scissors still in him!' She wrinkled her nose in disgust. 'It was horrible! Then I heard someone coming and hid in a doorway. It was all blocked up or I would have tried to go in.'

I remembered that doorway.

'And then *he* came along.' She nodded at Ridley. 'And starts laughing when he sees Mr N lying there.'

'Charming fellow,' Hugh said, looking for somewhere to wring out the cloth.

'And then he saw me.'

'That yellow dress,' Ridley said cheerfully. 'Pretty obvious, even in the dark.'

'I was scared,' Kate said. 'So I tried to run.'

'Into the other world?'

She nodded. 'And he grabbed me!' she said indignantly. 'So he came too!'

'And you ended up in that field.'

'And he had the scissors with him – I thought he was going to kill me!'

'I should have,' Ridley said, with a grin that was half snarl.

'He buried them. In a hole under the hedge.'

I looked at Ridley. He gave every appearance of enjoying himself, although I noticed he was leaning away from Heron's intimidating silent presence. The sword point was on the floor, but Heron was patently not relaxing his watch. Odd how being sodden merely made him look even more dangerous; I just felt ruffianly.

'You buried the scissors so you could use them to blackmail the person who'd attacked Nightingale,' I said. And then, I thought, he'd bought another pair afterwards; his attack on me with them had been opportunism – I suspected his real intent had been to flaunt them at Nightingale's attacker, to make it clear he knew how the attack had been carried out. But he must have had second thoughts and decided only the real article would be persuasive.

'He wanted to get them back again,' Kate said. 'That's why he wanted me to take him there tonight. Wrote me a note to say so.'

'Thought you couldn't read,' Hugh said. He pushed the cloth under the bed with his foot, leaving it next to the chamber pot.

'It wasn't a real note,' Kate said scornfully and fished a piece of paper out of the recesses of her dress. 'Here.'

Esther took the damp note, unfolded it and held it out for me to see. It was a sketch of a pair of scissors, drawn with a spluttering pen in thin greyish ink. The sort of inferior writing equipment usually found in inns. I remembered Ridley calling for pen and paper in the Old Man just as we were leaving; typical of him to flaunt his audacity in front of us, daring us to understand what he was doing.

'That's what he said he'd send if he wanted me to take him back for the scissors,' Kate said. 'If I got a note like that, I had to meet him in that alley off the Clothmarket.' She added again, 'What did you want to bring him back for?'

'I want to know the name of Nightingale's attacker.' I looked down at Ridley. He was brushing at the muddy knee of his breeches, apparently concerned about nothing else at all. 'The evening Nightingale was attacked, you'd been following him around, hoping to provoke him.'

'In the Turk's Head, for instance,' Hugh said.

'But what happened? Did you lose him?'

Ridley sneered; Heron's sword lifted slightly. Esther sighed. 'You really do not like to make things easy for yourself, do you?'

'Having lost him,' I continued, 'you went to the Fleece thinking Nightingale must go back there sooner or later. And while you were waiting for him, you saw someone hurrying out of the alley.' I glanced at the others and explained; 'The attacker must have followed Nightingale down the Castle Stair because Nightingale was attacked first from behind – an attacker coming from the street would have attacked first from the front. So, if the attacker came *down* the steps, it would have been natural for him to run off into the street – which is what Ridley saw. In fact, I think he saw the entire attack.' I stared down at Ridley. 'Am I correct so far?'

He grinned, sat back and folded his arms. The attempt at dignity was spoilt by the water trailing down his cheeks from his sodden wig.

'Then,' I said, 'you started your blackmail attempt. You've been following the attacker ever since – hoping to intimidate him.'

He said nothing.

'Or perhaps to get more information on his activities. At any rate, you were following him when he went into the Fleece and stole Nightingale's watch.' I reflected that I still didn't understand that incident; why had the attacker not finished Nightingale off then? 'And you saw me there at the same time and decided to tease me. By talking to the sailors and making sure I knew you'd been there, you not only made trouble, you also hoped to draw my attention away from the real culprit. Leaving him to your own tender mercies.'

Ridley grinned, looked round each of us in turn. The coldness of my clothes was beginning to make me shake uncontrollably. Heron's sword point, I noticed, was rock steady. 'Come on,' Ridley said. 'We're all sensible people here. What's wrong with trying to get a little money?' He smiled at Esther then looked up at me. '*You* don't see anything wrong in it. And while we're at it, how many people have seen the lady in such very *feminine* apparel.' He smirked, and his gaze lingered on Esther's breeches. '*Very* nice.'

I started forward but both Hugh and Heron stepped into my path. Esther sighed with melodramatic weariness. 'I suppose you will grow up at some point,' she murmured.

Ridley flushed brightly.

Hugh gave me a warning look. I bit back the anger, forced myself to return to the point. 'The attacker didn't like being threatened so tonight he tried to dispose of you. Only you were lucky and escaped his clutches. And your immediate reaction was to call for Kate and go and get the scissors. I presume he didn't believe you had any evidence against him.'

Ridley said nothing. Again.

'Well, here's my best offer,' I said. God knows it went against the grain to offer Ridley any kind of a deal, but I didn't see any other way of dealing with the affair. 'Give us the name of the attacker, and we'll pass it on to the constable and he can remove a dangerous man from our midst. And in return—'

I met Heron's eyes. Only he could make any kind of offer that would tempt Ridley. He looked stony-faced – I couldn't read his expression. Eventually, however, he stirred, said brusquely, 'An increase in your allowance and lodgings of your own. But no more help than that. Any trouble you get yourself into from now on is your own affair. After this, I wash my hands of you. And without my cooperation, you will get nothing more out of your mother.'

Ridley looked up at him. 'I want the whole of my inherit-
ance. My grandmother's money. *Now*.'

'No,' Heron said, uncompromisingly.

'That's what I want.'

'It is not legally possible. The money is held in trust until
you marry.'

'You can do it somehow,' Ridley said, grinning. He crossed
his arms and tried for a kind of damp dignity. 'If you want
the information, that is . . .'

And no amount of cajoling would shake him from that
position.

Forty

Be assured: anything to your discredit will sooner or later
become common knowledge.
                                 [*A Gentleman's Companion*, November 1732]

In the early light of day, I lingered at the door of Hugh's lodgings with Esther and Kate, talking quietly to avoid waking the
widow and her children. Kate was still inclined to be defensive,
kicking at the wall of the alley and staring out at the deserted
street as if she was eager to be off.

'Why did you go along with Ridley's demands?' I asked.
'Why didn't you tell me everything when we talked last time?'

She was as uncooperative as Ridley, hunching her shoulders
against me and mumbling something almost inaudible.

'Really, Charles!' Esther said. 'The answer is obvious.' She
looked at Kate. 'He threatened Charles, did he not? He said
he would hurt him if you did not cooperate.'

Kate flushed bright red, mumbled again.

'That's why she was out so late the night the watch was
stolen,' Esther said. 'You told her to go into the house but
she followed you down to the Fleece, just to make sure you
were safe.'

Kate refused to meet my gaze. I was almost as embarrassed
as she was. 'Thank you,' I said at last.

That brought her head up. 'Only did it cos I got an interest,' she said defiantly. 'If Mr N's dead, there's only you left to help me, ain't there?' And she flounced off into the street.

Esther was smiling. 'She refuses ever to let herself be caught at a disadvantage!' She lowered her voice. 'Charles, she is really remarkably good at that business, you know – *stepping through* into the other world. She knew exactly where and when you and Heron would be coming back; she had no doubts whatsoever – she led me there straight away.'

'I've no doubt she could teach me a thing or two,' I admitted.

'That is not what worries me,' she retorted. 'I think we need to teach *her* a thing or two, about caution and discretion!'

We went out on to the street; I was relieved to see Kate loitering outside the clockmaker's shop, peering through the shutters at the treasures inside. 'Here,' she said, her gaze settling admiringly on Esther. 'Can I have a pair of breeches too?'

They went off and I lingered in the warming day until Hugh came down behind me and stood looking out on Westgate and the early risers. A farmer came in to the market, a chapman walked stolidly out to the villages and the fairs. A single cow plodded down the street, urged on by a small boy with a bunch of twigs. It wasn't raining – I've never been so glad of anything in my life. A thin line of sunlight touched me and began to dry my clothes.

'Thought you had to play in church this morning,' Hugh said. 'Hadn't you better get some sleep?'

'It's hardly worth it,' I said. 'I'll have to be up again in an hour or two. Besides, I promised Heron I'd help him get Ridley back to the Old Man. He's given up trying to make him stay at his mother's.'

'He's still trying to get the fellow to talk,' Hugh said, rubbing at his left arm and adjusting the sling.

'Any success?'

'What do you think?'

'I think he's going to hell in a handcart and we might as well wash our hands of him and let him go. Nothing short of an act of God is going to stop him.'

'He's like a child playing games,' Hugh said. 'Having a wonderful time setting all the grown-ups in an uproar.'

'He's no child,' I retorted. 'He's the one who caused that baby to drown. That's what rankles, Hugh! An innocent, with no way of protecting itself – and he's going to get away with causing its death!'

Hugh nodded. 'But he didn't attack Nightingale.'

'No,' I admitted.

'So we'll have to look elsewhere. Who else might want to?'

I stared at the cow that had stopped to nibble at the grass beyond the railings of the vicarage gardens. 'Nightingale quarrelled with half a dozen people that night, and some of them were unsavoury characters. And he flirted with a good few married ladies at the concert, annoying their husbands. Philip Ord, for instance.'

'Good God! You can't think Ord attacked him!'

The idea was tempting but I shook my head. 'Ord would have done it face to face. Although, on second thoughts, he'd probably have thought Nightingale not a gentleman which means he'd never have dreamt of fighting him himself. He'd have sent a couple of servants to give Nightingale a thorough beating.'

'Then was it a robbery after all?'

'His watch wasn't taken until later. And he'd no money on him.'

'But if the robber was disturbed . . .'

'He'd have grabbed the watch at least.'

Hugh snatched at my arm. 'It's the watch, Charles! The watch is what he was after. He couldn't get it on the night, so he went back for it. There's something special about the watch!'

'It wasn't its monetary value,' I retorted. 'It was cheap and nasty.'

'Sentimental value then? It could have been some relative, someone come up from London to kill him.'

'It had to be someone Ridley knew,' I said slowly. 'How could he have blackmailed someone if he didn't recognize them? Which argues it was someone local.'

'Not necessarily! Ridley's just come north from London! Perhaps it was someone both he and Nightingale knew there!'

I had to admit this possibility. 'But how could we ever find out? Short of a trip to London – and even then it would be like trying to find a needle in a haystack.'

Hugh sighed. 'I've vowed off travelling.' He tapped the broken arm significantly.

'Until the next time you get restless feet.'

'No, no – never again. And particularly not on barges. You'll never get me on water again. Never.'

'I know how you must have felt,' I said. 'Too damn wet.'

'Your clothes feel three times as heavy as normal. And cold.'

'Clammy,' I agreed. 'We'd know if there was a Londoner in town. At least if he'd come into contact with Ridley or Nightingale.'

We were silent as the sky lightened. I rubbed my eyes. I couldn't remember the last night I'd actually spent in my bed; I was becoming nocturnal, forced into sleeping during the day. And even in the warming sunshine, I couldn't stop shivering.

'Scissors,' Hugh said with a frown. 'What kind of killer attacks with scissors? Knives are easy enough to come by, for heaven's sake!'

'Damn it,' I said. 'You're right. That's a very good question.'

Heron and I escorted Ridley back to the Old Man in the grimmest of silences, broken only by the squelching of our footsteps. He strode between us with a swagger, as if he felt he held a winning hand of cards. God knows what the passers-by made of us, all sodden, despite the brightening sunshine, and filthy.

At the door of the Old Man, Ridley turned to face us with a grin.

'The thing is,' he said as if we were resuming an interrupted conversation, 'you're not the fellows to let someone get away with murder. I know people, you see – I can read 'em like books. I know you inside out.'

'I doubt it,' Heron said.

'And I know you'll come round to my way of thinking sooner or later.'

'No,' Heron said.

'And leave Kate alone,' I added.

Ridley winked at me. 'Treading on your toes, am I? And you newly married as well!'

Heron gripped my arm and held me back. 'One thing is for certain, Ridley,' he said, coolly. 'You are not a man to live long.'

'A short life and a merry one!' Ridley grinned as he sauntered into the Old Man. We were left, wet and fuming, on the Key.

I was beginning to think I'd be the one to dispose of him.

I made it to All Hallows in time, without any sleep at all, and played by instinct, my only pleasures the feeling of good dry clothes and the mellow sound of the organ, about the only decent thing in a church that is rapidly falling down around everyone's ears. The church was crowded as always and the congregation were good-humoured and dozed discreetly while the Rev. Mr Orrick stuttered and stammered through his sermon. I thought of Cuthbert Ridley; I was convinced he'd taken his imitation of a bashful young man from the curate – but that was part and parcel of his cruelty.

I dozed fitfully and tried to keep myself alert by surveying the congregation through the small mirrors above the organ console. There was Esther, in her neatest and smartest clothes, with Kate sitting mutinously beside her, openly yawning from time to time. The servants were in a little row at the back of the church, just behind the landlord of the Fleece. And I spotted the Jenisons too. At least, Mr Jenison and Mrs Annabella were there; Mrs Jenison was absent; I wondered if she was still unwell. Mrs Annabella sat with her handkerchief to her face, occasionally dabbing at her eyes, but, thankfully, not audibly sobbing. I even caught her casting a quick glance at a young gentleman in a pew opposite; I fancied it wouldn't take long for her to recover.

I wandered off into speculation about Ridley and Nightingale and the death of the child and whoever it was that Ridley was blackmailing, so absorbed I almost missed my cue for the next hymn and was only brought back to my senses by everyone echoing the vicar's *amen* at the end of the sermon with some relieved force. I nodded to the bellows blower, the organ wheezed and I launched into the first lines of the hymn; the last thing I saw as I glanced into the mirror was Cuthbert Ridley's grinning round face.

Esther and Kate waited for me outside the church after the service so I could escort them home. Kate was behaving remarkably well, generally keeping quiet; my only fear was that she'd yawn in the face of some merchant or alderman. The sun cast long shadows from the gravestones across the path; two children and a dog were running about giddily, shrieking and laughing, and caring not a bit when they fell over. The organist's cat watched with disdain then began to wash itself.

As I approached, I saw Robert Jenison pause to speak to Esther before nodding rather wearily to her and walking away to his own carriage where Mrs Annabella was waiting in eager conversation with one of her cronies. Esther turned a thoughtful gaze on me.

'Mr Jenison was wondering if I could go and see his wife again, this afternoon.'

'On a Sunday?' I asked surprised.

'She is evidently far from well. He is very worried about her. He thinks she wants conversation, someone to confide in.'

'Will you take her another of your cordials?'

A mischievous smile touched her lips. 'I have very fond memories of those cordials.'

'So have I.' I held out a hand to her. 'Almost the first time we met you made one for me, after I'd been attacked.'

She pretended severity. 'And you got drunk on it! You are supposed to sip them genteelly.'

'I don't think I'm very good at being genteel,' I admitted.

She gave me a knowing look and rested her hand on my arm. 'And – in certain circumstances – I am very glad of that.'

'Esther!' I hissed, glancing round in alarm.

'Here,' Kate said. 'Ain't we getting back? I'm hungry.'

We went home, and Kate worked her way through a very large plate of cold meats in obvious good humour. She was meek when Esther talked to her and I had an uncomfortable feeling that she'd decided that working on Esther was by far the best means of influencing me. But for once everything was peaceful and I was happy to enjoy the fact. Tom was in a good humour; George was conspicuous by his absence. Which gave me time to consider whether I ought to apologize to him for ignoring what he'd said about Kate; he deserved an apology, but I rather thought it might encourage him to spy on her again.

After we'd eaten, Esther dressed in her best clothes and went off to the Jenison's house with her maid while Kate proved predictably recalcitrant about the thought of spending an afternoon listening to me reading from a book of sermons. As the prospect was no more attractive to me than to her, I dug out a book of suitably religious music – simple psalm tunes – and spent an hour or so teaching her how to play the harpsichord.

We'd have got on even better if George hadn't chosen at last to make his presence felt. He hovered just outside the library, loudly singing different tunes from the ones we were playing; my vague ideas of an apology disappeared abruptly. Kate responded by banging away at the harpsichord as if she thought she could persuade it to sound more loudly by sheer force of will. I started to develop a headache.

George stopped singing. There was a moment's eerie silence. Then he shot into the room, sizzling through the gap between door and jamb with amazing speed.

'Got a message from Mrs P!' he yelled. 'She sent it by the spirit in Mr Jenison's house. Wants you to go up there.'

My first thought was of Mrs Jenison; she was worse than anyone had thought – she'd died suddenly. But Esther would not have asked me to go there for that. There was only one reason she would have asked me to go.

It was connected with Nightingale's attacker.

Forty-One

No man of breeding would ever consider interfering in the private affairs of another gentleman.
                              [*A Gentleman's Companion*, May 1732]

Kate must have drawn the same conclusion because she wouldn't let me go without her. She was prepared to stand and argue over it, too, while I simply wanted to get away and find out why Esther needed help.

'He's out to get you!' she argued. 'You got in his way and he don't like that.'

'I'm going nowhere near Cuthbert Ridley.'

'Don't matter. He's going near you. And I'm coming.' She folded her arms and regarded me as mulishly as Ridley ever had.

'You can't take her, master!' George said stridently. 'The mistress didn't ask for her.'

'George—'

'She should stay here and read her Bible.'

Kate put her tongue out at the spirit. 'Can't read, so there.'

I could not do with this delay. 'You can come,' I said, 'on
the strict understanding you say and do nothing. If you utter
one word—'

'Shan't!' she said cheerfully.

'And tomorrow you can take me back to that field and we'll
find the scissors Ridley buried.'

'Why?' she asked blankly. 'They're just scissors.'

'Some people put their initials or their coat of arms on
cutlery,' I said.

'So they don't get stolen,' George said. 'By nasty girls who
worm their way into the household!'

'George,' I said. 'When I get back, we're going to have a
very long talk.'

'You mean the scissors might have the murderer's name on
them?' Kate said awed. 'Never!'

'It's a possibility.'

'Fancy attacking someone with your name on the weapon,'
she said. 'That's just plain daft!'

The Jenison household was in a tizzy. Servants came out
of doors with dusters, looked startled and embarrassed, and
disappeared again hurriedly. The footman who showed Kate
and myself into the drawing room was red-faced and slightly
dishevelled. 'Not up to snuff,' Kate said, in a wonderful imitation of Mrs Annabella. She spoke just a fraction of a second
before the footman shut the door and I caught a glimpse of
his angry face. I was far from sure Kate hadn't spoken
deliberately.

'Sit,' I said to her sharply. 'And remember what I told you
about not saying anything!'

She flung herself into a chair, then suddenly sat bolt upright
and tried to look demure. Esther had patently been teaching
her more than how to read music.

I could hear the servants muttering in the hall. Amazing
how a household could go to pieces when a mistress's firm
hand was withdrawn. I wondered where Mrs Annabella was.
Kate was peering at the paintings, and the ornaments, and
the great bowls of flowers. She picked up a china cat from the
table beside her, turned up her nose at it, and put it back
down.

'What's this?' She prodded at the box beside the cat.

'It's a sewing box.' I remembered Mrs Annabella sitting with her sister-in-law's embroidery opened out across her knees, trying to match the pinks and purples. 'Mrs Jenison's.'

Kate lifted the lid to sneak a look.

'Kate!'

She put the lid down again, unrepentant. 'She's got an awful lot of stuff in there. What's she making?'

'Cushions, I think.' I glanced around the room, feeling suddenly oppressed by all the clutter – the knick-knacks and ornaments, the feather pictures on the walls, the tapestry work on the chairs, the footstools scattered here and there. A huge peacock was staring at me from one of the chair backs, unnervingly cross-eyed.

I wondered whether to go in search of one of the servants. But if Mrs Jenison was really ill, it was unfair to make demands; the servants would be dashing about, trying to sort things out.

'Who's that sour-looking man?'

Kate lifted her hand to point at the picture of a long-dead Jenison over the fireplace. As she did so, she caught the edge of the workbox; it shot on to the floor, spilling its contents everywhere.

I sighed and put out a foot to stop a bobbin that rolled towards me. 'Kate, what did I say?'

'I know, I know!' she said irritably. 'I'll pick it all up.'

We scrabbled around on the floor. Amazing how much there could be in one small box: cottons, silk, needles, a pincushion fashioned like a grumpy-looking hedgehog, scissors, odd corners of material.

Scissors . . .

I took the scissors out of Kate's hands. They were a small delicate pair, with ornately engraved handles. Not the Jenisons' coat of arms, but a dragonfly with wings spread, one along each arm of the scissors. I opened out the blades; right at the bottom, where they met, was a slight stickiness.

And a faint brown stain.

Forty-Two

A gentleman should root out malefactors wherever he
finds them.

[A Gentleman's Companion, June 1735]

Kate was still crawling about, burrowing under chairs in search
of miscellaneous trifles. I stared at the scissors. If this was the
murder weapon, what had Cuthbert Ridley buried in that
other world? And were these large enough to inflict the wounds?
If only I could show them to Gale.

I sorted out the facts. Mrs Jenison had been in London with
her husband when they'd first encountered Nightingale; they'd
been in his company frequently. Nightingale was a man for
the ladies; he wouldn't have hesitated to have paid court to
Mrs Jenison, and she might have fancied he meant more than
he did. But he would not have done more than flatter and
flirt, surely, if Jenison had been in evidence. Or *had* there been
more than that? Had there been assignations? It would have
been difficult, though not impossible.

What could such a man offer Mrs Jenison to tempt her to
indiscretion? He couldn't compete with Jenison in terms of
money or social status. All he could have offered was love, and
would Mrs Jenison have thrown away all she had for that?
If she had indeed been prepared to do so, then any revelation
of his true character might have pushed her over the precipice
into madness. And if she'd then come to her senses again and
been appalled by what she'd done, that would explain her
malaise since the attack.

That afternoon concert was the key, I was sure of it.
Nightingale's behaviour had been outrageous. He'd flirted with
every lady in sight; even a woman head-over-heels in love might
have had her eyes opened. If only I could remember exactly
what had happened . . .

The door opened. Kate snatched the scissors from me, tossed
them into the box, pushed the box on to the table and threw
herself back into the chair, looking fearsomely innocent.

Mrs Annabella hesitated on the threshold. She was wearing one of her befrilled white dresses, and rouge made two bright spots on her cheeks. The handkerchief was not in evidence, thank goodness.

'How is Mrs Jenison?' I asked.

She burst into tears.

Kate sighed melodramatically. I took Mrs Annabella's arm, helped her into a chair. I would have liked to call for a footman to bring her some restorative but I didn't want to expose her to prying eyes. On second thoughts, she'd probably enjoy the encounter. I compromised. 'Shall I call for my wife?'

'I'll go!' Kate leapt up and was out of the room in an instant, unmistakeably relieved.

'I'm sure your sister-in-law will be all right,' I started, but Mrs Annabella turned up tear-brimming eyes. 'Mr Patterson . . .' She faltered, put a thin hand on mine. Her fingers were ice-cold. She said in a melodramatic tone, 'We both know that cannot be.'

I was startled, uncertain what to say. She gave me a watery smile. 'You have a reputation for catching malefactors, Mr Patterson. You cannot have— I mean, you must have—'

Now she came to the fateful words, her courage seemed to fail her. She took a deep breath, said, 'She met him in London, you know. And— and—' Her voice sank almost to inaudibility. 'Oh, she confessed all to me, swore me to silence!'

I was certain I would never have confided secrets to Mrs Annabella. But Mrs Jenison might have had no one else to talk to.

'And of course I said nothing. But—' Her voice sank. 'I thought that when we left London, all would be over, but it was not! He came here, you know.'

'When he first came to this town?'

'Before!' She sounded a little excited, and awed. 'Three or four days before. He rode up especially to talk to— I heard a noise outside and looked out of my window and there he was!' There was a pleasurable kind of horror in her voice; Mrs Annabella was enjoying all this excitement enormously, disastrous though it was for other people. 'And . . . and . . .' She took a grip on her emotions. 'I saw them together,' she said rapidly, staring at the floor. 'He kissed her hand! He said he loved her and would love her for ever, but their love must remain a secret, at least for the time being, and she mustn't say a word about it! Not at least until everyone had a chance to know him better.'

It did not strike me that better acquaintance would make local society more sympathetic to a man who ran off with another man's wife. Nightingale must have been panicking at that meeting. If he'd been lured into making rash promises in London, he must have felt secure he'd never have to carry them through; the Jenisons would leave London and he'd never see them again. But then he'd been tempted north, presumably by Jenison's money, and found himself in a difficult situation. No wonder he'd been urging secrecy! If Jenison found out what had been going on behind his back, Nightingale would lose the concert engagement *and* find himself saddled with a woman he didn't really want.

Mrs Annabella sighed. 'It was so romantic! Just like you and Mrs Patterson.'

I didn't see the cases were analogous at all.

She clutched at my arm. 'I've been so anxious, Mr Patterson. She went out several nights in succession, you know – she made an excuse, retired to bed early and then crept out. And later, when everyone else was asleep, I heard a noise and went out on to the stairs and saw her! Coming in through the servants' door.' She pulled me closer, said confidentially, 'I think she bribed one of the servants to leave the back door unbolted. I asked her where she'd been but she wouldn't say! She just told me to go to bed and mind my own business! I *knew*, Mr Patterson, I knew she must have been seeing— *him*.'

I thought of what Kate had told me of the night of the attack. She'd seen an 'old' couple go down the Stair from the Castle Garth: a man and a woman. She'd talked of the woman lagging behind and the man not helping her. But suppose they'd not been a couple; suppose the woman had merely kept close behind the man to suggest they were together. And suppose that woman had been at the concert, had seen Nightingale flirting and felt betrayed . . .

Mrs Annabella twisted her fingers in the fabric of her petticoats. 'What could I do? I didn't want to upset Robert.'

'He would have wanted to know if his wife was being unfaithful,' I pointed out.

'Oh, I couldn't, I couldn't,' she said tearfully. 'And then I heard the gentleman was *injured*, and I knew immediately what must have happened!'

Her hand went out to lightly touch the workbox. 'The scissors,' she whispered. 'I found them in her box when I was trying to match the silks. They were sticky, with— with—'

'Blood?'

She nodded. 'But what could I do? How could I tell anyone? Who would believe me?'

'And Cuthbert Ridley,' I said. 'Did she attack him too?'

'He tried to blackmail her,' she said, in a low voice. 'But she had no money of her own – what woman does?'

I thought of Esther.

'She asked me if I could help but I've nothing but a few poor jewels.' She gestured helplessly. 'We couldn't raise the money he was asking for.'

'So she had to be rid of him,' I said. 'The scissors again, I suppose.'

'Indeed,' she said earnestly. Her fingers gripped my arm convulsively. 'You mustn't think her conscience is not pricking her, for you can see it is. That's why she's so ill.' Tears ran down her cheeks; she opened the workbox, hunted through the disorder Kate had left, pulled out a scrap of lace and dabbed it to her eyes. 'She's sinking, Mr Patterson, I fear she's sinking. She's filled with horror for what she's done!'

She twisted the lace. 'I couldn't keep quiet any longer, could I? I mean, it's not going to stop, is it?'

'No,' I said gently.

The door opened and Esther came in with Kate close behind. Mrs Annabella looked up, said faintly, 'Oh, oh!' and plied the handkerchief again.

'How is Mrs Jenison?' I asked. There was an unpleasant interview to be had and I wasn't looking forward to it. But better now than later.

'She is not at all well, Charles,' Esther said. She cast a glance at Mrs Annabella, plainly moderated what she'd been about to say. 'I understand her husband is still with the churchwardens at All Hallows. I really think he ought to be sent for.'

'No, no!' Mrs Annabella protested. 'He must not know!'

'We have no choice,' Esther said firmly. 'Will you send a servant for him, Charles?'

I called for a servant and sent him off.

'She wants to talk to you,' Esther said, when the servant had departed.

'Oh no,' Mrs Annabella said earnestly. 'She's in her bed! That would not be proper at all!'

'She is very insistent.'

Mrs Annabella tried to protest again but I patted her hand; it was still ice-cold. 'Better to deal with this now.'

I summoned a footman, asked him to bring wine for Mrs Annabella. Under cover of her half-hearted protests and his murmured enquiries, I whispered to Kate, 'Go to the kitchens and see if you can find out if they've lost any scissors recently.'

Grinning, she dashed off towards the servants' quarters.

We left Mrs Annabella encouraging the footman to pour 'just a little more' and went into the hall.

'Charles,' Esther said uneasily, 'what is going on?'

I considered. 'A great deal of self-delusion.'

She sighed. 'I do dislike it when you are enigmatic!'

I ushered her ahead of me up the stairs. The wooden banister was as cold as Mrs Annabella's hand. 'Did it ever seem to you that Nightingale singled out any woman for attention?'

'Yes,' she retorted. 'Every single one of them.'

'Did you ever think any of them regarded it as more than harmless flirting?'

She considered, pausing at the top of the stairs with her hand on the banister. 'Well, the married women were all too sensible to make much of it, of course. The young girls swooned a great deal and I think a few of them took it very seriously indeed. Charles—' She frowned at me. 'The one person who took exception to it was Philip Ord.'

'No,' I corrected her. 'He was the one person who took *visible* exception to it.'

Rugs were thick underfoot, muffling our steps as we walked through a small dressing room, done out charmingly in the newest wallpaper. At the far end, Esther scratched on a closed door and – signalling to me to stay where I was – went in. I heard a murmur of voices, then Esther came out again and nodded to me.

When I went in, Mrs Jenison was sitting up in bed, a shawl wrapped about her shoulders and her grey hair pulled back into a long braid. Her face was white but she looked up at me with something astonishingly close to peacefulness.

'You know, don't you?' she said.

I nodded. 'I know.'

Forty-Three

Justice must be dispensed as the law demands.
[*A Gentleman's Companion*, February 1730]

As we walked back down the stairs, Esther silent beside me, Kate came running up. 'Lost a pair of scissors Thursday evening!' she said in a disastrously loud voice. 'Big things. Sharp.'

I heard a noise in the drawing room. I pushed past Kate, past a startled footman. Behind me, I heard Esther say, 'Stay here, Kate.' I ran into the drawing room.

It was empty.

The far door stood ajar, the feathers of the decoration still quivering; one had snapped and drooped askew. I edged round the furniture, moving back towards the wall so I could see through the half-open door into the room beyond.

'Mrs Annabella,' I called. 'I was wondering if I could talk to you.'

All I could see in the next room were a few chairs, the edge of a painting, a spray of purple flowers in a vase. No sound. I was seized with a fear that Mrs Annabella was running out into the next room, and the next, making her way round to the back of the house perhaps, to the servants' quarters and escaping from there. I dashed for the door, ran through it—

At the last moment, something saved me: a glimpse of movement, a flash of light. I ducked, flung up a protective arm and felt the sharp burn of pain. I jerked away. A scratch on the back of my hand oozed blood.

We stared at each other. Mrs Annabella had of course concealed herself behind the door. She clutched the little scissors, staring at me wildly. Two spots of bright red marked her pale cheeks. She was breathing heavily; she edged sideways, keeping a winged armchair between us.

'It's no good,' I said, 'I know.' The spectre of Mrs Jenison's face rose up before me, weeping with joy at her release from the secret she'd been nursing. 'I know how it happened,' I said. 'Mrs Jenison has told me everything.'

She glared, but there was something else there too – a touch of pride, perhaps.

'It happened exactly as you told me,' I said. 'The assignations, the meetings, the creeping in and out of the house by the servants' door, the confrontation between you and your sister-in-law on the stairs. Except it was not your sister-in-law who came in late but you. You were the one who idolized Nightingale and met him secretly.' I couldn't imagine Nightingale carrying his dalliance with Mrs Annabella as far as the bedroom but as far as extravagant promises – yes.

'She's lying,' she said, with a fine effort at unconcern.

I shook my head. 'I already knew you were the liar. The workbox is yours, not hers.'

'It is not!' she said with well-assumed indignation. 'I told you it was hers the other day.'

'I admire your foresight,' I said. 'You were confronted by Mrs Jenison when you came back in those two nights in succession – the night you attacked Nightingale and the night you stole his watch. You knew she suspected you, so you laid a little trap, just in case. The scissors are the ones you used to stab Cuthbert Ridley with, aren't they? No wonder he wasn't severely injured – those scissors are too small to do much damage. You put the scissors in a box of your own and then told everyone the box belonged to your sister-in law.'

Mrs Annabella maintained a dignified demeanour. 'You're wrong. It *is* her box.'

I curbed my anger. I'd just seen the pain and distress Mrs Annabella's actions had caused her sister-in-law and I was not in a forgiving mood. 'It was not a particularly good plan,' I pointed out. 'Mr Jenison, I daresay, would not know anything about such feminine trifles, but I rather think the servants would correctly identify the box as yours. And you'd already tried to deflect suspicion from yourself by pretending you thought Nightingale had been shot, not stabbed. Oh, and by inventing a fictitious aggressive man on the coach. Unfortunately for you, I was there when the coach came in – the only men on it were Nightingale and a boy of no more than sixteen.'

She stuck to her point. 'It *is* her box.'

'Then why was your clean handkerchief in it?'

She pushed past a chair, headed towards the far side of the room. There was another door there; I didn't know the layout of the house but it must surely lead towards the back. We sidled round on either side of the room, keeping the chairs, the little tables, the bowls of dried rose petals, the flaunting late summer blooms, between us. Esther came to the door into the drawing room, looking on with a frown. I saw Mrs Annabella glance at her and realize one escape route was now cut off, her face set in an obstinate, mulish look.

'I know you're being blackmailed by Ridley,' I said, trying to distract her and somehow give myself an advantage. 'He was waiting outside the Fleece for Nightingale and saw what happened. And being one to seize any opportunity to make money, he carried the scissors off and threatened to reveal the truth if you didn't pay him. You shouldn't have left the scissors in the body.'

'I had to,' she said, obviously irritated by this. 'I couldn't pull them out.'

I winced, imagining the scene.

'And the watch?' Esther advanced a few steps into the room. 'Did you take that too?'

I remembered Mrs Annabella fussing over Nightingale's room, making sure she knew where it was, making sure he wasn't moved. And hadn't she said she'd once got lost in the Fleece and ended up in the kitchens? She'd know where to find Nightingale.

'Of course I took the watch! As a memento of our love.' She looked momentarily wistful. 'It was so romantic. Such a fine man – and he wanted *me*! We were going to marry.' She turned a glowing face on Esther. 'If *you* could marry a penniless tradesman, why could I not marry Richard? He had noble relations, you know – baronets and viscounts in Hertfordshire.' She drifted off into a pleasant haze. 'It would have been so delightful. Marriage – at last . . .'

While she was distracted, I slipped round the edge of the room, hoping to reach the far door and cut off her exit. But I was grimacing all the while over her illusions. She'd no idea of the realities of marriage; romantic longing blurred her view of the real world. As perhaps it had blurred mine. I'd concentrated so much on the reaction of Society to our marriage, and the obstacles that lay outside our relationship, beyond our control, that I'd never envisaged those obstacles within. I'd imagined that if the outside world could be satisfied then all would be well, when in fact the biggest obstacle to our happiness was me, and my stupid stubborn pride over money.

Esther shifted further into the room, stood with her hands on the back of a small sofa, engaging Mrs Annabella in conversation to keep her attention. 'Why did you not take the watch when you first attacked Mr Nightingale in the alley?'

'I didn't think of it then,' Mrs Annabella admitted. 'It was only later, when I remembered the delightful times we'd had. If only circumstances had been different,' she said passionately. 'If only he could have brought himself to defy Society and reveal our love!'

I eased around a last small table; the door was within reach. And Esther was still between Mrs Annabella and the drawing room, using the sofa to keep well clear of those silly little scissors. Now, if I could only summon a burly footman or two . . .

'What about the poor boy you hit over the head?' Esther asked.

Mrs Annabella looked disconcerted as if she didn't quite remember Joseph. 'I did so want to see Richard. A last fond look. And everyone was so busy, I knew they'd not see me. Though,' she added, vexed, 'I did tear my petticoats climbing out of the window. I'm not as young as I once was, you know, and I was a little clumsy. Most annoying.' She giggled. 'But it was so exciting!'

I began to think she wasn't in her right senses.

'Why did you not attack him again?' Esther prompted. 'One more stab and he would have been dead.'

'I couldn't!' Mrs Annabella was shocked. 'He wouldn't have been able to defend himself! I gave him a chance, you know,' she added earnestly. 'In the alley, I pleaded with him to come back to me. But he just laughed. He stood there with blood dripping from his shoulder and laughed at me! He said *you know you can't do it, little Annabella* – that's what he always called me. *Little Annabella* – no one else ever called me that—'

I reached the far door and clicked it quietly closed. Cutting off every avenue of escape.

'*Why should you want to hurt me?* he said. *Why should you want to destroy our love?*' Mrs Annabella said indignantly, 'It was not *me* who destroyed our love! It was *him*. At that concert, I saw him for what he was – a philanderer, making up to every woman there. And he snubbed me!' Her face wrinkled in fury. 'He cut me off in the middle of a sentence and went off to be ingratiating to that odious little Mrs Ord! And *she's* no better than she should be!'

I began to realize that Nightingale's objectionable behaviour at that concert had not been on account of Philip Ord or the clash over Kate. He'd been frightened of what Mrs Annabella might let slip. He'd lived with that hanging over him throughout his entire stay in the town. And it had acted upon an uncertain temper and caused disaster.

Mrs Annabella looked smug, touched again with that odd glow of pride. 'I've never had the chance to do anything before, you know. Everyone else has such exciting lives and for once I'd made up my mind to do something and I *did* do it. I'd been wronged. He tricked me, promised me marriage and then deserted me. And I defended my honour!'

I must have made a noise at this. Mrs Annabella's head snapped round; she stared at me on guard at the door.

'You can't prove anything!' she said fiercely.

'I can,' I said. 'Because last night, Mrs Jenison found this in your room – and she had a maid as witness.'

I held up Nightingale's watch.

She threw the scissors at me.

I ducked, and they missed by a considerable distance but by that time Mrs Annabella was already making a dash for the drawing-room door. Esther went after her but she lost time negotiating the small sofa. Mrs Annabella threw down a small table, laden with potpourri and Chinese porcelain. Esther stumbled trying to avoid it, went down in a tangle of hoops and skirts and cursing.

I vaulted a footstool, dodged a chair but was then forced to divert round an armchair and a huge vase of flowers, and by that time Mrs Annabella was in the drawing room. When I reached the door, her petticoats were disappearing out of the far door into the hall.

I heard a screech and a yell, saw a flicker of white skirts. I burst into the hall. A footman was standing open-mouthed.

'They— they—' He stared wildly at me. 'Gone! They just disappeared!'

Kate. She must have taken hold of Mrs Annabella and stepped through into the other world. Devil take it – in full view of a witness! She'd been wrong – sometimes people couldn't help but notice. 'Nonsense,' I said and cut off the footman's protests. 'Is your master not back yet? Go and fetch him.'

He hesitated. 'Do it!' I snapped.

He stared at the place where the women had been, plainly beginning to doubt. 'He's still at the church,' he said, uncertainly.

'Get him!' He lingered, still confused. 'Now!' I roared.

He went like a frightened rabbit.

Forty-Four

A gentleman instructs his inferiors to carry out necessary tasks, not failing to supervise them with assiduous care.
[*A Gentleman's Companion*, March 1733]

I closed my eyes, took a step forward. A moment's coldness – and I was through and opening my eyes to dazzling candlelight.

'Damn it,' a voice snarled. 'Who the devil are you, sir?'

The owner of the voice was a portly man who in another year or two would be simply fat. His face was obscured by the dazzle of the candles, but as he took a step forward, I saw he was probably thirty or thirty-five years old with a bald head devoid of wig; he was wearing a dressing robe very like the one Mr Handel is reputed to wear. The room stank of smoke.

He had a pistol in his hand.

He roared for the servants. I put up my hands quickly. I needed to find out how Kate was so precise in her stepping through; this was the second time I'd fallen into difficulties! 'I assure you, sir, I'm a respectable man. I'm on the track of a fugitive . . .'

He snorted with laughter. 'You're a burglar, that's what you are, sir. We saw you in the garden the other day!' He frowned, peered at me more closely. 'Damn it, do I know you?'

In heaven's name – he was acquainted with my counterpart here! I said, uncompromisingly, 'No.'

I reminded myself I was in no danger, even though I could hear the thunder of servants' footsteps on the hall floor: a step would take me back to my own world and safety. But I was impatient. The few minutes I'd taken to talk to the footman in the Jenisons' house might have set me hours behind Kate and Mrs Annabella, and to go back and start again would reduce my chances of catching Mrs Annabella to nothing at all.

'I'm looking for my aunt,' I said, in a desperate rush. 'And her granddaughter. I had a message to say they'd be here.'

'A likely story!'

'An elderly woman and a girl of about twelve,' I said. 'They were both wearing white.'

'I don't want to hear your ravings, sir!' he roared. 'James! Thomas! Apprehend him!'

Two large footmen jumped on me.

James and Thomas were *very* large; I'm not short but they towered over me. And the plum-coloured livery concealed strong muscles; one twisted my right arm painfully behind my back. Beneath the powdered wigs, they sneered at me.

'I'll go, I'll go!' I gasped out, bending almost double as pain shot through my shoulder.

'You will,' the gentleman agreed. 'When the Watch arrives! James, has the boy gone for the Watch?'

'Yes, sir.'

Someone knocked on the front door.

'Damn me!' The gentleman pushed himself up. 'They're alert for once!'

But it was female voices I heard in the hall, and I sagged in relief. A servant flung open the door and in walked Esther, Kate demure at her side.

'That's him!' Esther said melodramatically, pointing a finger at me. 'That's the rogue who stole my purse!'

'He knocked me over,' Kate said indignantly, with a smirk, and clung on to Esther's arm. 'Didn't he, mama?'

'I knew it!' the gentleman said with glee. 'Clap the fellow in irons! Jail him! Transport him!'

'Devil take it,' I started. But another figure was emerging

from the shadows of the hall. 'I am a justice of the peace,' Claudius Heron said. '*I* will deal with this.'

We walked briskly away down the chill moonlit streets and didn't stop until we were out of sight of the house. I was breathing heavily, not sure whether to laugh or be angry. At last, I halted under a tree out of the reach of the torches in the street and turned to face the others. Esther was looking amused, Kate smug, Heron exasperated.

'So,' I said, 'Kate went back to our own world and brought you both here.'

'I can think when I need to,' Kate said smugly.

I stared her down. She might have just rescued me but that didn't obscure the fact that she'd caused the mess we were in, by carrying Mrs Annabella off in the first place. 'Where's Mrs Annabella? And why did you leave her?'

'Because you didn't follow me!' Kate protested. 'Not for ages! And then when you did come, you got yourself tangled up with that old gent!'

'She is *very* talented, Charles,' Esther said. 'When she saw you were having difficulties with the old gentleman, she came back to collect me and insisted on going for Mr Heron. I was frantic with worry but she kept saying we had all the time in the world – and then she brought us back here precisely.'

I stared at Kate. I'd been in that house a matter of minutes and Kate had done all that? She knew how I felt about it too – she was smirking. 'Well, Mrs P said I could use it in emergencies!' she pointed out. '*When the occasion demanded*, she said. And it did, didn't it?'

Heron's hand was on his sword. 'We had better sort all this out later at our leisure. We have a dangerous woman to catch.'

'That's why you're here,' Kate said grinning. I thought for a horrified moment she was going to prod Heron in the arm, but she contented herself with poking at his sword hilt. He looked intimidatingly down at her but she didn't seem to notice.

'I had to grab her quick,' she said. 'So I just jumped through, without deciding where to go. And we ended up outside St Nicholas's church. She was really upset. Tried to hit me. So I let her go and just followed.'

'Didn't she wonder where she was?' I asked.

'Nah. She was just ranting and raving. Yelling. She's mad.'

'Where did she go?'

She grinned. 'Home. That house where the angry gent was.'

'But she was not there,' Esther said.

'She would have found it much altered,' Heron said. 'I spoke to one of the servants before coming in to you. Robert Jenison in this world died six months ago and the house has been sold, the servants dismissed and new ones hired by the new owners. Even if Mrs Annabella Jenison exists in this world – of which we have no knowledge – no one at that house would recognize her.'

'So where would she have gone after that?' Esther asked.

'Never saw,' Kate said. 'Came for you.'

They all stared at me as if expecting me to produce an answer out of thin air. And I had no doubts. 'To the cause of it all,' I said. 'To Nightingale. At the Fleece.'

The quickest way down to the Keyside was via the Castle; we walked across the open expanse of the Castle Garth towards the postern gate and the Stair that led down from it. The Garth was well lit with torches that cast flickering shadows. Three drunken miners ogled Esther but she ignored them and sailed coolly on. 'You do realize we do not know whether Nightingale exists in this world,' she pointed out. 'And if he does, whether he was attacked?'

I was in a hurry, would rather have left them and plunged on down the Stair, flight after flight, twisting and turning past the old decrepit houses down to the alley beside the Fleece where Nightingale had been attacked. 'That doesn't matter. Mrs Annabella believes this to be her own world. She knows Nightingale to be at the Fleece. That's where she'll go – for one last look.'

Kate tugged at my arm. 'Why don't we just go the quick way? You know, stepping through?'

'Because we don't know what we might find when we arrive at the other end.'

'Stepping through,' Esther said firmly, 'is to be used only for emergencies.'

Half a dozen people wanted to accost us; Heron carried off the attempts with high confidence, nodding, bowing, once exchanging a few words with a complete stranger who appeared to know him – the weather is always an unexceptional topic of conversation. I lost patience, clattered on down leaving the others to descend behind me. Torches burned on the Stair, and one showed the alley empty except for shadows. But there was a gleam and flicker of candlelight from the window of Nightingale's room. Or the room Nightingale occupied in our own world. I stooped to look in.

And there stood the man himself, obviously hale and hearty and well on the way to getting drunk. A tankard in his hand, a red sheen on his cheeks and a puzzled frown as if he was trying very hard to work out what was going on. He was staring at someone just out of my view.

'Mrs Annabella.' He was prepared to be extraordinarily gallant, bowed a little too deeply and had to put out a hand to the table to prevent himself toppling over. 'If you'd warned me you were going to call, I would have— have— have—' Triumphantly, he found the right words. 'I would have ordered wine!'

I shifted so I could see the other person in the room. Mrs Annabella stood with her back to me. I could see only her dress, muddied a good foot from the hem, and her grey hair which was escaping from her cap and straggling, pitifully thin, around her shoulders. Her voice was so quiet I had trouble hearing it through the window. 'You're dead,' she said.

'I assure you,' he began bewildered, but she interrupted, her voice rising in volume and pitch. 'You deceived me!'

'I assure you—'

'You said you would marry me!'

Horror spread across Nightingale's face. 'Marry!' he squeaked. 'But my dear lady, you are in error!'

'You gave me a ring!'

'I did not,' he said indignantly.

'You said you would buy a licence.'

I scrabbled at the window, hoping to throw it open and climb through. It appeared to be slightly ajar but it was merely ill-fitting; a narrow gap was allowing me to hear the exchange of words. I peered inside and saw it was firmly latched.

'But I already have a wife,' Nightingale was protesting. 'A delightful young creature!'

Mrs Annabella shrieked with rage and flung herself at him.

Forty-Five

A lady is at all times reasonable and gracious, soft in
manner but adamant as steel in her devotion to duty.
[*A Gentleman's Companion*, August 1731]

Esther came up behind me and handed me a large stone. I
swung my arm back and smashed the stone against the window.
Ages-thinned glass shattered; inside the room, both Nightingale
and Mrs Annabella jumped, stared wildly. Heron was already
bending to give me a boost over the windowsill.

I landed on bare floorboards amongst shards of glass.
Nightingale stared in horror at the broken window. 'Mr Patterson!
The landlord will charge me for that!'

By the door of the room, Mrs Annabella picked up a candlestick. A very large candlestick. The candle burning in it tipped
at an alarming angle, dripped wax on the floor. She tore the
candle out and dropped it on the rug she stood on, where it
guttered then brightened.

Nightingale hadn't the slightest idea what was going on
behind him. I said quickly, 'I'll leave you payment for it. Mrs
Annabella, I think you should come with me.'

'She's mad,' Nightingale said, waving his tankard. 'She says
I agreed to marry her but devil take it, sir, I have a chit eighteen
years old waiting to warm my bed in Clerkenwell. Why should
I want a dried up old piece like her?'

She charged. He staggered round, yelped as she swung the
candlestick at him. He dropped the tankard, spraying beer everywhere. 'Madam!' he squeaked. The candle flame licked at the
rags of the rug.

Nightingale retreated. 'Madam, I beg—'

She swung again, he ducked, stumbled and fell back against
me. We both went down in a tangle. Nightingale caught hold
of the bedpost and managed to drag himself up again as the
candlestick whipped through the air inches from his head.
The room was beginning to stink of smoke.

The table at the bedside was just above me; I got on hands

and knees, grabbed up a jug and threw it at Mrs Annabella. The water it contained sprayed across her and she shrieked. The jug smashed on the floor.

Flames leapt suddenly from the rug; perhaps I ought to have saved the water for the fire. Nightingale flung a book at Mrs Annabella but his aim was beyond lamentable. The book smashed against the far wall.

I crawled backwards on to floorboards, grabbed the edge of the rug and tugged.

The rug rippled. Flames snapped. Mrs Annabella staggered backwards.

And Claudius Heron stepped through the door of the room and took the candlestick out of her hand.

'My apologies for being late,' he said. 'I came the long way round through the yard.'

For a moment we were all surprised into immobility. Then Nightingale, galvanized into action, slapped Heron on the back. 'My dear sir, my greatest thanks!' And while Heron was looking appalled at the familiarity, Mrs Annabella slipped past. I yelled, Heron spun to seize her – but Esther and Kate were blocking the doorway.

Mrs Annabella stopped in baffled fury. Heron took hold of her wrist. 'Time to go.'

She looked at him outraged. 'How dare you! Unhand me!'

'Oi,' Kate said. 'You do as you're told.'

We let Nightingale rave about Mrs Annabella's being a madwoman. I gave him some money for the damage to the window and the rug, and got out a shilling or two to give to the servants who ran in from the kitchen passageway. 'Mr Patterson, sir,' Nightingale said, fingering the sovereigns I'd given him. 'You're a gentleman.'

Heron and I exchanged glances. 'I'd be grateful, sir,' I murmured, 'if you'd say nothing of this to anyone. The family . . .'

'Don't want it known she's mad, eh?' In his relief, Nightingale positively glowed with good humour. He tapped the side of his nose. 'Rest assured, sir, I shall be dumb. Not a word shall pass these lips.'

'Rogue!' Mrs Annnabella said, in a tremulous voice. 'You shall not escape, sir. Your miraculous recovery will not help you for long.'

'Miraculous recovery?' he said, wavering.

I gave him another shilling or two. 'Buy yourself more beer, Mr Nightingale, and sleep well.'

His face lit up.

'And,' I added, 'a long life to you.'

Forty-Six

Fine clothes are an ornament, not the substance, of man.
[*A Gentleman's Companion*, October 1734]

In the middle of the next week, I went back to the Fleece. As I came under its arch, I saw a private coach being loaded, half a dozen children dashing about excitedly. Spirits looked on with good-humoured and voluble interest as a middle-aged man anxiously watched his boxes being stowed on the roof. The man was curt with the servants, obviously used to being obeyed; by the look of him, he had a few guineas to spare.

He glanced round as he heard me walk into the yard behind him, looked for a moment, then nodded. 'Good day, sir.'

Sir. I nodded back. What a difference a new coat and breeches made. In the eyes of the world, at least. Nightingale had summed me up by my frayed cuffs and was over-familiar. This man was respectful to my new expensive coat.

Esther, still in her nightgown and sipping hot chocolate in bed, had made me turn round several times for her approval. 'Very fine, Charles! Mr Watson is an excellent tailor.'

'I agree,' I said, sitting on the edge of the bed and bending to kiss her forehead. 'So I've ordered three more coats.'

She stared at me in amazement. '*Three?*'

'Don't you approve?'

'Well yes—'

'But?'

'They are not *all* brown and green, I hope?'

I laughed. 'I allowed him to persuade me to a dark plum colour, on Hugh's recommendation, and a buff-coloured coat, on Heron's. Esther . . .'

'I agree entirely,' she said promptly. 'Whatever it is you propose to buy next, I concur. And can I order those seven shirts now?'

'I thought you would have done so already. The provision of linen is after all the housewife's duty.'

She sighed. 'I was intent upon taking things slowly, getting your agreement.'

I winced. 'Have I been so unreasonable about it all?'

She cocked her head on one side. Her hair was loose and fell about her shoulders like sunshine, trailing fine strands across her shoulders. I ran my fingers through it. She smiled and kissed the palm of my hand. 'Yes, very unreasonable.'

'I was wondering,' I said, accepting this rebuke meekly, 'if we shouldn't spend some time this afternoon going through the estate records.'

She stared then said hurriedly, 'Yes, yes indeed!'

'On condition,' I said, 'that if we disagree about anything, your opinion prevails.'

She raised her eyes to heaven – or the roof of the bed, at any rate.

'Charles, you will never be master in your own household if you behave like this! Yours must be the last word – they are your estates, since we married.'

'I will never be master in my own household,' I retorted, 'if I don't acknowledge what a superior wife I have, who knows more about estate management than I ever will.'

'Flatterer,' she murmured.

'They're your properties, Esther, and you're the most fit to manage them. But I'll do my best to help.'

She thought about it for a moment. 'If that is the way you want it, so be it.'

'I want peace in the household,' I said. 'And neither of us will have that if I have sole management of those estates. I'd lose every penny of them, you'd be hard put to keep them from going to rack and ruin.'

She laughed. 'Ridiculous!'

I caught my breath. I loved the way the skin around her eyes crinkled as she laughed, the way her eyes lit up, the way she tilted her head back and showed me the long line of her throat . . .

'I must be off to the Fleece,' I said, sighing. 'Hugh will be there already and getting impatient.'

'And I must deal with Kate,' she agreed. 'Although I do not have the least idea what we are going to do with her.'

I bent to kiss her again, on the lips this time, contenting myself with a mere peck because I knew that if I indulged myself, I'd never get away. She said, provocatively, 'How soon do you think you will be back? Shall I trouble myself to get up?'

I grimaced. 'I have to see Heron afterwards too.'

She sighed. 'Then I will see you tonight. Charles—'

I turned back.

'What changed your mind? About the estates?'

'Mrs Annabella,' I said. 'We had certain – ideas – in common.'

'Nonsense!' she said, outraged.

I shivered in an unexpected chill as the wind idled through the Fleece's arch. I suspected we were in for a hard winter. Hugh came up behind me, peering over my shoulder at the private coach without a great deal of interest. He was in his favourite blue and the sling was very white against the darkness of his coat.

'The coffee house rumours,' he said, without preamble, 'are that Mrs Annabella has gone quite mad with grief and been packed off to the countryside for her health.'

'The rumours wouldn't be far wrong,' I said. The ostlers were leading out a matched pair of black geldings.

'Is she going to be safe there?' Hugh asked. 'Devil take it, Charles! The last thing we want is her breaking out and hotfooting it back to town with her embroidery scissors!'

'I've seen the two – er – *companions* Jenison has given her.'

'Hefty, were they?'

'Fine figures of women,' I said.

'And Ridley?'

'I'm meeting Heron in Nellie's coffee house after we're finished here. Messages have been sent to his father in Narva though God knows when we'll hear back. But I'm not going to let it rest, Hugh. That boy killed a child and ought to pay some penalty for it. At the very least he should be brought to realize the enormity of what he did.'

'You always did hope for the impossible,' Hugh said.

We walked round the edge of the chaos, ducked into the passageway that led to the Fleece's kitchens. Mally was bearing a huge pie along the passageway and stopped to glare at me.

Then her gaze drifted over my shoulder and her smile broadened invitingly. I glanced round to find Hugh grinning back.

'That arm hamper you much?' she asked, nodding at his sling.

'Not a bit of it.'

She leant closer as she passed. 'You could prove that to me. Tonight?'

'Hugh,' I said wearily.

He grinned. 'You're becoming a staid married man, Charles!'

We went up the stairs off the kitchen passageway, and stood on the threshold of what had been Nightingale's room, looking at the stripped bed, the clothes tossed on to the trunk.

'There was a good turnout for the funeral,' Hugh said. 'He'd have liked that.'

I thought of the Nightingale who'd faced Mrs Annabella in that other world. I'd rather liked him; I wondered if under all the sham and pretence our Nightingale had been similar. 'I think he'd have much preferred to be at someone else's funeral.'

'I wonder why his spirit hasn't disembodied yet. It's been three days since he died.'

I couldn't guess – three days is the general length of time it takes for a spirit to appear but it can take longer. I was, in truth, glad Nightingale's spirit was not yet here; to turn over his belongings in its presence would not have been a comfortable experience.

Hugh picked up a ruined waistcoat, stiff with blood. 'What are we supposed to do with all this?'

I began to sort through the paraphernalia of everyday living on the bedside table: a razor, a ring, a few coins. I put Nightingale's watch amongst them, picked up a thick bundle of letters. 'The clothes he was wearing when he was stabbed will have to be thrown out. The rest are to be kept until his landlady in London replies to my letter. If there are relatives we'll send them the trunk; if not, it'll all go to the poor.'

Hugh was trying to fold clothes one-handedly. I held out the bundle of letters. 'Here, you go through these. I'll see to the clothes.'

Hugh sat down on the bed and used a nail to flick up the heavy blob of wax on the first letter. 'These just look like business matters. Jenison's letters are here.' He whistled. 'Have you any idea what Jenison was proposing to pay him?'

'London prices. And even then he wasn't satisfied.' I tossed aside the blood-ruined clothes, looked down on a trunk that was already neatly packed. 'Do I need to repack this, do you think?'

Hugh glanced across. 'There might be more letters there – even a miniature or two – some clue as to his relatives.'

'True.' I started lifting clothes from the trunk, trying to disturb them as little as possible. Some of the clothes were very fine; Nightingale had plainly been intent on cutting a figure in the neighbourhood. The colours were all rather too strong for me – there was a particularly bright purple that tried my eyes.

'There's a letter here from Durham,' Hugh said. 'Unopened. Looks like it came after he was attacked.' He lifted the wax with a fingernail. 'Good lord, it's from Peter Blenkinsop. You know, the fellow who sings through his nose.' He did a quick, and accurate, imitation.

'Was Nightingale inviting him to perform?' What a concert that would have been, I thought.

'No, it's in his other capacity, as landlord of the Star and Rummer Inn. Charles,' Hugh was sounding very puzzled now, 'it's a bill – for four nights' accommodation and the devil of a quantity of beer, wine, spirits. You name it, he drank it. He must have been stupefied the whole time he was there!'

I stared at him. 'Does it say the nights he stayed in Durham?'

'Friday night till Monday night.'

'That fits in with what Mrs Annabella said.' I leant against the bed post. 'She told me Nightingale had come up to town several days before he officially arrived on the coach. He was trying to persuade her to keep quiet about their dalliance in London.'

'He must have led her on quite as much as she suggested, if he felt he had to come up and plead for secrecy.'

'He must have been here on the Friday, ridden back south to Durham – that wouldn't have taken him more than an hour – then stayed in Durham four nights until the coach came through. Devil take it, Hugh! I heard one of the women on the coach say to him he'd given her a wonderfully entertaining *end* to the journey. I should have realized then that he couldn't have come all the way from London on the coach. He caught it in Durham!'

'There's another bill attached.' Hugh struggled with pieces of paper that didn't wish to be unfolded. 'For stabling a horse for four days.'

'He must have ridden up from London. Quickest way.'

'Blenkinsop says that if Nightingale doesn't pay his bill by the end of the week the horse will be sold.'

'Let him sell it,' I said. 'It's the simplest way of getting his money.' A horse, I thought; Nightingale had come north on a horse to Newcastle, seen Mrs Annabella, ridden south again . . .

I lifted out the folds of clothes. A pocket knife fell into my fingers. A folded newspaper with an advertisement marked.

'There's a letter to someone else entirely,' Hugh said. 'A man by the name of Richard Crowe.'

'Crow?' I stared at him. I'd heard that name before. No, someone had said that Nightingale sang like a crow. Ridley – at that drunken fracas at Jenison's house.

Hugh started to laugh. 'You'll never guess, Charles! His name wasn't Nightingale at all.' He waved the letter at me. 'This is from an old inamorata. She says, *You'd better change your name, Dick, whoever heard of a singer called Crowe?* Charles, are you all right?'

'Crow,' I repeated. 'Richard Crow.'

'With an "e" on the end.'

'Cuthbert Ridley,' I said. 'Richard Crowe.'

'What?'

'That's the trouble with monograms, isn't it?' I said. 'You never know which way round they are. *CR* or *RC*?'

'What are you talking about?'

I started digging amongst the clothes left in the trunk. I was barely halfway down and the coats were thick. There was a pair of boots and some shoes, a copy of an almanac, a book of stories of a very unsavoury kind. And something that chinked amongst the folds of a waistcoat. I threw back the folds and coins chinked, louder.

'He was bound to have cash somewhere,' Hugh said.

I tucked back the skirts of the waistcoat and there it was. A leather purse with a drawstring fastened securely. And the monogram *R* and *C* intertwined.

The bag was heavy in my hands. Hugh stared. 'It can't have been him! Maybe Ridley hid the purse here to implicate him.'

'Ridley doesn't have this kind of money. And he wouldn't part with it if he had.' I was busy pulling the story I'd built in my mind apart and putting it back together again. 'Nightingale came up on the Friday to see Mrs Annabella,' I said. 'He must have been furious at having to humour her but he had to – if Jenison had found out Nightingale had been leading his sister on, he'd have lost his engagement here. Nightingale would have been angry at even finding himself in that kind of a situation. What would you have done then, Hugh?'

'Get drunk.'

'Exactly. He was a stranger in the town and Jenison had recommended the George to him. I wager he went there, Hugh – the stable boy saw someone that night who matched his description. Or the description of his horse, at any rate. That's why he refused Jenison's offer of rooms there – they'd have recognized him, and he didn't want it to be known he'd been in the town before he was supposed to be. The stable boy gave him directions to the bridge; he was riding south to Durham to wait for the coach there. But he went the wrong way, probably got lost. Which would have made him even more angry. And when he ended up on the Key, being Nightingale, he had one more urgent need to satisfy.'

'The whores.'

'But he was too drunk to perform properly – which worsened his temper yet further. He rode off without caring who or what was in his way – and knocked the woman into the river. He may never even have realized what he'd done. He was too preoccupied with thoughts of Mrs Annabella.'

Hugh sighed. 'He was playing a dangerous game.'

'No,' I said, 'a fatal one.' I dropped the purse back into the trunk. 'But he should have known. He spent all his life dancing on ladders, after all. He must have fallen off more than once.'

A silence.

'So Ridley's innocent after all,' Hugh said.

I grimaced. 'He didn't precipitate the child into the river, certainly. But innocent, no. Ridley's not dancing on ladders, Hugh – he's on the edge of a precipice.' I tossed the clothes back into the trunk. 'Let's throw all this in together and leave it for Jenison to deal with. I'm sick of it all. I just want to get home.'

Hugh gathered up the bits and pieces from the table and tossed them on top of the clothes, together with the letters. I looked at the heavy bag in my hands, the intertwined initials.

I buried it deep in the pile of clothes and turned my back.

HISTORICAL NOTE

Every effort has been made to be geographically accurate in a depiction of Charles Patterson's Newcastle. In the 1730s, Newcastle upon Tyne was a town of around 16,000 people, hemmed in by old walls, and centred on the Quay where ships moored to carry away the coal and glass on which the town depended. The single bridge across the Tyne, linking Newcastle with its southern neighbour, Gateshead, was lined with houses and shops, a chapel and even a small prison; from the Quay, the streets climbed the hills to the more genteel, and cleaner, areas around Westgate and Northumberland Street. Daniel Defoe liked the place when he visited in 1720, but remarked unfavourably on the fogs and the smells that came drifting up the river. Places such as Westgate, High Bridge, the Sandhill and the Side did (and still do) all exist, although I have added a few alleys here and there to enable Patterson and his friends to take short cuts where necessary, and invented a stylish location for Esther's house, Caroline Square.

Musically, Charles Patterson lives in an atmosphere that the residents of Newcastle in the 1730s would have recognized instantly. The town had one of the most active musical scenes in England, after London, Bath and Oxford. From 1735, inhabitants could hear music in a weekly series of winter concerts (and occasionally during the summer too), listen to music in church (plain simple music if you went to St Nicholas, much more elaborate and 'popular' music at All Hallows), attend the dancing assemblies in winter, and listen to the fiddlers, pipers and ballad singers in the street. Nationally – and internationally – famous soloists often visited, but sadly there is no evidence to support the story that the most celebrated musician of the period, Mr George Frideric Handel, ever visited Newcastle.

A number of real people fleetingly appear in Charles Patterson's world. Solomon Strolger, organist of All Hallows for fifty-three years, is one, as is another organist, James Hesletine of Durham Cathedral. Thomas Mountier, the bass singer in *Broken Harmony*, was a singing man at the Cathedral for a short while until drink intervened. The Jenisons and Ords were real families with a particular interest in music but the specific individuals who appear in these books are fictional.

Strange though it may seem, ladder dancers also existed in real life; occasionally advertisements for such acts appear in London newspapers. None, however, ever seem to have found their way north to Newcastle. In addition, a 'Signor Rossignol' (an Italian 'Mr Nightingale' from Naples) enjoyed enormous popularity in the second half of the century, 'singing' concertos, symphonies and other pieces, as well as imitating birdsong, but nevertheless died penniless and forgotten in Yorkshire.

Charles Patterson is entirely fictional, but the difficulties he finds in making a living would have been entirely familiar to musicians of the time. If he has an *alter ego*, it would be Charles Avison, a Newcastle-born musician and composer who was well known in his time and who dragged himself up by his own efforts from obscurity to wealth and respect, even being invited by local gentry to dine at their tables. If Patterson's career follows the same path, he will be extremely happy.